MW01413822

STRAND PRICE
$ 1.00

LAS VEGAS ILLUSION

by

CAROLYN SLICKER DeFEVER

Paisley Publishing Company
San Antonio, TX

Las Vegas Illusion

Copyright © 1993 by Carolyn Slicker DeFever

All rights reserved, which includes the right to reproduce this book or portions thereof in any form whatsoever except as provided by the U.S. Copyright Law.

Printed and bound in the United States of America

Excerpt from "Macbeth (Witche's Chant)"
by William Shakespeare.

Except for any known figures, the characters and events in this book are fictitious. Any similarity to real persons, living or dead, is coincidental and not intended by the author.

Cover design by Mark Oehlert

ISBN: 0-9626117-6-X

Library of Congress Catalog Card Number: 93-83080

First Edition

Published by Paisley Publishing Company
1802 Paisley Drive
San Antonio, TX 78231

For my husband, Rodney, who, after 16 years, can still make me laugh.

PROLOGUE

The blazing Nevada sun mimicked a face pinched in anger, nostrils flaring white hot vapor.

Or so it seemed to one lone man—a man fallen from favor—a man sent to redeem himself.

He fell in step with a crowd of tourists in an effort to become invisible, a useless gesture on his part for he was not an average-looking man. Eyes from the crowd fell on him admiringly, some, blatantly inviting.

He scoffed, stuffed his hands deeper into his trouser pockets, and quickened his gait. He had the uncanny feeling that 1976 was to become a black hole in his memoirs.

A different kind of heat assaulted him as he stepped under the brilliant marquee of the Golden Nugget Casino. His gaze sprang upward in protest, taking in the expansive clustered bulbs spanning a full city block.

As far as he could see in every direction a neon wonderland blinked and winked at him, seeming to say, "Your secret is safe with me."

Las Vegas, Nevada, a real-life fantasy, he thought sardonically. He strode quickly inside the open doors. The relief of cool air swathed his face. White-blond hair matted his brow in unfashionable disarray as he lifted his shoulders up and forward in an effort to dislodge the closely-fitted sport coat from now clammy skin.

His square jaw was set in determination while sparkling eyes, blue as the ocean's depth, held a promise of retribution.

If this is to be my destiny, then let it be a successful one. With that thought, he zeroed in on his target.

CHAPTER ONE

The horseshoe-shaped "21" pit was formidable in presence. Behind each half-circle table stood a blackjack dealer in uniform of starched white shirt and black pants. There the sameness ended.

A fiery redhead stared daggers at a rotund, abrasive player.

"Cheating bitch!" he mumbled, not entirely to himself. "Probably dealing from the bottom of the deck."

A smile twitched at the corners of the seasoned dealer's lips as she extended her middle finger, hesitating just long enough before raising it to her forehead, rubbing in an up and down motion, never taking her eyes off the player.

Beads of sweat framed the puffy features of a face growing purple with rage, spawned of a known impotency to change the situation. Feeding his agitation were the bemused smiles of his co-players. He uttered one last obscenity and threw his cards on the table, knocking the chair over as he fled.

At another table the dealer, decidedly bored, yawned.

At yet another table, cards fired from the dealer's hands like poison darts.

Farther down the pit, a campy blonde smiled demurely at her single gentleman player. Her signals were spiced with innuendo.

This was Leah Aston's world. The world of competition—us against them—the House against the player. At the Golden Nugget, often man against woman, for nearly eighty percent of the dealers were women.

Leah leaned against a slot machine, fingering the black cotton half-apron embroidered with the Golden Nugget insignia in gold and green threads. Several tables away, she could see her friend, Jenny, leaving her table, flame-red hair swinging across her shoulders, a defiance in her walk.

Jenny, oblivious to anything about her, walked straight past Leah, her eyes fixed.

Leah, forced to a half-run to catch up, said in a breathless voice, "I really like your style."

Jenny looked up quickly, her slow smile a begrudging one. "Oh, you saw that. The big baboon! He's lucky I didn't punch him in the mouth!"

"You'd better grow a foot or two first." Leah laughed at her friend of meager height.

Jenny disregarded the gibe, knowing full well that it was meant with the greatest of affection, and let out a deep sigh. "I should be more careful...that clown could have been from the Gaming Commission. Sometimes I act like a damn amateur."

Leah put her arm around Jenny's shoulders. "Come on, I'll buy you a cup of coffee."

They walked to the snack-bar at the end of the casino—a long walk, for the Nugget took up the length of a full city block. They quickened their stride and rushed to claim the last remaining seats at the bar.

Leah ordered coffee for them, laying the money on the counter.

The snack-bar, almost hidden at the far end of the casino, was a desert jetty of white shirts and black pants, full and overflowing when the dealers broke, and just as quickly, an undiscovered oasis when they left. It was open to the public, but the dealers monopolized it most of the time. Patrons happening upon this almost secluded area of the casino often fell privy to the innermost thoughts and reactions of dealers being shared, sometimes boisterously, with one another. The language wasn't always mild.

Jenny's eyes scanned the expansive length of the snack-bar with an expression of resignation. "I feel like a member of a secret cult. Tahoe was never like this."

Leah sat silently, this last remark unsettling her resolve to be a sounding board. "Do you realize that it's been almost a year since we walked through those swinging doors almost simultaneously? You were so incredibly arrogant. I wasn't sure I even liked you."

"What brought on this reminiscence?" Jenny asked.

"You're the best friend I have and I don't like to hear you talk about Tahoe or any other place in preference to Vegas. You find jackasses everywhere, more in gambling towns, granted."

"Okay, so it's just a bad day. I get tired of being treated like the enemy. Do you suppose anyone ever looks at me standing behind that table and thinks, 'Gee, I'll bet she's someone's mother'? Hell no they don't!"

Leah studied Jenny with an exaggerated scrutiny. "No...you don't exactly depict *Mother of the Year*. A short show girl, perhaps."

"Oh, go to hell!" Jenny nearly sputtered her coffee in a spasm of laughter.

Leah smiled contentedly. The spell of bad humor was broken. It was tough to shake it off sometimes. Taking on an air of inhumanity often begot inhumane treatment. Maybe someday they would be replaced with robots. It seemed to be the kind of behavior that was expected from blackjack dealers.

They sipped their steaming aromatic coffee from heavy white mugs, all the tensions of only minutes before forgotten.

The dealers around them were standing now, preparing to return to the pit, their fifteen-minute break over. Leah watched another of her friends, Carmen, slip a White in her mouth. Another pitfall of the job, Leah thought. It was imperative to remain alert. The casinos were keenly aware of this, and as a result, dealers worked only 45 minutes out of every hour.

Jenny sprinted ahead of Leah, having a farther distance to go. Leah couldn't help but smile for, Jenny, with her full hips that were not capable of a straight forward motion, swung from side to side like the exaggerated motions of those sometime athletes seen alongside the roads doing their *fast walking*.

Leah didn't waste any time either. In contrast, her long legs made the distance shorter. In another setting, one might have thought she was a fashion model on her way to a shoot. She had an air of sophistication mingled with an almost unique kind of beauty. But there was a softness and warmth to her angular face that belied the facade of worldliness, ivory complexion and pale blonde hair creating an almost ethereal illusion.

She smiled at the pit boss, snapping her brief black apron around her narrow hips as she went. Leah had a way of seeing through the rough exteriors of people. She tried to remind herself daily that people were much more alike than they were different, and that thought helped her through many difficult situations. She walked directly up behind her relief dealer and tapped him on the shoulder.

He finished out the hand he was dealing and spread the cards in a perfect arc on the green felt table. He clapped his hands, held them palms up, shrugged his shoulders and stepped to the side. Leah moved one step up and took control of her table again. It always embarrassed her when a relief dealer acted that way. After all, she thought, she was the one who had to face them. The palms up and shrug indicated that he didn't have a toke to show for his fifteen minutes' effort.

The hand-clapping exercise was required every time a dealer left the table—the purpose being to indicate to the eye-in-the-sky, and any observing pit boss, that one wasn't walking away from the table with money or chips from the rack. His fulfillment of that requirement was a soundless haphazard effort that hardly met the criterion.

One never really knew if the players were being tight or just didn't know that it was protocol to tip the dealer, or better yet, put a bet up for them. She hoped the players at her table didn't realize they had just been insulted.

Leah had become so adept at her job that she did it automatically. She could look at a group of cards and know the total immediately. She knew all her combinations of 21—6,7,8; 5,7,9; 9,3,9; etc.—all the little tricks she had learned at Dealers' School.

Suddenly, a single, long-stemmed red rose was thrown across a vacant betting square. She looked up, automatic pilot shut down, the majestic blue of her eyes meeting and holding the matching blue of his. He brought to mind a magnificent palomino stud. His white-blond hair lay across his golden-tanned forehead as mane would on a shiny coat.

Leah's reactions were conflicting. Foreign objects

were strictly not allowed on the gaming table. She opened her mouth to protest just as he plunked a silver dollar in the square beside the rose. Somehow that seemed to legitimatize the transaction and Leah made a swift decision to deal, hoping to get rid of him as quickly as possible before undue attention was brought upon her table.

She dealt: silently, expressionlessly, her heart pounding. She knew this was raising havoc with the eye-in-the-sky in spite of her hopes of anonymity. In her mind's eye, she visualized the scanning camera doing a double take and bearing down hard on her.

She repositioned the deck in her left hand and indicated to the first player on her left, who was still holding his cards. He finally made his decision and slid the cards under his chips.

The second player scratched his cards on the table. She gave him a card, he scratched again, another card...satisfied, he slid the cards under his silver dollars.

The third player was good, indicated by the cards already neatly tucked under the chips.

Leah looked at the rose, then up to its donor. He was standing, his hand resting on the green felt, still holding his cards, looking thoughtfully into his hand. She waited patiently, taking the opportunity to study him more closely. This was a new tactic. She was convinced that she had heard every conceivable variation of every line imaginable during this last year at the Nugget. None had worked so far. Why should this?

Every eye at the table was focused on him. The other players were silent, amused, she sensed. *Thank God this isn't a serious game with big money.* Leah felt the presence of the pit boss now behind her right shoulder.

The man with the rose smiled, put his cards under his silver dollar and looked into her eyes. She quickly averted her gaze and continued the hand. As she came back around to the rose, she slid her hand around it and turned over his cards. A 4, a 5. 9! He stayed on a 9...when she had a 10 showing? Either he was tremendously stupid or he intended to lose.

"You win," he said, easing away from the table, smiling with those gorgeous teeth. *Six Foot Two, Eyes of Blue.* The thought sprang into Leah's head as she watched him blend into the crowded aisle and disappear. She gathered the cards, ignoring the rose, and slid them into the discard rack. *What am I going to do with this obtrusive rose!*

After a moment's hesitation she picked up the rose and slid it beside the discard rack where tokes normally go. She began shuffling, taking half the standard time, her cheeks flaming. All the players were watching her, exchanging looks, half smiles. No one spoke.

It was like that. Players were not usually friendly with one another. They loved the magic moments of Vegas, though, and this had been one, a good story to take home.

The pit boss ambled back to his podium and everyone settled into his or her private battle against the House. She smiled to herself, wondering how they would split a rose 30 ways.

Leah drove home in silence. Her foot was heavy on the throttle, but she didn't care. Her Lincoln was older than her children, to whom her thoughts were directed now. As the vehicle chugged and coughed its way down Fremont Street, Leah made a mental note that another trip to the garage was imminent. The only consolation was that the final payment had been made. She admonished herself yet again for walking out of a lucrative marriage with only her pride, when she could just as easily have had cash in her hand. That was a mistake, but hindsight is always so flawless.

Leah considered herself a mother first, everything else was secondary. She devoted every spare moment to her twin daughters, Carrie and Sherry.

But in spite of that always present conviction of priority, her mind drifted back to the man with the rose. He was devastatingly handsome. More than that, there was a certain...intrigue about his manner. If she had not been so taken aback by the uniqueness of the situation, she might have been able to judge him better. But Leah was barely coming out of the novice stage, with just a year's dealing behind her. She still had a healthy fear of dealing, born of inexperience and the tales overheard in the dealers' lounge—a secret sanctum, to be sure.

What did it mean...just a lark? Had he singled her out? The man had simply vanished, swallowed up by the crowd and never spit back. She thought that on her next break he would approach, ask her out—she would say no—end of story. But that had not happened and it made her wonder. But not for long. She had decided that after her last failed marriage, she was not even vaguely interested in another, and she was not one to have casual affairs. When she had the urge to accept a date, she would weigh the merits of spending her evening with a total stranger against spending time with the delightful and inquisitive Carrie and the beautiful and prim Sherry. How could her decision be otherwise? There was an ache in her heart when she thought of those loving and trusting babies just waiting for her to pick them up at the nursery school. Leah's decision was always the same. The twins would be starting school in September and, even though it was early in the year, Leah knew how fast the precious years were slipping away. She didn't want to miss these last months of utter innocence and discovery.

It was a sad thought. And as she often did, when she thought of the twins, she thought of their dear father, in heaven now, if that's where the worthy went. She liked to think so in Bill's case. He died while rescuing a neighbor's child from an ice pond. But in spite of her best efforts, anger still lingered. He was the all-time "good guy", often sacrificing his own family's needs to help others. There was a small child alive today because of him, but the gruesome circumstances made it a bittersweet memory. Those terrible mid-western winters were something she never wanted to experience again. His passing was untimely, to say the least, and left Leah with more debts than assets. But she couldn't blame him. Who could have predicted such a thing? And how perfect was she, rushing into a second marriage for all the wrong reasons—as if a father for her children was so easy to replace?

The next day a single red rose adorned with baby's breath and a red ribbon was delivered to the pit for Leah Aston. There was no card. Leah wondered if it was from the handsome stranger. She enjoyed the intrigue, to her own dismay, and found herself wondering if he would show up again.

The mornings in the casino were usually quiet. Sometimes the dealers stood at an empty table for two or three 45-minute stints without a player. Since the dealers were not allowed to talk to one another while positioned at their tables, it was a good time to think.

Leah stood at ease at her table, not turning to one side or the other, as was the rule, arms folded. She thought how strange it seemed that she was actually here in Las Vegas, Nevada. A blackjack dealer, of all things!

Foolish as it seemed to her now, she had done it on a bet. Her, then "new husband", Damon—the twins always pronounced it Demon, as if somehow they knew it was more appropriate—had taunted her...she could still hear his words. *You, a blackjack dealer! My dear, you could no more be a blackjack dealer than I could be a prima donna. Let's all stick to what we do best, shall we?* The challenge was irresistible, and had he really known her, would not have made the remark so lightly.

The fact of the matter was, he made an excellent prima donna. What he did best was spend money. He was involved in one scheme after another in such quick succession it was hard to keep up with them. There were land deals and oil investments and, as if that wasn't enough to keep him interested, Leah found that there were mistresses that followed and changed just as frequently.

The final straw fell when he slapped Carrie and sent her flying across the room. Tears came to Leah's eyes as the memories flooded back. He had never been affectionate to the children, and to her horror, she came to realize that he actually hated them. She had become extremely protective of them ever since. The marriage was a disaster from beginning to end, lasting only a year. The pain was still fresh in her mind and heart— not for lost love so much as from self reproach.

But Leah believed in destiny, and holding on to that belief made it easier to accept when she had to move out of her luxury home, with the swimming pool and sauna, to a little three-bedroom apartment. The rent was not bad, and now that she was a dealer, she was making decent money. She had topped out on salary, and tokes were often more than salary. And she went one step further to reduce her overhead, one, sometimes controversial, step.

Leah's reminiscence was interrupted as a dowdy couple walked up and plopped down at her table. Her immediate thought was that they were from Iowa—unpolished and underfinanced. Every part of the country seemed to feel superior to another, and Vegas was no exception. Leah didn't really understand why people from Iowa had that reputation except that, in comparison to high rollers, they did seem grossly outclassed. But then, so did everyone else. The couple bought in for five dollars.

Every day, all week long, Leah received a single rose, delivered by a local florist. It was in the pit waiting for her each morning at ten o'clock as she went on duty. Today's offering was on the podium. Her curiosity was heightening daily. She felt sure the roses were being sent by the tall, blond stranger. She thought about the symbol of a single red rose—true love. It was kind of nice, she thought, like someone saying to her every morning, "I love you." For some strange reason, that thought, although pleasing in its own way, was equally disturbing to Leah. Perhaps it was the threat of a possible disruption of her well-organized life. Or maybe it was the unwritten obligation to one who says, "I love you."

In the final analysis it didn't matter. She wouldn't let it matter. She wasn't ready for a relationship, nor, might she ever be. She wanted to be free, she told herself. It didn't matter that she was 32 years old, had two five-year-old daughters to support, and a savings account hardly worth mentioning. She was free and she was happy. Her daughters were paramount in her life and she didn't need anything else. She refused to let herself feel the emptiness and loneliness that sometimes tried to surface.

"Good morning, beautiful lady." He slid gracefully into the first chair to the right of her.

It had been a week since she'd seen his face but she recognized him immediately. It didn't go unnoticed by her that he sat at third base. The best players always sat at third base. If they knew the game, they really could affect, even control, to a certain extent, what the dealer would draw for her hit card.

"Good morning," she said, smiling, drinking in his stunningly masculine presence. He wore a tan silk suit and cream-colored shirt, open at the neck. With his coloring, the combination was remarkable.

He retrieved a stack of MGM chips from his coat pocket and placed them in the middle of the table.

Leah scooped up the cards, spread in an arc on her table, and proceeded to shuffle. The shuffle was a set pattern. She could do it with her eyes closed. With the vantage of peripheral vision, she noted him playing with his chips as poker players do. On his left hand, covering half his finger, lay a huge turquoise ring set in silver. Without looking up, she knew that it perfectly matched the pressed turquoise chain around his neck. She wanted to ask if he was responsible for the *rose-a-day* program, but thought how embarrassing it would be if he was not.

Leah reached for the chips, drop-counted five and cut into them three times. One hundred even. She didn't ask how he wanted them, since he gave her fives, she assumed he wanted fives back. She exchanged them for Nugget chips and dropped his into the slot-box. His forearms rested on the thick, red leather padding surrounding the outside of the table.

"My name is Jim," he said, in a deeply melodious voice.

Just Jim, she thought to herself, no last name? She half smiled and pointed to her name tag, then pitched the first round of cards.

He grinned sheepishly. "Didn't you like the roses?"

His intensive blue eyes appeared almost vulnerable under heavy mysterious lashes. She softened and smiled. "Does any woman not like roses?"

His expression seemed to be that of boyish satisfaction but his next question was cautious and presented in a humble manner: "Do you think you might consider dinner with me sometime?"

Leah did not hesitate. "I'm sorry, I don't date." *Stock answer.* She shuddered inwardly.

Jim was not daunted by the rejection. The game went on. She was dealing to him heads-up—a strange way to refer to dealing to one player. Leah had been more familiar with the term in association with horses or golf courses. She watched him now, knowing that he was sitting there losing his money simply for the sake of talking with her—or trying to. Somehow that made her feel sorry for him. That was her downfall, she reminded herself. She was always feeling sorry for someone. Rules were rules and whether she thought they were fair or not didn't matter. One did not just sit at a gaming table talking to a dealer. If you didn't play, you didn't sit.

Jim wasn't losing badly, but his stack of chips

came alarmingly close to depletion before taking an upward swing again. He was actually a good player, she observed. He knew when to stay and he knew when to hit. He doubled down and split at all the right times but, unfortunately, being a good player didn't guarantee one of winning.

Leah studied his hands. She knew that hands could tell a lot about a person. His were large, well-manicured—not a working man's hands. She wondered who he was. Another player wandered up and sat down and Jim immediately rose and played out his hand.

"Leah, may I ask you again sometime?" His voice was even and matter-of-fact, and he looked her straight in the eyes.

She was taken aback by the simplicity of the request. He seemed to be making a habit of surprising her. He wasn't asking her to make a real decision, she rationalized. He was asking permission to take a chance on being rejected again. She swallowed hard and with a half smile, answered, "Sure, why not?"

Relief washed over her as she watched him walk away. The muscles in his long legs virtually rippled through the thin fabric of his trousers as his long strides took him quickly out of view.

Leah looked at the trembling hands in front of her and, astonishingly, recognized them as her own. Her knees felt weak and her pulse raced wildly. What was this? Delayed reaction? Did she only allow herself to feel, after the fact? When she stood behind that formidable half-circle table of padded red leather and green felt, she was virtually *on*, no different from an actress on a stage. The practiced expressions of indifference, the much, much practiced pitch of the cards, the calculated smoothness of motion—and yet...it was only a facade that sometimes managed to be penetrated.

He was out of view now, but not out of mind as Leah reflected on the magnetism of this mystery man with the oh, so, measured actions which unduly intrigued her, an unwelcome intrigue. Somewhere beneath the conscious shield of steel a cord was struck, a nerve touched. Leah felt as though she had been holding her breath.

The lone player impatiently scratched his cards on the table, silently demanding a hit. Leah reluctantly directed her thoughts to the game at hand, but it was with great effort, for she kept hearing her name on Jim's lips and it gave her a warm feeling all over.

All through the next week, Leah felt let down. There was no rose to greet her in the mornings and she found herself thinking about the mysterious stranger more and more. Maybe she should have gone out with him, she told herself. Then again, maybe he was a dealer, too. She had seen too many of her friends suffer hardships as a result of getting involved with other dealers. It seemed that most of the men dealers were also gamblers. They would pick up their toke envelopes, run to a casino next door or across the street, and lose the money before their shift started. They were not allowed to gamble in their own casino, that fell under the restriction of dealing to friends or relatives.

They were allowed to play the slot machines, however, and that was the one weakness Leah allowed herself occasionally. But only occasionally, for she had come to abhor the gambling personality and wouldn't have been able to bear to think of herself in the same category. She considered gambling a weakness beyond comprehension, unless it was for entertainment or under strict control. Control was the key word.

But, she herself, wasn't immune to the lure of sudden riches. When she picked up her toke envelope, if she had any quarters in it, she would put those quarters in the slot machine at the end of the casino which she passed every day as she entered the pit. It was the slot machine where you could win a car. There was a fabulous, chocolate brown, Lincoln Continental, sitting there right in the casino, beside the magical slot machine that had the power to, for only a quarter, ring its triumphant bell and put you in the driver's seat. Sometimes she laughed at herself for doing it. But, she would think of the farmer from Iowa whom she had seen put four quarters in and win a beautiful sailing sloop. Or the secretary from California who had won the four-wheel drive jeep, after only four or five dollars.

Some players would stand at the machine all day long pumping quarters into it and go away disappointed and broke. The Continental was just too beautiful to pass by. Glistening in the artificial light of the casino, it seemed to whisper, "Try me, just one time, try me, I could be yours."

There was a dealers' meeting called by the management this morning, requiring the entire day-shift dealers of all games to come in an hour earlier than usual. It was their annual "Why you shouldn't join the union" meeting. The cocktail waitresses and food servers were unionized, but as yet the dealers were not and management wanted to keep it that way. The unions in Vegas were strong, and organizing the dealers had become their top priority. The Golden Nugget wasn't in any real danger in Leah's opinion. Their dealers were loyal, with good cause, they were treated well. The casino manager was kind and always understanding when someone needed time off for personal business or to care for a sick child. It really felt like family. It was a rare place to work in a city as callous as Las Vegas.

The meeting was brief in duration and successfully served to endear staff to management once again. No small credit went to Steve Wynn, the power behind the Golden Nugget, who made a rare appearance. He was the personification of charisma, and the dealers responded to him positively. How could anyone not respond to a man who dressed up like an old hermit miner and passed himself off as Zachariah, the Golden Nugget's founder of 1847? He would put on the shoulder-length salt and pepper wig, round, wire-rimmed spectacles low on his nose, and mustache that seemed to blend and become a part of the beard that matched the hair in length. The shaggy brow was barely visible under the beat-up old hat worn sideways on his head.

These occasions were rare, but memorable. The huge portrait of Zachariah was as much a part of the Nugget as the *Girl on the red velvet swing* suspended from the ceiling high above the bustle of activity below.

Leah left the meeting, winding her way down the narrow stairwell that led to the main casino. The familiar ringing of slot machines reached her ears and the odor of money reached her nostrils—that's what she thought it was anyway. She had tried to identify that special aroma that one smelled when entering the casinos from the street. It had escaped her for a long time. Then one day without thinking about it, it came to her. She remembered the times she helped her mother do the books at the end of a busy sale day at the store. She would count stacks and stacks of money. There was no doubt about it, it was the smell of money. She was pleased that she had finally identified it.

Leah's life was orderly and she liked to have control of things around her. She categorized and identified and dealt with her environment in a logical and calculated manner. Perhaps that was why Jim disturbed her so much. She had not been able to classify him. He was still an enigma to her.

"Leah, don't forget, we're doing tokes tonight," Jenny called to her from behind.

"Okay," she shot back absently.

Leah walked to her table. She was midway down the pit—Table 17. She dropped her purse under the table beside her feet and waited for the pit boss to unlock and remove the cover from her rack. The game had been closed during the graveyard shift. Only about 7 out of 30 tables remained open from two a.m. to ten a.m. The pit boss spread a new deck of cards on her table and Leah immediately picked them up and started the standard shuffle.

"Lucky today?" a booming voice interrupted her tranquility.

Leah looked up and smiled. "I don't know yet, I just got here." It felt good to be able to answer a question honestly. She couldn't possibly answer with a yes or no. Repercussions might occur either way. *Yes, I'm lucky as hell, sit down and let me take your money. No, I'm giving money away hand over fist. Sit down and I'll give you some, too.*

"Good," he said, and plopped down on the chair directly in front of her, motioning to the woman with him to sit.

The woman sat two seats away from him. Leah didn't like the feel of this. She could sense the tension in the air. The man was wearing a white undershirt, wrinkled dress pants, and was unshaven. That didn't bother Leah by itself, except that any ordinary man wouldn't have the gall to amble through the casino with no shirt on. He was certainly no tourist.

The woman was the one who captured Leah's attention. She was wearing what must have been a five-caret diamond ring, gold bracelets, and her hair looked freshly styled. She wore an evening dress which almost transcended into day, but not quite. It was not unusual to see women adorned in full evening dress in the middle of the day, after all, this was Vegas. There was no distinction between day and night here.

The player pulled out a wad of hundred dollar bills that would choke the proverbial horse. *Oh, damn! And so early in the morning, too.* The scenario was typical. He had probably been gambling all night and was trying to get even with one grand gesture. It was not an uncommon psychology with gamblers. Leah's heart was pounding and she wished she hadn't eaten breakfast. She dreaded this kind of player. They could get to you in a hurry, which meant that the casino manager would be called down and she would have 18 bosses standing in the pit, outside of the pit, and in the ceiling, watching her. God forbid, if she made a mistake...the wrong payoff, dropped a card, or worst of all, lost!

Her hands started to sweat. The player placed a one hundred dollar bill in each of two betting squares in front of him. The woman was obviously not playing, just sitting. This was an exception to the rule—she was with him. Besides, he was playing more than one hand, which entitled him, officially, to more than one seat.

Leah called out, "Money Plays," and waited until the pit boss came to her table. He nodded for her to go ahead. It was his job to keep track of how much the player bought-in for, and how much he won or lost.

Leah busted the first hand, paid off, and waited for him to place his second bet. He hesitated, looked her over cautiously—the cat appraising the mouse—and then started peeling off hundred dollar bills, three in every spot on the table. At seven spots, that was 21 hundred dollars! She saw the pit boss head for the podium. She knew that he was calling the shift boss. In seconds they were both standing, arms folded, one on either side of her. She knew too, that black chips had been ordered from the cage. If she lost the hand, she wouldn't be able to pay him off with what was in her rack.

She was hardly breathing as she dealt the first round of cards. She gave herself a king, face-up. She dealt the second round of cards, and with precision, checked her hole card for an ace. *Saints be praised!* She flipped over her hole card and with cool matter-of-fact control, said, "Blackjack."

The player hadn't yet checked all his hands. He sputtered, "Son of a bitch" as he glared at Leah. He turned over each hand and threw the cards face-up on the table. He sat there while Leah picked up the cards and shoved his money down the slot with the paddle.

She could tell he wasn't sure what to do next. She waited. The pit boss waited. The shift boss waited. The security guard waited—holding the tray of hundred-dollar chips. The standers-by waited.

Leah held her breath. She was going to be in trouble now if he played another hand because she would have to decide whether or not to shuffle. It could make a big difference. She didn't know whose favor the deck might be in. She was not a card-counter, and she didn't think he was either. Known card counters were 86'ed from all casinos in Vegas. There were pictures of them on file in the security office. If any of them were spotted, they were asked to leave and never return. Some card counters gained a certain edge over the house, but Vegas couldn't prosper unless the edge was always in its favor.

He stood up, picked up his still thick wad of bills and placed the whole lump on one square. Leah thought she would die, right then and there. She wasn't accustomed to dealing to this kind of money. Worse fear gripped her now. He was betting like a counter. To protect herself she should shuffle, but doing so now would be so obvious given the fact that she had sufficient cards left, and he was just as aware of this as she was—probably counting on it. The risk was, and it happened all the time, that he might pull back his bet and walk away. It was a judgement call which Leah didn't relish making.

She reached for the money to spread it out, lest he be over the limit.

"Don't touch it!" he bellowed.

Leah jumped back, visibly shaken. Suddenly she felt a hand on her arm; a soft voice spoke, "It's okay, deal." It was Murrey, the casino manager. He had a calming effect on her, and she felt a surge of new confidence.

She dealt. He turned his first card face up, king. Leah dealt herself a 4. She felt her heart sink. He turned his second card up with a triumphant snap, 10. He straightened up and stepped back from the table a ways to hike his trousers up. Leah thought she would faint. How could she beat 20? She turned her hole card over, 9. Nine and 4 equaled 13. She dealt herself another card, 8. "Twenty-one," she announced, managing not to show an ounce of emotion.

The man with that fleeting smirk of victory was gone

almost before she looked up, with the woman trailing behind him.

Leah picked up the wad of bills and started spreading them across the table. The pit boss needed the count and the camera in the ceiling was recording it, as well. Two uniformed security guards were shielding the outside of the table now. Leah counted six thousand dollars which had been riding on that one hand. All were satisfied now.

Murrey patted Leah on the shoulder. "Good work."

"Nice going," said the shift boss, smiling.

Thumbs up sign from the pit boss. It felt good to be the fair-haired child but, Leah knew only too well what it would have been like had she lost.

A few minutes later Leah's relief showed up. "You didn't do very well for the dealers, I see," he said while observing the absence of gratuity beside the discard rack.

"No," Leah sighed, "but I did great for the House."

It was funny, having a choice, she would always rather win for the House. Only problem with that was, losers didn't tip. Maybe sometimes, as a bribe. A dealer could try to change the run of the cards by using a different shuffle, but there were never any guarantees. Luck, that's what it all boiled down to, in Leah's opinion.

The day progressed without further incident. At one point in time, Leah thought she saw Jim leaning against a pillar in the Keno Lounge, but when she looked closer...there was no one at all.

Jenny met Leah as she left the pit for the last time of the day.

"Phew! I'm glad this day is over," Jenny sighed. "If you'll get the toke boxes from the "21" pit, I'll pick them up from roulette and the crap pit."

"Okay, I'll meet you in the dealers' lounge," Leah said. She swung her purse strap over her shoulder to free her hands and collected the heavy metal boxes.

Leah and Jenny spent the next hour in the dealers' lounge counting the tokes and placing them in money racks to be taken to the cage and converted into green money. They worked out the mathematics and determined how many of what denomination bills would be needed to stuff the envelopes and sent a list of them to the cage.

"Jenny, do you think there's any truth to the rumor about someone in the cage keeping records of our tokes?"

"Can you think of anyone more qualified for the job? I told you before, keep a record of your tokes." Jenny pulled a small black book from her purse and made an entry. "This is my copy," she said with a wry smile. "The IRS copy is home on my dresser, in plain view."

The numerous deep lounge chairs in the room were all filled. The television hummed in a monotone and the dealers were starting to amble up the stairs from the bar to see if the tokes were ready.

Leah and Jenny stuffed the small brown envelopes as quickly as they could. A line was already forming and Jenny started passing them out.

Leah was glad that poker and baccarat stood alone and were not included in their split. It would have taken another hour to complete the tedious job, had they all been together. Actually, it wasn't much fun counting tokes. It spoiled the suspense of opening that gratuitous brown envelope. Their turn only came around once every three months, so it wasn't that bad. But when it did, it meant getting to work early and staying late. Sometimes very late, if they had trouble getting the count to come out even. The casino took a strictly hands-off view of the matter. They didn't want to know how much tokes were. It was the responsibility of each dealer to report and pay taxes on tokes.

Jenny stood up and stretched. "Is that it? Anyone else want their tokes?" There was silence. "Okay, Leah, let's get out of here."

They walked down the narrow stairway and exited through the swinging door that led directly into the restaurant.

"Why are we going this way?" Leah asked.

"I'm meeting someone. Just wanted to give you a peek." Jenny had that familiar twinkle of mischief in her green eyes.

"Another new boyfriend?"

"If at first you don't succeed..."

"Yeah, yeah, I know. Where does this one deal?" Leah didn't even try to hide her disapproval.

"The Stardust. Baccarat."

"Is he at least single?" Leah asked skeptically.

"To hear him tell it." Jenny laughed.

"I really have to give you credit. You do keep, keeping on." Leah smiled benevolently.

"There he is! Around that post!"

"The dark-haired one with the red shirt and gold chains?"

"That's him. What do you think?"

"He's a real knock-out, but it looks to me like you'd better go protect your interest before that keno runner latches onto him." Leah gestured toward the young girl displaying her wares in obvious seduction.

"Ah, it's a dog-eat-dog world." Jenny snickered as she strode confidently across the room to claim her conquest.

Saturday had finally come. Leah decided to take the twins to Circus Circus to play the games and watch the pretty girls in their sparkling costumes on the flying trapeze. They loved to try and catch the balloons the performers threw down into the crowd. Circus Circus was the only casino in Vegas that *welcomed* families with children. They took great strides, however, to keep them out of the gaming areas—in keeping with the law. There was a mezzanine arcade where they could spend as much money as they could pry out of their parents. It had the full flavor and variety of a carnival midway, including refreshment stands.

As they sat on a low railing watching the performing girls in the air, Leah noticed Carrie's attention was elsewhere. She was watching a man who had a little girl, about her size, heaved up on his shoulders, and another sibling holding onto his leg. Carrie had such a sad look in her eyes. Leah felt her heart wrenched from her chest. She had heard it before and now she heard it again, in her mind's eye, as tears fought to surface. *Mommy, why can't we have a daddy like everyone else?*

They were only two when their father died. They seemed to have no memory of him at all. Leah wondered if it wasn't some kind of survival mechanism in children that protected them from painful memories. It was the same with Damon, her second husband. As far as the children were concerned, he never existed. It was as if they never had a father. In Damon's case, she understood the memory block. But Bill was a loving, generous father, a memory that she fell back on with yearning reminiscence, even though she knew full well the inevitability of remembering only the good times.

They spent the entire day together, mother and children. Leah cherished these times and it served to reinforce her resolve to make up for any deficiency the lack of a father might create.

Saturday was behind them and Sunday announced its arrival with a flourish of sunbeams. It was a spring day so warm it might easily have been the middle of June. Leah invited Jenny and her children over for the day and they swam in the heated pool and shared a picnic lunch. They were not alone, for everyone else seemed to have the same idea. The pool area was soon colorful with white bodies and bright swim suits. Nearly all of the apartment complexes, and houses for that matter, had swimming pools. The summers in Vegas had temperatures that soared to as high as 115 degrees. Anyone with children would say that *no pool*, automatically meant a summer of pure agony.

Jenny's girls were six and seven years old, and in spite of the age difference, were Carries and Sherry's best friends.

Jenny and Leah spent a great deal of their off-time together. They were among the few lucky ones who had weekends off. To many, it didn't matter, because Vegas was a 24-hour town. The grocery stores never closed. The nursery schools were open 24 hours. Day ran into night. There were no windows or clocks in the casinos; time stood still. It was very carefully planned to be that way.

Leah watched the lapping ripples slap against the blue tiled sides of the pool as one diver after another shot off the springboard. She lifted her head to gaze tentatively at Jenny.

"Jenny...sometimes I feel like such a failure, and worse than that, I feel so guilty."

"Ah, yes, the 'no father' syndrome." Jenny smiled at Leah's shocked expression. "I've been watching you watch your girls. It's written all over your face. Hon, I know the feeling. I've been there. When you've been divorced as long as I have, you tend to get guilt under better control. But then, I guess I have a different outlook on life than you do." Jenny turned over and untied her bikini top, letting the sun soak into the lighter line across her back. "Leah, why don't you loosen up? Being a hermit just isn't healthy. Guys are forever trying to get me to fix them up with you. Why don't you try it sometime? If for no other reason than to go out and have a good time."

"A crap dealer? A blackjack dealer? That's all I need—someone who will blow all his money at the tables and then take mine, too. No thanks."

"Leah, they're not all like that. Look at you, you don't gamble. Besides, most of them have college degrees. They're not dummies; they're here on a lark, sowing a few wild oats, making some good money before they continue with their careers and their lives."

"I know that," Leah mused, "but look at the ones that never leave. The money is too easy. They get caught up in it. It gets in their blood." Leah's expression turned pensive. "I wonder if it's not happening to me, too; I love to win. On the table I'm a winner. No matter what's happening in my personal life, I'm in control, complete control of my game, and I know I can beat the best of them."

"Sure, if they sit there long enough." Jenny laughed.

"Well, how many of them walk away a winner, oh wise one?"

"You have me there. Greed is alive and well in Glitter Gulch."

Jenny knew about the *Rose-Man*, but since there hadn't been anything all week, figured Leah had blown another golden opportunity. She never gave any of them a fighting chance. Jenny thought how sad it was that Leah chose to be alone. People came from all over the world to Las Vegas because it was a place where they were sure to have a good time. It was a town of excitement and unlimited entertainment. Yet Leah didn't seem to see it in that light. She wasn't affected by her environment as so many others were. She definitely took a more serious view of life. Jenny couldn't really discount her for it, in fact, on reflection, perhaps it was why they were such good friends. It made for a good balance between them.

Jenny had her own short-comings, of this she was quite aware. She had been shocked and dismayed when she walked in on her husband and caught him in the act with another man. Far from homophobic, Jenny had no problem with alternative lifestyles. But in the aftermath came the realization that she had been used to closet his true self. Oh, the lengths he had gone to present a conventional facade. Her anger only grew with time. The healing process oft referred to hadn't reared its head in her direction. But in spite of the hurt and scars, Jenny had an inborn spirit of fun. She loved to laugh. She cherished a good time. And if some of these natural character traits magnified themselves for other reasons these days, it served, nevertheless, to make her a much-liked person. In the last six years of single life, Jenny rarely thought of her dreadful past, but subconsciously, she was aware that her, sometimes outrageous, behavior was a response to the anger it triggered.

Leah stood up and stretched. The sun was past its zenith, nearing the hottest part of the day. "Let's get wet, I'm about to cook."

They dove in, in unison, and swam the length of the pool. The children were playing on their plastic rafts, diving off of them and playing water games. They all knew how to swim expertly, it was a prerequisite to growing up in Vegas.

Leah heaved herself up and over the edge of the pool with practiced ease. Her short-cropped hair was plastered to her head like molten gold, and her angular face took on qualities of celestial radiance. Leah pushed the turmoil and anxiety seething within her, deep inside. She lay supine on the edge of the pool wall, oblivious to the many envious eyes devouring her. Soon, she would have to take the twins out of the sun. But for now, she just wanted to be suspended in time—not to think, nor plan, nor regret...just float in oblivion.

Monday morning Leah and Jenny met early in the casino restaurant to have breakfast. It had become a ritual. There was a special section for dealers only, and they had their own waitress. Dealers were highly respected and even envied by the general citizenry of the casino; in terms of hierarchy, next in line under the casino management itself. The keno runners, the change girls, the security guards, the floor sweepers, the cashiers, the cocktail waitresses—it was one of the small rewards dealers enjoyed.

Jenny arrived before Leah that morning, coming in the side door and passing by the large, horseshoe-shaped pit on her way to the restaurant. There, on the middle podium, was a huge bouquet of red roses. It was not rare for flowers to be delivered to the pit for dealers, but then again, it was not everyday fare either. A bouquet of roses that size was extremely impressive. Jenny had a feeling about these. She asked the pit boss who they were for, and it was as she suspected, Leah Aston. She wondered now what she could do, or say, to encourage Leah to be more receptive should her "Jim" reappear, and surely this was a sign that he would.

"Jenny, you're so quiet. Something on your mind?" Leah asked.

"Oh...no...not really." She could have kicked herself. Why couldn't she be more imaginative? She normally just told it the way it was, but this was a delicate subject to broach with Leah. She might cause a reverse effect if she pushed. Besides, this guy just might be a jerk anyway, she thought. Her own experiences with tourists had not been good. The last one she went out with arrived at her door with his suitcase. He assumed that he would go to the airport the next morning directly from her house. He found out differently—in a hurry!

Leah pushed the remains of her hastily-eaten breakfast aside. "Well then, come on Kiddo, let's go kill 'em," Leah quipped.

Leah took her position at Table 5 as the pit boss spread a new deck of cards on her table.

"Looks like it's getting serious," he said, with a sly grin.

"What's getting serious?" Leah inquired, with only half interest.

He nodded toward the roses.

Leah gasped, "Are...are those for me?"

"Don't look so shocked," he chortled, "lots of men like fat, ugly girls like you." He continued down the pit chuckling at his own joke all the way.

Damn! Why didn't he tell me before I went on the game? Now it will be 45 minutes before I can check the card...if there is a card. She wondered if it was another anonymous offering.

CHAPTER TWO

Leah clapped away from her table and approached the podium where the gigantic bouquet of vivid roses sprawled in grand splendor. She pulled the card from its holder and headed for the snack-bar.

As she sat drinking coffee, she read, *As intense as the rose is red, is the desire in my heart to touch your hand, Jim.*

Jenny plopped onto the stool next to her. "Love letters?"

Leah held out the card.

Jenny clasped both hands to her bosom and squealed, "My God, how romantic. I can't stand it!"

"Yes, too romantic. It sounds like something he copied out of a book."

Jenny sighed. "I give up. There's no hope for you. You're going to die a lonely old maid, and your children..." Jenny stopped. She had crossed the line. "I'm sorry, Leah. Open mouth, insert foot, that's me."

She looked so genuinely unhappy, Leah couldn't help smiling. "That's okay, forget it. You're probably right. If I wait much longer no one would have me on a bet."

"Now you're talking!" Jenny beamed.

Leah pondered the words Jenny spoke, as she walked the well-worn path back to the "21" pit. Was she letting life pass her by? Was she cheating her children out of a father? Did she really want her freedom as badly as she contended?

Leah didn't want to answer these questions. She was confused and unsure. She hadn't been with a man for so long, the idea frightened her. On the surface, Jim seemed to be controlled, sensitive, almost capable of vulnerability. But it was what lay behind the smoldering blue eyes that frightened Leah—and attracted her, too.

By the end of the day she had decided it didn't matter. Jim had not shown up. All that worry and soul searching for nothing. She exited the pit for the last time of the day, her mind filled with a multitude of tumultuous events that went by the name of work.

Never a dull moment, she thought, as she ran smack into a pale blue linen suit. Her face was nearly buried in his chest. Then she felt two strong arms help her regain her footing.

"Oh, I'm so sorry," she sputtered. "I'm...I'm..." She looked up into Jim's tanned face. Mirth twinkled in his eyes. "I'm so embarrassed. I almost knocked you down." A swell of crimson highlighted her face.

"Not to worry," he said. "It would take more than..." he gave her an appraising look, "115 pounds to do me in."

"The roses are beautiful," she recovered.

"For a beautiful lady. Would you do me the honor of having a drink with me at the bar? Please," he added.

His piercing eyes captivated her. "Yes, I could use one."

Jim took her by the arm and guided her through the crowded casino, past the "21" pit and through a maze of slot machines, until finally the crowd thinned, only to build frantically again as they approached the busy bar. People were standing three deep. Half of them were off-duty dealers, a shift change situation that was short-lived.

Jim spotted someone leaving and lunged for the open seat, staring down a Local who dared to challenge him.

Leah was amazed to see the gentle blue eyes turn fierce, and with a smile, visualized jungle animals stalking one another over territorial rights.

Jim quickly reached for her arm, not taking his hand off of the heavily padded back of the bar stool, and pushed her gently toward it.

The noise level rose. Two harried bartenders strove to fulfill everyone's needs with quick deft hands.

Jim stood close beside her, simulating a protective barrier, keeping the wild animals at bay. He lifted his hand into the air and immediately caught a bartender's attention.

"What would you like to drink, Leah?" Jim asked.

"A Vodka Gimlet, please," she answered, as she watched Jim's hand come down and briefly meet with that of the bartenders. A patch of green passed hands. Suddenly the bartender acted as if he had but two customers. Nothing in Vegas was more powerful than the almighty dollar.

Jim ordered a Scotch on the rocks and turned his attention exclusively to Leah. "This is a wild world we live in. Wild..." he repeated slowly, the word obviously taking on a new meaning to him as his sultry blue eyes leveled on hers.

Leah felt uncomfortable beneath his intense scrutiny.

The solicitous bartender broke the spell, informing

them that he had two seats reserved for them at the end of the bar.

Jim gave him a nod and helped Leah down from the tall bar stool. Taking her arm again, he made a path clear, and they eased comfortably into the new location. Leah sat protected, with the wall on one side, and Jim on the other. It was quieter at the end of the bar. Their drinks were placed before them.

Leah withdrew a cigarette and Jim swiftly reached for a match from the bar. The flame danced with the tremor of his hand.

"Leah, I've been watching you for some time." He appraised her openly. "You're sheer poetry in motion. You control your game with such ease. I've watched you shut a player off with your eyes. I've seen those same intense blue eyes give another, hope. You're truly incredible. I've never seen such communication without words."

"Why have you been watching me, Jim?" Leah asked softly.

He lowered his eyes briefly, then raised them to meet hers. An intensely haunting gaze threatened to unnerve her.

"You're extraordinarily beautiful," he almost whispered. His words fell like a cloak of fine silk. "You've cast a spell on me...I keep seeing your face, and I feel drawn to you as if I've lost control of my own actions." He spoke in low intimate tones and Leah leaned closer to hear. His index finger went tentatively to her chin and slowly traced the line of her jaw. "I'm glad you agreed to see me."

Leah felt a shiver run down her spine. She couldn't remember the last time she heard words of endearment. And as she searched her memory she knew well that they all paled in comparison. She remained silent, compelling him to bare even more of his soul to her.

"I've asked around about you. I know you don't date." He weighed his words carefully. Now, he waited for a response, playing the same game of silence that she did.

"I won't bore you with my life story. Overall, I'd say you know a great deal more about me than I do you." Leah was nearly trembling and her breath was coming up short in her lungs. Something about the prolonged closeness to him was having a strange effect on her. She had the urge to flee.

Jim swiveled on the bar stool to face her more directly. In doing so, his long legs bumped against hers, causing her chair to swing outward. His hand shot out and clamped over her knee, pulling her back to face him. His muscular legs flanked hers—without touching—yet Leah felt the intimacy of the position. His hand lingered on her knee long enough for her to feel the intense burning sensation it created.

Leah's cheeks burned hot.

"I'm sorry," Jim said lightly. "I have trouble fitting into small places. Are you comfortable now?"

"Y-Yes. I'm fine, thank you."

"I live in Reno," Jim proceeded to tell her. "I work for Harrah's as a shift boss. I've been finding myself in Vegas quite a lot lately—on business for the hotel." He surveyed his surroundings with an appreciative attitude. "I like the Golden Nugget. There's a warm, friendly atmosphere here. I usually stay on the strip, at the Grand. The atmosphere is so different there, cold, tense, and the dealers are nothing more than machines."

"They're under a lot of pressure," Leah said. "And too, they grow hardened. You know that. They've paid their dues in a downtown casino, and in the natural progression of things, moved on to a better job. Sometimes, better means tougher." A wistfulness filled her eyes. "I wish I were ready to move on to the strip. But, even if I were, I don't have strong enough juice."

"Ah, the magic word in Vegas."

"We're a clandestine society, all right." Leah laughed, shaking her head at the absurdity of the rules of her own community. Suddenly, her eyes turned serious, melancholy. "I'll never forget my first days in Vegas. I'm still embarrassed to think of my incredible naïveté."

"Tell me about it. I love stories of naïveté," he prodded, his slow grin becoming full blown.

Leah grinned self-consciously. "Well, when I moved here, the only thing I knew about Las Vegas was what I had heard from occasional customers who came into my mother's dress shop. I used to help her on weekends. Her clientele were affluent—well traveled. They talked about the fabulous rings dealers wore, about the lifestyle of the working class. But in all their conversation, I never truly grasped the magnitude of its splendor. I was so overwhelmed! I mean, I must have walked around for days with my mouth gaping open. Everything here is so different—so glamorous. I had to get a job right away. I racked my brain trying to figure out what exactly I could do. The only work that I had done prior to coming here was in retail, and that was in my mother's store. But I didn't come here to stay in a low-paying field. I knew that I had to get into a casino to make the big bucks that I had heard so much about. So, I decided to get a job as a cocktail waitress, since I had done a little of that in my college days. And, as my mother had taught me, I went straight to the top. I called the casino manager of Caesars Palace and inquired about a job. He said, 'What do you deal, honey?' I was confused by the question. I wondered why he immediately assumed that I was a dealer. I let it pass and answered confidently, 'Oh, I don't deal. I'm a cocktail waitress.' He had the decency not to laugh in my face and politely directed me to the union. Oh, the humiliation I felt, once I'd learned the rules."

Sheer amusement flickered in Jim's eyes. "So then what did you do?"

"The first thing I did was ask questions. When I found out how the union's white-card, pink-card system worked, I decided I had chosen the wrong path. I couldn't afford to pay my dues in that field. Starting out in a dive was too unpalatable to me. Besides, I had a family to support. That's why I came to Vegas. I had heard that it was the one place a single mother could comfortably support her children."

"Go on," he prompted.

Leah blushed. "I promised that I wasn't going to tell you my life story. And look at me."

"You can't stop now. So then, is that when you decided to be a dealer?"

"No, it wasn't. But I'm not going to bore you another minute with my mundane tales." Leah looked at her watch, suddenly aware of the time. "I really have to go. My girls are waiting."

"How old are your girls?" Jim ignored her inclination to leave.

"They're five. Twins."

"Are they as beautiful as you?" His eyes bore down on her.

"They're more beautiful than I could ever hope to be."

"I wish I could meet them." A strange kind of tender

sadness crept into his voice. "I wish too, that you would have dinner with me tonight. And while I'm wishing..." He reached casually for her slender hand and brought it gently to his lips. He kissed her fingertips and, gently releasing the pressure, directed them across the length of his full lower lip.

An electric shock shot through Leah with such intensity that she paled. She eased out of her chair with tempered dignity, slowly retrieving her hand.

Jim's gulf-stream blue eyes blazed with a fiery passion barely contained. "Another time," his throaty voice promised.

"Maybe," Leah said, hoping that the fear in her heart didn't transmit into her voice, as she quickly walked away.

"Mommy! Mommy! You're so late. Where were you?" Sherry wailed.

"Where were you?" Carrie echoed.

Leah hugged them both. "Mommies need time for themselves sometimes, too, you know." No, they didn't know, she thought. They were too young to understand. Leah wondered if it was worth the guilt. Their sad little faces made her feel like a deserter.

Thoughts of Jim lingered in Leah's mind. She liked him, but something inside her screamed, *Watch out! Be careful! He wants to own you, like all the rest. He'll want a receipt, 'paid in full, property of Jim...'* Damn, she thought—she still didn't know his last name.

The week went by slowly and Leah found herself looking for Jim, but not finding him. Throngs of people crowded the casino every day. With each tall blond man that turned out not to be Jim, a pain of regret pierced Leah's heart.

Then, just when she least expected it, Leah felt a firm hand gently grip her arm from behind. A deep voice simultaneously uttered her name.

Leah brusquely pulled away from the too familiar touch and, with blazing eyes, she confronted the perpetrator.

Jim's lips curled in amused delight. "You're not the trusting sort, are you?"

"Jim!" she sputtered in complete surprise. The anger in her eyes swiftly turned to pleasure. "I was just on my way for coffee."

"How about some company?"

Leah flashed him her most charming smile and gestured toward the snack-bar.

They found, to their dismay, that all of the seats were filled. Jim quickly took control of the situation and ordered coffee in to-go cups. He directed Leah to two empty, short, backless stools in front of some slot machines nearby.

They sat down, setting their cups on the shelf between two machines.

"Our time here is limited." Leah grinned, nodding to the paper cups hanging loosely over the levers of the two slot machines.

Jim's eyes went momentarily blank. He quickly offered, "I know you don't have a very long break. I won't take up much of your time. I made reservations at the Jockey Club for dinner tonight. If you don't go with me I'll have to eat alone."

Leah was enchanted by his arrogance and impressed with his stark admission that without her he would dine alone, if indeed that were the truth. "Your persistence is overwhelming." Leah studied his face, finding only sincerity there. "I wouldn't want to be responsible for you dining alone at the illustrious Jockey Club."

"Good," he beamed, "I'll pick you up at eight. What is your..."

"N-No," Leah interrupted, "I'll meet you there."

Jim's eyebrows furrowed in puzzlement. "Okay...eight o'clock then?"

Before Leah could answer, two heavy-set graying women came stalking directly up to them, with blood in their eyes.

Leah jumped up quickly, explaining, "We were just borrowing these seats." When the women continued glaring without a response, Leah again tried to assure them. "We didn't play your machines, really." She turned toward Jim, who was slowly easing up from the stool, a baffled look on his face. Leah reached for his hand and pulled him away with her.

"Jim, I have to run. I'll be late. I'll meet you at the Jockey Club tonight at eight o'clock."

"Good, I'll see you there." His hand reluctantly dropped away from hers.

Leah ran double-time back to the pit. Something wasn't quite right. Jim didn't seem to have any idea what the encounter with the two women was all about. Everyone in the casino business knew that devout slot machine players frequently took over a machine for the entire day, and when nature called, or they took out time to eat, they reserved the machines by turning a paper cup over the handle. Reno was no different from Vegas in that respect. There was no doubt in Leah's mind that Jim was not aware of this phenomenon. And that being true, he couldn't possibly be a shift boss in a casino. That voice was in her head again. The one her mother had always told her to pay heed to when she felt it there. But it was only intuition, after all. Sometimes it was right and sometimes...well, how could one make decisions based on such an ambiguous thing.

Upon her return, Leah systematically deprived every player of their chips and now found herself standing at an empty game. Her mind was in a whirl with this new suspicion, and the anxiety of keeping Jim away from her home. She couldn't let him find out about Jason—her well kept secret.

Jason had been one of Damon's closest friends. He spent a great deal of time with them when they were first married. As the marriage got stormier, Jason stayed away more and more. It was six months ago when they accidentally ran into each other. Jason had lost all his money on one of Damon's, sure-thing, oil investments in Oklahoma, and had been forced into taking a job as a crap dealer at the Horseshoe Casino. He told Leah about his search for an inexpensive apartment and she told him about putting the girls into one bedroom and converting the third bedroom into a housekeeper's room. She had been interviewing for weeks for a live-in who would care for the twins and do light housekeeping. The applicants had been a disappointing array of misfits. Most of them looked like old show girls well past their prime. The nursery was charging an exorbitant amount and it was all she could do to keep her head above water.

As it turned out, she and Jason struck a deal and neither one of them had ever been sorry. The twins loved him. Jason would write their names with mustard on ham sandwiches, and make chocolate pudding for them, and run to the pool and play. He was the perfect playmate and friend. To Leah, he was the brother she never had.

To Jason, Leah suspected, she was the mother he always wanted. There was just one flaw in the plan. It was hard for some people to believe this was a platonic relationship. Leah told her landlord that he was her brother. That worked out well enough and the neighbors seemed to accept it. The children called him Uncle Jason, which helped. Jason had arranged to work straight graveyard shifts so he and Leah seldom were awake, or at home, at the same time—only in passing. They well might have been strangers passing in the night but for the history they shared.

Jason had agreed not to have any girls sleep over, for the children's sake, but occasionally would have someone over for a drink, or take the twins along on an afternoon date. Jason was a good-looking man and exactly the same age as Leah. He was also the same height—five-foot-six. He was constantly looking for short girls. He wouldn't date anyone as tall or taller than he was, which narrowed the field considerably.

The big advantage of having Jason around went deeper than the obvious. His residency gave Leah a sense of security. She was no longer a woman living alone, with all of the vulnerability attached. At the same time, he provided the twins with a father figure—of sorts. Jason didn't discipline them, however, like a father would. Reflecting on their relationship, Leah decided that Jason never really saw anything that they did as wrong, or bad—if anything, only amusing. No wonder they loved him so much. To the twins, Jason was their friend. Leah loved him, too, as a friend, a brother, a nursemaid, and a protector. Given the small amount of time Jason was really there, she realized that the security she felt because of his presence was mostly psychological. But it made her feel more secure and that was the overriding factor.

Leah hurried home after her shift. She had never been to the Jockey Club, but had heard of it. It was reputed to be one of the most elegant private dinner clubs in town.

Leah had pangs of guilt as she hugged the twins. She had already called Jason and he was willing to watch the girls. It was his night off and he had planned to stay in with a book, something new on trivia that he had recently obtained. *Bambi* was playing at the Red Rock Cinema and Jason immediately made plans to take the girls. Leah suspected that he was really the one who wanted to see *Bambi,* and was probably delighted to have the twins pave the way for him.

Leah ran a tub full of hot water, added lots of bath crystals, and collapsed into the endless foam. Jason had already left with the girls and she was alone with her thoughts. The hot water was steaming all around her and she felt her muscles begin to relax. "Jim," she sounded his name with her lips. She thought of his handsome, tanned face, his blond hair that seemed to get lighter every time she saw him, and his tall lithe body. She remembered the sensation she felt when her body was so close to his. A shiver ran through her from head to toe. She closed her eyes, feeling again the softness of his lips on her fingertips. She could see his face as vividly as if he were right beside her—his intense gaze holding her.

What had happened that she agreed so readily to see him? She had surprised herself. Had she already made an unconscious decision to do just that? A new fear struck Leah's heart as she considered her position logically. It had been over a year since she had been with a man. Until now, it hadn't been a problem. But Jim, oh Jim, she thought with a panic, how he touched her senses. There was such a powerfully magnetic force between them that it made Leah weak just to think about it. He could play her heightened sensitivity like a violin if he chose to.

She had to protect herself against herself.

Then, suddenly, she remembered the two women and the slot machines. Could she have read his reactions wrongly? And if he weren't a shift boss from Harrah's, then who was he? What was he? What could his purpose for pursuing her be? That answer could be simple enough. The outside world had a misconception of Vegas in general—the people who worked there, in particular. Many gamblers coming to Vegas had the idea that dealers were part of the comps...a complimentary dinner, a complimentary show ticket, a complimentary dealer.

No...if that was the reason, Jim would have tried the straight-forward approach. Why would there be any need for charades?

It didn't make sense. Leah decided that she simply misread him. But still, she felt apprehensive, almost foreboding.

Reluctantly, she drew herself from the tub, chose a thick, pink towel from the bar, and held herself tightly in it. She was having serious second thoughts. She considered putting her nightgown on and curling up in front of the TV for a quiet evening at home.

No, you fool, the other side of her fought for survival. *Go out! Have fun!*

Leah was becoming fatigued from her own inner struggle. She threw the towel to the floor and, with great resolve, chose her finest white evening gown. The back plunged to the waist and the front draped loosely from the neck to a cinched waist. The skirt fell gracefully over her narrow hips to the floor. She said a silent thank you to her mother, who occasionally sent her a stunning designer original. She had made a plea for black slacks and white blouses, but was promptly ignored. She slipped into gold high-heeled sandals and was soon on her way.

Leah pulled up in front of the Jockey Club where a valet quickly opened her car door and helped her out. She felt like Cinderella, whose Fairy Godmother had forgotten to turn her pumpkin into a regal carriage. She accepted a claim ticket for the *Gray Bear* and entered through the imposing ornate doors.

With long strides, Jim approached her. "Leah, you look ravishing! I'm so glad you came. I was afraid you wouldn't."

"Thank you, I-I'm glad I came, too," she said softly.

"I have a table waiting for us. Shall we?" He extended his arm to her.

"By all means." She took his arm as they entered the dimly lit lounge. They were shown to a settee with a low lacquered table in front of it. A small band played soft music and several couples danced on the large parquet dance floor. Everywhere she looked, red velvets with gold ornate decor abounded.

"What would you like to drink?" he asked.

"White wine will be fine." She didn't want to drink anything too strong. She wanted to be sure to keep her wits about her.

"They seem to be extra busy here tonight. I'll get them at the bar. Be right back," he said over his shoulder. "Don't go away."

Leah settled back into the overstuffed velvet settee. The room had a warm glow about it, almost a melancholy feel. She began to relax.

Jim returned with a glass of wine in each hand. "A

modest vintage," he said apologetically. His expression of irritation swiftly changed to humor. "To Don Quixote." He raised his glass.

"Don Quixote?" Leah laughed.

"Don Quixote," he said. "Anyone who pursues a dream the way he did deserves my undying respect."

"Even if it was only windmills," she agreed, raising her glass to his.

"I'm afraid I'm a hopeless romantic," he confessed, staring into the glass of wine. "Did the Civil War ever strike you as a romantic era?"

"I'm afraid not. Was it?" she asked.

"It's been my life's work. I think that probably some of the world's greatest love stories might have been written of the era."

"You don't sound like any casino boss I've ever known." She looked at him with aroused suspicion.

"I'm probably the exception," he confided.

In spite of Jim's obvious attempts to be entertaining, he appeared to Leah to be somewhat on edge. Maybe just trying too hard, she thought.

The maître d' appeared and informed them that their table was ready. They were escorted to the dining room and shown to a large round table with deep upholstered chairs.

The table was set with sparkling platinum-trimmed china. A whole artichoke had already been served at each of their places. As they were seated, a waiter brought a long-stemmed red rose and laid it across Leah's lap. Moments later another waiter appeared with a bud vase half full of water for her to put it in. Behind him came the waiter delivering their drinks from the lounge. Leah was impressed with all the attentive service.

All through dinner they were catered to like royalty.

The waiters delivering food wore white gloves. The Caesar salad was ceremoniously prepared for them at the table and as it was served yet another waiter presented them with chilled salad forks from a silver tray. They ate lobster and Jim ordered a bottle of white wine—apparently one more suitable to his refined taste buds than the bar wine had been. Dinner was climaxed with a flaming Cherries Jubilee.

"How about an after dinner drink in the lounge?" he asked.

She nodded assent. "If I can make it that far. I'll have to jog every day next week to make up for this."

"I have a better idea. How about going dancing every night next week instead?"

"Sure, let's do. Shall I pick you up at the airport every evening or will you just walk over from Reno?"

"You really are a terrible realist, aren't you?" he chided.

They strolled back to the cocktail lounge where the evening had begun. The dance floor was full now. The lighting was soft and there was the smell of expensive perfume in the air. Jim took Leah's hand and guided her onto the dance floor. His hand went around her waist and he pulled her close to him. A shock of excitement so shook Leah that she thought she would swoon. This man is dangerous, she thought, and the way he makes me feel is dangerous.

"I've waited so long for this moment." Jim's voice was a melody. "Having you in my arms is more wonderful than I imagined." He held her even closer and she felt the tension in his body grow stronger.

"I knew from the first time I saw you that you would be my lady." His voice took on a sensuous quality. He touched her face tenderly and slowly let his fingertips slide down her neck and over her shoulder as if caressing a fine piece of art.

"Jim, I don't know what to say," she said softly.

"Don't say anything, my darling. Don't say anything." His hand moved up from her waist, pressing against bare flesh provided by her backless dress.

They continued dancing silently to the enchanting music. Finally it came to a stop. Jim escorted her back to their table.

She took her place on the settee and Jim eased in close to her. Leah reached for her drink but the trembling of her hand caused her to pull it back. She blushed deeply under Jim's intense gaze. She felt as if her emotions were transparent for all to see.

Jim's eyes turned gentle as he reached for her hand. "It's not just me, is it?" he said softly. "You feel it, too."

Leah's thick lashes lowered, casting a shadow over her tormented expression.

"I have a problem being with you, Leah."

Her eyes shot open. What was he saying? That this beautiful exhilaration would end before it began?

Her expression caused him to smile widely. "My darling, Leah, how you bewitch me. I haven't even tasted the sweet nectar of your lips." He studied her silently for a moment. "Leah...I want to be with you." His grip on her hand grew tense as he tried to pull her closer to him.

"Jim, no," she whispered, in a faltering voice. "We're in a public place."

"Then let's go somewhere else," he said hoarsely.

How dare he suggest...did he think she was that easy! Leah pulled away from him, straightening herself erect as a noble goddess. "I've had a lovely evening." She deliberately evaded his eyes. "I have to go now." She lifted her chin with regained decorum.

"Let me see you home then," he offered quickly, reaching in his pocket and pulling out a money-clip thick with bills, his eyes searching frantically for the waitress to bring a check.

"I drove my own car, thank you." She moved smoothly out from behind the table and sent him a fleeting smile as she walked away.

Jim slumped back against the red velvet as he watched Leah disappear through the door. His right hand clenched into a fist. *Damn! Damn! Damn! This isn't going the way I planned it at all.* He leaned forward and pulled a cigarette out of Leah's forgotten pack and lit it. He had quit years ago. Drawing deeply, he let his head fall back, and then let it ease forward to fall into his hands, elbows resting on the cold lacquered table.

"Your check, sir," a waitress chirped.

"Forget it," he growled. "Bring me a double Scotch on the rocks."

Alone in the tranquility of sea-blue and ivory that constituted the make up of Leah's bedroom, she admonished herself for being so enraptured with Jim. The short-lived indignation was just an excuse to escape. She knew it and wondered if he had figured it out, too. Lust, she thought—not denying the passion she felt for him. Her mind drifted, remembering the strength of his arms...the feel of his body as they danced, the touch of his hand on her face, the gentle, gentle touch of his hand on her neck. She wanted him, she allowed herself to admit. Oh, did she want him. She wanted to throw all care to the wind and let her body and soul be enveloped in the warmth and inviting aroma of his total being. A shiver racked her body. She tried to think of other things but his forceful presence wouldn't be shut out. She found herself wondering what his lips would taste like, how his touch would feel on her body.

She immediately reprimanded herself. The unknown

always created its own excitement. She needed to remember that. Still, the depth of feeling she experienced with Jim was so entirely new to her. Could it be that her feelings for him were becoming something more than physical?

Leah was awakened the next morning by the sound of the telephone ringing. "Hello," she mumbled into the phone.

"Good morning, Sunshine."

"Jim? My God, the sun isn't even up yet."

"Don't tell me, you're not a morning person. And here I had a great day planned. Thought I'd take the twins on an outing. You're invited, too."

"What kind of an outing? Wait a minute, I'm not even awake yet."

"Okay, I'll call you back in ten minutes." He hung up.

"Damn," she muttered, stumbling out of bed. He certainly didn't lack when it came to persistence. She started a pot of coffee, all the while weighing the risks of going with him. She wondered how wise it was to involve the children with this man. On the other hand, maybe it would be good for them. She seldom took them to do anything really interesting or different, and to have a man in the lead, a father figure...well, maybe it would be good.

The telephone rang and Leah looked at the clock. Ten minutes almost to the second. Was he watching his clock, too?

"Hi! Awake now?"

"I'm just pouring a cup of coffee. Umm, now, ask me anything." She sipped the steaming coffee and lit a cigarette.

"Wish I were there having coffee with you. I'll bet

you're barefoot and wearing a blue robe," he said wistfully.

"Jim, you're crazy! Absolutely crazy. And you're wrong. I'm wearing a white robe." She laughed. "You do let your imagination run away with you."

"It's all I have when you're not with me. How soon can you be ready?"

"What did you have in mind, Jim? I'm not sure..."

"Leah, I won't take no for an answer. I found a great place for lunch. There's a lake and ducks—the children will love it. Ten o'clock okay?"

"You drive a hard bargain." She hesitated. "Okay. Ten o'clock it is."

"I'll pick you up. What's your address?"

Leah hesitated perhaps too long, but finally gave him the address and apartment number. She calculated that Jason would soon be home, but he usually went straight to bed. She was taking a chance. It would be impossible to keep Jim away from her place if she continued to see him. He would learn about Jason soon enough, but not yet.

No time for the customary leisurely coffee and newspaper this morning, thought Leah as she hurriedly got the twins ready. She set the table and fed them a light breakfast. In the meantime, Jason came home and went directly to bed, with barely a hello. Leah took a quick shower and hurriedly donned a pale yellow sundress and matching flat sandals. She carefully applied makeup and touched up her hair with a brush. She was glad at times like these that she wore her hair short. It required very little maintenance. She stood back and appraised the results. Most of the dealers wore false eyelashes. Leah had chosen the individual lashes which had to be applied at a beauty salon. They were modest and natural looking, but lent a glamorous touch, too.

The doorbell rang and Leah ran to answer it. She thought that in the brightness of day the sparks between Jim and her would dim, but she was so wrong. The sight of him was awesome. He wore white trousers and a shirt the color of blue that hinted of clouds and lakes and skies blending into a softness that invited touching. His shoes, in contrast, were of a rough grain white leather. It occurred to Leah that she always took notice of his shoes and was never disappointed in the rightness of his selection or of the unexpected quality apparent in the styling.

It was a mutual appraisal and as their eyes met and held, Jim suddenly grabbed her, pressing his mouth down on hers. Leah was taken by surprise and, operating strictly on emotions, melted into his embrace.

Then, just as suddenly, he released her. Smiling broadly, Jim walked past her into the apartment. He turned back to where she still stood breathless and with those twinkling eyes, said, "I just had to get that out of my system."

The tension eased as their day progressed. If one took the time to investigate such things, there were to be found in the surrounding Vegas areas many interesting out of the way spots. Jim must have been one of those people who had such leisure time, for the quaint and charming log cabin restaurant adjacent to a wooden dock flanking a small lake sprinkled with colorful exotic ducks was such a place. The children were enchanted, not only with the exciting new sights but with Jim, too. He had a natural way with children, completely at ease and even appeared to strive to be the center of their attention. It wasn't hard. The twins were not accustomed to being around men, other than Jason. That in itself lent to novelty, but Jim was charismatic. Leah understood the fascination the girls held for him. He was able to communicate on their level and injected excitement into the simplest pleasures, like walking along the old wooden dock without touching the cracks. Or by choosing to feed just the right duck so that none were close enough to challenge it for the morsels. Such wonderfully simple pleasures and such carefree laughter were high points in this memorable day.

If Leah was impressed with the day's activities, the ride home was even more so. Jim displayed a new talent: Storytelling. The children were mesmerized with his vivid stories of animated forest creatures. Leah found herself as anxious as the children to hear what would happen next. But in a striking thought of reality, Leah had to ask herself why she was allowing this obvious bonding to happen. Of course she hadn't known it would turn out like this, but she should have considered it a possibility. The last thing she wanted was to give her children something wonderful just to take it away. She would have to be more careful in the future.

The girls had dozed off in the back seat and they rode now in silence.

"Leah, I have to go back tonight." He watched the road in front of him. "Will you save next weekend for me?"

"Let's wait and see, Jim. Today has been wonderful but I don't like to plan too far ahead." Leah felt panic stricken. She wasn't the most worldly person but she could recognize a rush when she saw one. The declaration of love, however thinly disguised, and the wooing of her children fell too neatly in line. But how did she feel about him? Oh, there were strong emotions there, but they needed sorting out. Is it possible he could be sincere? And why not "love at first sight?"

"May I call you again?" Jim had taken a step backward in his pursuit.

"Yes, Jim. I would like that."

Leah watched the cactus and Joshua trees rush by as they sped back to the sweltering city. Las Vegas rested in a valley surrounded by treeless mountains. What a pleasure it had been to be out of it for a day.

When Jim delivered the trio to their door, Leah didn't ask him in and he didn't anticipate it. Instead, he deposited a gentle kiss on her cheek. It was his intention to back off a little, put a rein on his emotions. But he was once again overpowered with the very essence of her. The clean fragrant aroma of her hair and skin assaulted his senses. As simple a gesture as a kiss on the cheek sent his animal instincts skyrocketing. He cupped her face in his hands and gazed inquiringly into her eyes. "Leah, why do you do this to me? All of my good intentions melt away when I touch you." His lips parted and his mouth lowered to take possession of hers.

Leah trembled as his hands traveled from her face, down her neck and around her shoulders.

His lips moved tenderly against hers, soft and gentle and intoxicating. A tormented moan escaped from somewhere deep within him as he abruptly pulled his mouth away from Leah's. She pressed her face against his chest, all breathless emotion. His hand pressed her head closer to him, as one would a child to console.

"I can't do this...I can't do this." His voice was thick with emotion.

She wasn't sure she heard him right.

He pushed her away from him and abruptly left.

Leah stood trembling in the doorway. *That was some strange good-bye.*

CHAPTER THREE

It was a Monday morning tainted with the wild desert gusts that caused sagebrush to dance across the highways. Leah dodged a number of them and then, to her dismay, caught one under her wheel. By the time she entered the casino, through those same swinging doors that she had every day for the last year, she was thoroughly irritated. She traveled the familiar route to the stairway that led to the dealer's lounge. She had the same feelings of anticipation, edged with fear, that had been present that first day.

But today felt different. Leah sensed an undercurrent that hadn't been there before. Dealers huddled in small cliques sharing hushed exchanges. An unrest permeated the air.

"Where the hell have you been?" Jenny's voice sounded from behind her.

Leah swung around, startled. "The same place I am every morning this time. On my way to work," she barked back.

"All hell has broken loose around here."

"What happened?" Leah whispered, a contagious fear gripping her.

"The blasted IRS had a plant in the crap pit, that's what happened! That tall, good-looking dealer that started about a month ago...what *was* his name? Anyway, they fired him yesterday."

"Smoky? Damn, who would have guessed? How did they find out he was an undercover agent?"

"Who knows? The point is, they did, and he's gone. I'll tell you, between the union organizers and the IRS informants, you don't know who to trust anymore."

"He was here a good month, long enough to get a clear picture of how much we're making in tokes. This will surely mean trouble for us."

"We have one hope. If this class action suit against the IRS goes to court before the end of the year we just might be okay."

"I don't know why it couldn't just stand on the lower court ruling. That judge said tips are gifts and not taxable. That decision fits my finances just fine. At least I don't have to struggle to put food on the table." Leah sighed.

"Don't I know it," Jenny exclaimed in exasperation. "Incidentally, there's another meeting with the attorneys tonight. They've rented a hall downtown. All of the dealers in town are supposed to be there, except the ones on duty, of course. You are going, aren't you?"

"Oh, God. Do I have to? All this cloak and dagger." Leah rolled her eyes.

"You'd better be there," Jenny warned. "This is important. Damn important! And be careful who you say what to these days. The IRS isn't going to take this lying down! It wouldn't surprise me if Smoky wasn't more than just the run of the mill *plant,* but an agent gathering information for this case. By the way...what were you up to this weekend? I tried all day Saturday to reach you."

"I spent some time with Jim, but he had to go back Saturday night."

"He must have a strange schedule at Harrah's. Do you notice how he's here sometimes during the week, and then sometimes on weekends? It seems like a peculiar schedule for a shift boss."

"Oh, Jenny, for Christ's sake, you're getting paranoid. You'll suspect me next."

"Well, maybe I am. What's his last name? Did you ever find out?"

"Henderson. He gave me his card. Does that satisfy you?"

"Henderson. Jim Henderson...well, at least he has a last name." There was something familiar about that name.

Leah went on to her game with a heavy heart. The specter of doubt had once again shadowed Jim's credibility. It was bad enough that she herself questioned his motives but for Jenny to voice suspicion, when it was she who encouraged this liaison in the first place...and to make matters worse, Leah was feeling defensive—wanting to defend Jim against her best friend. This wasn't going to be an easy day, Leah thought. And she was right, it wasn't.

Leah took Jenny's advice and went to the dealers meeting that night. It turned out to be just one more, of many, geared to keep the dealers all of one mind. They were adamantly instructed not to claim any tokes on their income tax returns. There was power in numbers, they were being led to believe.

Leah was glad when it was over and drove home tired and a little confused. She was not convinced that the dealers weren't all going to be in serious trouble over this stand. In the past, dealers had claimed a small percentage of their tokes. To blatantly ignore their existence altogether was quite another matter. The telephone was ringing as she opened the door. Jason must not have heard it, she thought.

"Hello?"

"Leah? I didn't wake you, did I?"

"Oh, Jim! No, in fact, I just walked in."

"Late date?"

"No. Not a late date," she said coolly. She didn't like being questioned. The one glorious thing about being single was the luxury of not having to answer to anyone.

There was an uncomfortable silence on the other end of the line. "I just had to hear your voice. I miss you."

Leah's irritation immediately vanished. "It's been a long hard day. I didn't mean to be testy."

"Is anything wrong?"

"No, just a dealers' meeting tonight that I wasn't crazy about attending." She kicked off her shoes and sank into the welcome softness of the sofa.

"What was the meeting about?" he asked cautiously.

"Oh, you know, that suit the dealers have going with the IRS. The attorneys were just in Reno, weren't they?"

"Seems like I heard something about it, but you know management tries to stay out of that sort of thing. What's your position on the issue?"

"That's a strange question. It's hardly one person's opinion that counts anymore. We've gone far beyond that. It's really more a matter of loyalty, I think. I wouldn't sabotage the efforts of the dealers as a whole even if I did disagree with what they were trying to do."

"Leah, it's an ill-advised thing you're pursuing. And you're wrong about one person's opinion. It's a lot of one person's opinions that make up the whole. How do you know that it's not just the attorneys that are advocates of this nonsense? You can't fight the IRS and win."

"Jim, it's not my fight. This has been going on for years. I walked into this. Whose side are you on?"

"I'm just being realistic. I don't want to see you get hurt."

"How could I get hurt? You mean physically? Is the IRS going to send out hit men?" Leah knew she was being facetious.

"Not likely," his tone sounded grim, "but if you're making ninety dollars a day in tokes and end up having to pay taxes on all of that at the end of the year, that's likely to hurt, isn't it?"

"I don't have to worry *that* much! Damn! We're not a strip hotel. We're just a downtown casino. Is that the kind of money the dealers at Harrah's make?"

"About that," he answered evasively. "It doesn't matter how much. It's just that you'd be better off claiming tokes on your check each week. That way it would be easier on you in the long run. Leah, I'm worried about you," he said softly. "I wouldn't want to see you in trouble."

"It's not that big a deal, Jim, really. I appreciate the concern, but you seem to be ruling out the possibility that the dealers might win. The lower court ruling could stand. Tokes might be considered gifts."

"You're right. I do seem to be rejecting that possibility." There was a ring of discountenance in his voice. "I must be terribly pessimistic tonight. I didn't mean to lecture, but I care about you. You know that."

"I know, and I'm grateful. Thanks for the advice, Jim. I really mean it. Thanks for caring."

Leah feigned fatigue and brought the conversation to an end. There was a tightness in her chest and her mind was swimming. How strange an attitude he took about all this, she thought. He was very different from other casino workers, management included. He never talked about his work, almost as if it didn't exist for him. But on the other hand he was always asking about her day; always anxious to hear about funny happenings or tense moments or just dealer gossip. That was a very appealing trait of course, but on reflection, also very one-sided. It was not that Leah didn't ask, he just chose not to share his day's ups and downs. Or was that the real reason?

She didn't sleep well that night.

It was the evening of the next day that Leah arrived home to find a package waiting for her. She smiled when she noticed the return address was a Reno boutique. Hurriedly she tore the brown wrapping off and opened the box. Inside was the delicate blue silk robe that Jim had envisioned her wearing. The initial L was monogrammed on the lapel in ivory thread. Jim certainly knew how to court a girl, she thought. *Next, he'll want to see me in it.* The idea was becoming less remote to her, in spite of her continuous suspicions. She was looking forward to seeing him again, even as she reflected on his possessive nature. That did disturb her. But he seemed to back off when he sensed that he pushed her too far. She liked that about him, that, and his gentle way with the children.

Leah couldn't push the conversation of the night before from her mind. Was he prying? He might have been trying to get information. It seemed strange to her that he didn't sympathize more with the dealers. Most pit bosses, and shift bosses were once dealers themselves. Leah contemplated the puzzle and suddenly came to a decision: It was time to see if Jim was who he claimed to be.

Leah enlisted Jenny's help, and together, they devised a plan. Jenny had not met Jim. It was uncanny the way they seemed to have avoided each other.

When Jim called again Leah informed him that they were invited to Jenny's house for dinner. He seemed delighted. She felt apprehensive but she wasn't going to back out now. She had to know if he was being straightforward with her. There were too many incongruities.

The allocated day was Friday and it seemed to drag by in slow motion. Leah stole a glance at her watch as she dealt to the three accountant-types at her table. She was approaching the last break of the day. Butterflies were multiplying in her stomach from anticipation of the evening to come. She felt the tap on her right shoulder and with a sigh of relief finished out the hand. She squared the double-deck of cards and set it on the green felt table. Then, with her palm flat over the deck, expertly spread the cards in a decorative zig-zag arc, clapped her hands absently together and moved away from the table. Her relief dealer gave her a bemused glance and muttered over his shoulder, "Nothing like doing it with style."

Leah ignored his appreciation and quickly made her way to the snack-bar.

Jenny was waiting there. "I ordered hot tea for us. I thought you'd appreciate a change." She studied Leah closely. "Look, Babe, you're getting uptight over nothing. We're not going to tar and feather him, just find out how much he knows. If he's really a shift boss there are certain things he would have to know that the average person wouldn't. We'll try to make it as casual as possible. By the time the evening is over we'll have a lot better idea of just what we're dealing with. I invited Drake over. You remember him, from the restaurant."

"Good. How are you two getting along?"

"He's fun to be with. Drinks a lot, though." Jenny lowered her eyes, then stealing a sideways glance at Leah, said, "I really don't understand why you can't just call Jim at Harrah's. Then, there would be no mystery."

"Jenny, I don't call men! If I had some good reason to, I might. But I can't think of a reason in the world to call him." Leah's voice took on a high pitch of frustration.

"Okay, Babe. Look, don't worry about it. We'll handle it tonight. Let's just take it one step at a time." A wry grin spread over Jenny's face. "From what you tell me about him, it should be an interesting evening. Does he really *radiate sexuality?*" Jenny teased. "Or is it simply in the eyes of the beholder?"

"Don't make fun of me, Jenny Graham. Anyone that's turned on by body hair the way you are doesn't have any room to talk. Let's face it, in a dark alley, Drake could pass for a gorilla!"

Jenny cocked her pixie face to one side, her red locks falling over one shoulder. "What can I say? So I have a passion for hair. If there's anything I can't stand it's a bald chest. Now, come on." She put on an air of indignity. "Let's get back to work and leave Drake's body hair out of this."

Leah's three players were still there, playing a popular

system. When you win, double up. When you lose, pull back. They had each bought-in for one hundred dollars and weren't making any progress. Up and down, up and down. They were all playing the red (five dollar) chips, but never really got up to more than five chips per hand. To an onlooker it might appear as if some significant money was trading hands. But it really wasn't, which was further evidenced by the pit boss who was at least six tables down the pit, cleaning his nails for all Leah knew.

The game at hand was boring for Leah. It didn't make the adrenaline flow.

An oriental girl slithered up to the table. With the grace of a cobra she slid onto an outside chair beside the player with the highest stack of chips. She laid a small clutch purse on the table.

Leah immediately stopped the game. "Miss, you'll have to remove your purse from the table." Leah waited.

The attractive girl responded to Leah as if she didn't understand the language, then uttered an undistinguishable word.

Leah sighed with exasperation and made a second effort. "Miss, please, no foreign objects are allowed on the gaming table. Only cards and drinks. You'll have to remove your purse before we can continue."

The pit boss strolled up behind Leah and appraised the situation. He made no effort to intercede. He stood jauntily, his hands clasped behind his back. He scowled at the sagacious violator, his stance reinforcing his expression of authority.

Under his gaze, she immediately complied and removed her clutch from the table.

Leah resumed dealing the hand and the pit boss walked away.

Instead of producing money or chips, the provocative girl fingered the breast zipper of her flimsy jumpsuit. She leaned closer to the gentleman player and whispered seductively, "You play for me?" She eased the zipper down to well below her breasts, almost fully exposing bountifully full, bronzed mounds. Her erect nipples stood out daringly through the thin film of fabric that barely covered her.

The player flushed and shifted uncomfortably, his eyes frozen on her tantalizing breasts.

Leah sighed heavily, turned her head and looked down the pit until she caught the eye of the pit boss. She nodded for him to approach. Leah dealt around the girl.

The pit boss made a flash evaluation of the situation, then, quickly summoned a security guard to remove the chip-hustler.

Chip-hustlers were in a class by themselves, shunned by their counterparts. Unlike a hooker, who produced value for value, a chip-hustler simply seduced men into putting up bets for her. Win or lose, the hustler systematically slipped chips into her purse. The casinos found it necessary to banish them for two reasons: The most obvious being that they didn't want their players disturbed, and secondly, the chips going into the hustler's purse had no chance of returning to the dealer's rack.

The security guard approached and clamped one giant hand over her frail arm. "Let's go," he demanded in hushed tones.

She struggled violently to free herself from his grip. "Okay, okay, I'm going, you pig!" she screamed in perfect English.

In the struggle one heavy breast fell free and grazed fleetingly across her intended victim's shoulder. He turned quickly, his chin brushing against the jutting nipple.

She seemed delighted with his bulging eyes. "You

want little lick, pigeon?" she teased, falling back into her broken English.

The security guard picked her up, threw her over his shoulder and marched down the aisle and out the door, depositing her on the street.

Her victim blazed red under his collar and tie.

One of his companions looked conspiringly to the other and then back to him and said in a teasing sing-song mimic, "You want little lick, pigeon?" The two men laughed uncontrollably, at the expense of their friend.

The poor man had all he could endure and with this final jab, wrenched himself out of the chair and stomped away.

The six o'clock shift came on duty and Leah gave up her table with a sigh of relief.

On the twenty minute drive home Leah pondered the plight of the chip-hustler. She had mixed emotions about having had the girl thrown out.

Vegas was a melting pot. There was a comradeship here unlike in any other city in the country, because in one way or another they all made their living off of the tourists. It was that common denominator that created an invisible bond. But that bond wasn't without limits. There was still right and wrong. And even though Leah believed that what this girl did for a living was wrong, she couldn't help feeling sorry for her, sorry that she had to resort to such a level to sustain her existence. But then, knowing full well how Vegas operated, it wasn't unlikely that this girl just didn't have any juice.

As Leah drove into her apartment complex and parked, she knew she had very little time to get prepared for the evening ahead. She took a quick shower and slid into lightweight camel slacks, then flipped through her closet until she found just the right top, a cotton, popcorn knit sweater of pale ivory. She had bought it at the *Broadway* only a week before, shoved it in her closet between some other sweaters and completely forgot about it, until that very moment.

She applied fresh makeup and touched up her hair with a brush.

She bathed the twins and dressed them in identical pink sundresses with boleros. They wore white patent leather shoes and lace-trimmed anklets.

As if right on cue, Jim rang the doorbell.

The first thing Leah noticed was his black alligator shoes. Somehow, they seemed to match his arrogant good looks tonight. His gray trousers held a firm crease that didn't break before touching his shoes. A sensuous gray silk shirt sheathed his broad shoulders.

Leah wondered how he could afford to dress so expensively. He obviously had a penchant for fine clothing.

In Jim's hand he held two brightly colored books. He greeted Leah with a kiss on the cheek and turned his attention to the twins. "I brought you girls a present." He smiled a beguiling smile. He knelt to their height and holding the books behind his back, said, "So that there's no conflict, I'm going to let you each choose a hand."

The twins danced around him excitedly, finally deciding who would choose which hand.

Jim presented them with autographed copies of the latest best sellers in children's literature, Boston Potter's *Bunny Lake* and *Turtle Tree*.

"Jim," Leah puzzled, "how did you manage to get

autographed copies of these books? I've been watching the book stores for months. They sold out the first shipment in a day."

"I have influence in high places," he said in a teasing voice. "Actually, my sister knows Boston Potter very well. I managed to talk her out of these copies. I know that she can get more."

"That's great. You couldn't have thought of a more perfect gift. They have all of his earlier books. You should see them, they've almost returned to pulp they've been read so much."

"Good, I hope they enjoy them. How about you? Is Boston Potter your favorite author, too?" Jim's eyes twinkled and that jaunty grin was in place again, the one that signaled Leah that he was making fun of her.

"He's running a close second. Actually, I've been into non-fiction lately, trying to improve my mind. I can't remember the last time I read a book of fiction."

Jim walked over to the coffee table and picked up the book lying there. "I would say this is *pure* fiction. *Taxes are Voluntary*. Where did you get this piece of..."

"I don't intend to get into this discussion with you again, Jim." She smiled warmly to take the edge off of her words. "Please...not tonight. We'll be late if we don't hurry."

They left the apartment looking like the average all-American family. Leah thought how lucky she had been that Jason was sleeping when Jim showed up.

When they got in the car, Leah noticed a brown paper bag in the front seat. Jim had brought two bottles of Chardonnay. "I didn't know whether to bring red or white, so I just took a wild guess," he said.

"You guessed right. Lobster tail is on the menu. It's Jenny's specialty. I hope you don't mind having it again so soon after last week."

"It sounds wonderful to me. I never tire of the finer things in life."

His appreciative glance made Leah feel guilty in the face of the evening's plans. She hoped Jenny wouldn't be too hard on him.

They arrived at Jenny's a little before seven. She had a pitcher of daiquiris already made up and had a good head start. Introductions were made and Jenny dove right into casino talk. She was exchanging techniques of complicated pay-offs with Jim. Drake contributed to the drama, too, although he didn't know what the real purpose was. Jim was no amateur. He knew the casino business. Leah could see that Jim was passing the test.

"Jim, how did you ever become a shift boss at thirty-five? I don't believe you're only thirty-five years old," Jenny teased.

"I'm just a lot more intelligent than the average person." He gave it right back to her.

"I think I'll have to have you prove it to me. Let me see your driver's license."

"You'll have to take my word for it, Red, because I don't carry a wallet, too bulky," he explained.

Jenny didn't seem to be put off by the proclamation. It appeared that she liked him and they fell into an easy repartee. Drake seemed equally impressed with him, although it probably didn't take much to impress Drake.

Dinner progressed smoothly with the inquisition out of the way; everyone relaxed and enjoyed the rich food and good wine. The evening was coming to an end.

"Jenny, my sweet, you're a marvelous hostess, a

fantastic cook and cute as a bug." Jim tweaked her cheek. "Thanks for asking me."

"Oh get out of here, you big flirt." She smacked him on the arm playfully.

Jim scooped a twin up in each arm and they left.

Leah felt a warm glow as they drove across town on the freeway. The evening had gone well.

"Leah, will you have dinner with me tomorrow night?" Jim asked.

"Yes." Her response was immediate.

"We'll be going to the Alpine Village, across from the Hilton. Have you ever been there?"

"Yes, I love it! German food is my favorite," Leah exclaimed.

"Good. Let's take the girls for dinner and if you can get a sitter, we'll drop them off and go to a show later. The Grand has a good one, if you like magic."

"Sounds interesting. I'll be looking forward to it."

He pulled into the parking lot and turned off the engine.

"Jim, don't bother getting out. We can see ourselves to the door."

"Don't be silly. I wouldn't dream of letting you out alone at night. Come on angels," he called over his shoulder to the twins in the back seat.

The strapping muscles in his arms barely flexed as he lifted them once again, one in each arm. He carried them up the outside stairs to Leah's apartment.

Once inside, Leah instructed, "Okay kids, hit the tub."

They scampered obediently out of sight.

Leah stood uneasily in the middle of the room. The last thing she wanted right now was another lusty encounter with Jim. She didn't trust herself. What she felt for him was all-consuming. If he touched her she felt she would melt submissively into his will.

"Leah, are you tired? Do you want me to leave?" Jim asked softly.

"No...yes. I-I mean..." Leah wrung her hands distressfully.

Jim gripped her shoulders, gazing meaningfully into liquid pools of fear. "I hate it that I can be here so seldom. I enjoyed tonight. Jenny is a real kick. But, I don't feel like I've been with you. Not in any significant way. Could we just talk? I won't touch you." He suddenly dropped his hands from her shoulders, embarrassed from the contradiction his hands suggested. "Don't be afraid of me, Leah."

"I'm not afraid of you, Jim." *I'm afraid of myself.*

"Good." His sensuous lips curled in a victorious grin.

"I need to help the girls get their bath started. Ah...do you want to sit down?"

"Do you have any coffee?"

"Yes, sure." Leah headed for the kitchen.

"I'll make it. Just point me in the right direction."

Jim made the coffee while Leah helped the twins. His eyes took in the freshly lined cupboards and neatly stacked china and crystal. He surmised that she had known more prosperous times than presently. Her entire kitchen was highly polished and immaculately kept. A sign that she spent more time there than most would. Most of the women that he had known, anyway.

He passed by the fine blue rose, platinum-trimmed china cups and opened a cupboard door that offered an everyday variety. He chose two matching cups—pure white with a teddy bear emblem painted on them, surrounded by tiny red hearts. The letters underneath the bears read: "Love is all around us."

A grin played at the corners of Jim's mouth. This was indicative of the real Leah, the one he found under the Vegas facade—sensitive, vulnerable, sentimental, and needing. Needing his passion and fire as much as he needed hers.

A fresh pang of guilt stabbed his heart. *Why me? Why did I have to screw up and show compassion for an old woman who meant nothing to me?* The Vegas assignment was meant to be his punishment. If his superiors only knew how much of a punishment it really was, they would probably be pleased as hell, he thought.

Being with Leah was like playing with fire, drawn irresistibly to the flame, yet knowing full well that it could destroy him. His involvement with her was at a dangerously high level, above and beyond the call of duty. So much at stake, so much to lose. Still he broke all the rules. His desire to possess her overpowered his will, dangerously close to overpowering his duty. *What the hell am I doing here?*

"Find everything?" Leah's softly spoken words shook him from his reverie. "Jim...are you all right?"

Her warm, soothing concern washed over him like molten lava. He wanted to scream, *No, I'm not all right. I'm being consumed by your flame. My desire for you is a torture beyond endurance.*

His eyes undressed and caressed every inch of her body.

Leah watched the tortured expression on his face turn to one of pure animal lust. She could almost feel the caresses exuding from his eyes.

They stood for what seemed like eons. Leah felt warm inside, almost as if they had shared an unspoken experience.

Jim slowly walked to her and pulled her into his

arms. He held her for a long time. Words didn't seem to be necessary.

"Mommy...we're finished, the twins chanted from the now open bathroom door.

"Go put the girls to bed," Jim said, his voice tender.

Leah extracted two small glasses from the cupboard and filled them with milk. "Have some coffee," Leah said, her blue eyes, smoky. She took the two glasses of milk and walked out of the kitchen.

Sherry and Carrie came galloping into the living room, half dressed, with their new books in hand. "Jim, Jim, read us a story. Please read us a story," they pleaded.

Jim was enchanted with the beautiful little twin girls and, smiling down at them, offered each a large hand to grasp. "Into bed with you and I'll do better than read you a story. I'll tell you a story. A brand new story."

Leah watched as Jim followed them into their bedroom. Her heart swelled to see her beloved children and her almost lover in such a warm, loving relationship. Her heart went out to Jim with a new intensity. *Love me, love my children.* A new rule she swore to live by.

Leah lay down on the sofa.

Jim told the twins a story, but they wouldn't be satisfied until he had also read both new books that he had given them. Toward the end of the second book they both dozed off. He kissed them gently on their foreheads and turned out the light. He was beginning to feel possessive toward them. A dangerous emotion for a man in his position, he reminded himself.

He found Leah asleep on the sofa. With a deep sigh, he kissed her on the forehead, as he had the children. Their time would come, he consoled himself, and he walked out of the door, closing it gently behind him. Tomorrow evening wasn't so far away, he thought.

"Jason, when Jim comes to the door, you go hide in the bedroom. Damn it, don't give me any trouble! I'm not ready to explain you."

"Oh, come on, Leah. I want to meet him. I'll explain me. I'll say I'm your broad-minded lover." Jason had the most contagious smile and now he was grinning from ear to ear. "You're just getting a taste of what I've been going through for months. How do you think I've explained you to my friends?"

"I hate to think! How do you explain me?"

"Sometimes you're my sister. Sometimes you're my mother. It doesn't really matter as long as they don't see you. But if I ever take anyone out more than three times I suppose I'd be in trouble." Jason laughed.

"You're an enigma, Jason. Why don't you take anyone out more than two or three times?"

"A lot of reasons. Mostly because I just haven't cared that much about any of them. But, I have to admit that I'm scared shitless of falling into the alimony and child support trap. I'm just very content with things the way they are. I have Sherry and Carrie...and I have the perfect wife. You don't bitch at me or ask for money, or demand to know where I've been. I think it's great." Jason snickered.

"Jason, you're impossible. Just a little boy who doesn't want to grow up. But, I like you just fine. We make a good pair." She laughed.

Leah chose a lilac voile dress with billows of flair in the skirt, which made her waist look tiny. She dressed the twins in similar shades of lilac. They were striking, all pastel and blonde.

Jim had rented a Cadillac Eldorado convertible for

the evening. When he arrived, he had a large package for each of the girls. They squealed with delight. Carrie opened her package to reveal an *Ernie* doll. Sherry got a *Bert* doll. They insisted on taking the dolls with them to dinner.

"You may," Jim said, "but you have to leave them in the car when we go in to eat. Okay?"

They reluctantly agreed.

The evening was balmy; palm fronds swayed lazily in the breeze. Dancing neon signs lined Las Vegas Boulevard for as far as the eye could see. Caesars Palace was a mirage of lighted fountains and graceful, full life statues.

The traffic was heavy and moving slowly. Suddenly, Carrie screamed, "Ernie! Ernie! Ernie!"

Leah turned to the back seat, horrified. "What's wrong?" The agony in Carrie's voice was frightening.

Carrie was leaning over the side of the car, looking woefully into the distance. She turned tearfully to her mother, "I dropped him."

Leah was disgusted with herself for not having considered that a possibility in view of the fact that they were in a convertible. But then how could she think of everything?

Jim spent the next half hour backtracking, but Ernie was no where to be found.

They arrived at the Alpine Village to find the usual half dozen picketers holding vigil in a slow moving circle. They wielded signs in varying degrees of heights which sent out their message: *Unfair labor practices. Let the union in!* It was one of the few remaining restaurants that refused to accept the union.

They decided to eat in the Rathskeller since it was more informal than upstairs. They descended the darkened stairway to an atmosphere of charming storybook wonder. The decor depicted a colorful German cottage. The lighting was dim and the twins were hushed in the domain of adults.

Dinner was served and the children were on their best behavior, Carrie, still sullen over the loss of Ernie.

They had just finished when a man came hurriedly up to Jim and whispered in his ear.

"Leah, get Carrie. Quick!" Jim lifted Sherry up in his arms and promptly shuffled them up the stairs and out the door. A loud explosion sounded as they walked into the clear night air.

"My God! Jim...what was that?"

Patrons stampeded out of the restaurant in a panic. Leah could hear bits and pieces of conversation as they headed for the car. The word "bomb" was on everyone's lips. Leah noticed that the picketers were gone.

"Jim, what the hell happened?" Leah nearly screamed.

"It's all right. Don't panic," he nodded toward the girls. "The union was just trying to make a point."

They drove home in silence. Leah wondered how it happened that Jim had advance notice of the bomb, little as it was. She thought again about his declaration that he didn't carry a wallet because it was too bulky. Of course he must have his identification in the glove box of his car when driving, as Jenny had surmised. Then again, he always paid in cash—never used a credit card. That was unusual. Something just didn't add up.

"Jim, let's just call it an evening. I don't think I'm up to any more excitement tonight," Leah sighed.

"Okay, Leah. I'll call you tomorrow." Jim seemed relieved. Leah wondered what he would do after he left her. Did he have something to do with the union after all? Why was it that she felt he was not what he claimed to be? Intuition? She had felt it from the very beginning. Something mysterious. It wasn't the first time ESP had served her, but unfortunately, like many people, she often chose to ignore it.

Leah had a sleepless night. She was anxious to talk with Jenny. Maybe she could shed some light on the problem. She had a sharp analytical mind and, in addition, was distanced from the problem, unlike Leah.

"Jenny, come over for breakfast. Bring the girls. I'll make French toast with strawberries."

"Should I bring champagne?" Jenny responded into the telephone.

"Only if I don't have to change the entree' to Eggs Benedict. The twins can't abide the cheese sauce."

"Same here. French toast sounds good. We'll be there in half an hour." Jenny hung up.

Leah ran her fingers along the smooth silk of her new robe. So beautiful, she thought. Tailored and simple.

She reached for the vodka and *Snappy Tom*. A Bloody Mary sounded like a good way to start this Sunday. She couldn't bring herself to get dressed yet. Her ivory silk pajamas were too comfortable to give up. She loved elegant sleepwear.

In what seemed like no time at all, Jenny was at the door with her girls, who immediately took off for the twin's room.

"God! Leah, you're getting crocked. Fix me one of those, will ya?"

"Sure thing, Red," she teased, remembering the name Jim had called her.

"All right, out with it," Jenny demanded.

"Out with what?" Leah inquired innocently.

"Cut the crap. I know when something is bothering you." Jenny plopped onto the plush beige sofa. She loved Leah's apartment. It was small, but decorated so tastefully. It was done in earthtones and seemed to be designed with total comfort in mind.

"All right, all right, I know you think I'm crazy but it's Jim. Last night we had dinner at the Alpine Village. There was an explosion..."

"An explosion! I didn't see anything about it in the paper. Are you okay?"

"We're fine. The girls were with us and they didn't even realize what had happened. But that's the point. Some guy came over to Jim only moments before and apparently warned him. Jim got us out before it happened. But only by moments. I didn't see any signs of the explosion from the outside, so it must not have done a lot of damage. I don't know if anyone was hurt."

"Sounds like the union. Probably just a scare tactic."

"That's what Jim said. I think he's involved somehow."

"If he were involved with the union he would have known about the bomb well in advance. Do you really think that he would have taken you, not to mention the children, there if he had known?"

"I don't know what to think. I just have a feeling...even if there is a logical explanation."

"Jim's a lot of fun, Leah, and he seems to adore you and the children. Are you sure you're not looking for a reason to reject him?" Jenny asked softly.

"Let me fix another pitcher of Bloody Marys and I'll contemplate that," she said with mock seriousness.

"Contemplate, my ass, and who will make the French toast if we finish off another pitcher of that stuff."

"There's always *Fruit Loops* in the cupboard." Leah laughed.

"One of my favorite..." Suddenly she stopped, listening. "Was that the doorbell?"

"Probably one of the neighbor kids. Get it for me, will you?"

"Well, hi, Big Boy," Jenny giggled as she looked miles up to greet Jim's smiling face.

"Hi, Red. Fancy meeting you here. Am I interrupting a party?"

"Yes, you are. But now that you're here, come on in."

"Jim! Is that you?" Leah called from the kitchen. "For heaven's sake, I didn't expect to see you so soon."

"You're breathtaking. I knew blue was your color." He looked down at her bare feet, laughing. "Was I right?" He took her in his arms and held her tight. "Do you need some help out here?"

"I'm doing fine," Leah swayed to one side, giggling.

"I can see that." He swept her up in his arms and deposited her on the sofa next to Jenny. "You crazy Las Vegas women. I'll take care of this."

Jim proceeded to make breakfast, sipping a Bloody Mary as he worked.

Later, as they sat around the table eating breakfast, Leah quizzed, "How did you learn to make strawberry sauce?"

"You would be surprised at my many talents."

Leah would normally have been upset had anyone just shown up without any notice, but the truth was, she liked the way Jim acted as if he were a part of their lives; it all seemed so natural.

"How many little girls would be interested in going

to the zoo?" he asked the children.

They jumped up and down with excitement. Carrie jumped on his lap and hugged him. Jenny's girls chimed in enthusiastically.

Jim directed a roguish expression toward Leah. "Tonight is for us." And in those eyes Leah saw a promise of ecstasy.

CHAPTER FOUR

"Jim, you're so good with the children. They had such fun today at the zoo."

"I'm glad, I like them a lot. I've always wanted children of my own but...I do have Flower, my Saint Bernard. He's two or three kids all wrapped up into one."

"That could be good and bad." Leah laughed. "But a Saint Bernard! I'll bet he eats his weight in food."

"Sometimes it seems so. He has this little personality glitch, though. Not only does he think he's human but he's developed a taste for booze—leftover champagne and crepes, stale beer and peanuts, any kind of party leftovers he'll devour with the passion of starvation. I'm afraid he's cultivated a taste for the finer things in life. I think he's what is referred to as a 'Party Animal'."

"Sounds to me like you're teaching him bad habits," Leah scolded. "That reminds me, we never did get around to that champagne that Jenny brought this morning. Want some?"

"Sounds perfect, let's do." Jim opened the bottle of champagne and poured two glasses full. "A toast to the most beautiful girl in the world, inside and out." He raised his glass to hers.

"You're too flattering." Leah smiled, getting up to turn on the stereo.

"You're very special to me, Leah, and I want to be a part of your life."

Leah's mind raced from the implication of his words. Was what she felt for him more than physical? He would make a marvelous father for her girls but, was that enough? No, she had traveled that gamut, mistakenly so, at that. She knew it wasn't enough. She wasn't going to settle for second best—never again. She would be absolutely certain the next time. The fact was, she didn't need a husband. But that little voice inside her echoed, *Your girls do need a father.*

Leah turned from the stereo and walked back to the sofa where Jim sat. She took his hands in hers and spoke softly. "Jim, when I came to Vegas I was fleeing a way of life that to me was no longer bearable. I don't like confinement. I thought that being in a new place, so far and so different from anything that I'd known before would set me free. Then, I made a terrible mistake. I was working at the Hilton as a keno runner. That's where I met my second husband, Damon, and we were married within a month. I thought I needed him. I thought that my children needed a father. The marriage lasted only a year. As it turned out, he wasn't the person he led me to believe he was. I felt tricked; betrayed. That's why I haven't dated since the divorce. I have a problem trusting people, especially men. I was forced to question my own judgement and motives. In the year that followed my divorce, I came to realize that I didn't need anyone. I became financially independent and emotionally independent, as well." Leah lowered her eyes to stare at her hands still holding Jim's. She released them, letting out a deep breath.

"Oh, I don't have much, that's true. But my girls don't want for anything. That's what my life is all about now, making my children happy."

Jim's eyes clouded over. "What about you, Leah? What about your happiness? You need someone to care about you, to touch you, to love you."

"No, I don't need that. I don't!" She jumped up from the sofa in exasperation.

Jim followed, grabbing her roughly by the shoulders. His icy blue eyes challenged her. "You need me, Leah." He pulled her body tight against his, lowering his mouth to her parted lips.

Leah's inclination to fight immediately dissolved as his strength enfolded her. Her heart pounded. There was nothing more she wanted at that moment than to be embraced by him. Her feelings were a preponderance of contradictions.

Jim's breath was hot on her ear as he whispered her name. "Leah...Leah...my love." His hands lowered from her shoulders to the small of her back.

Suddenly the front door opened. Jason stood in the doorway, a momentary look of surprise on his face, quickly replaced with a bemused grin. "Hi guys," he said brightly, continuing through the living room to the kitchen.

Leah stood speechless, a crimson blush on her cheeks.

Jim stared at her in disbelief.

Jason sauntered back into the living room with a tall glass of milk in his hand. "I just have to change clothes before I go to work," he offered apologetically.

"Jason," Leah managed to control her voice. "I would like you to meet Jim Henderson. Jim, this is Jason."

"Pleased to meet ya." Jason thrust his hand out to Jim.

Jim stared at the hand in front of him. Slowly he offered his, an expression of puzzlement frozen on his face.

Jason ambled out of the room and down the hallway to his bedroom.

Out of the corner of her eye Leah saw the laughter Jason suppressed. Once behind his closed door he would probably have the best laugh he'd had in a very long time. At that very moment she wanted to kill him. She wondered if he came home deliberately. He knew she would more than likely have Jim there. She had left a note on his dresser before leaving for the zoo that day.

Jim's voice turned bitter. "I understand now—why you don't feel like you need anyone."

"Jim, it's not like that. It's not like that at all. Jason is just a friend, a very special friend," she added in a challenging voice, suddenly irate at having to explain anything to him, or anyone.

"I would hope that he is special. Does...does he live here?"

"Yes, he lives here," Leah said defiantly.

"I was obviously concerned over nothing." Jim made his way to the door and left without turning back.

Tears of fury filled Leah's eyes. "How could you, Jason? How could you do this to me?" she muttered incoherently as she sequestered herself in her bedroom.

Monday morning Leah found herself assigned to the five-dollar minimum table, reserved for the best dealers. She was not pleased with the promotion because she knew it was a vulnerable position to be in. The pressure was greater.

She and Jason had a confrontation that morning and she was feeling miserable about it. She had vented her anger at his expense before finding out that he hadn't seen the note on his dresser. Even then, he took it good-naturedly. A little hurt, she knew, but still laughing about Jim's shocked expression. Jason tried to convince her that Jim would be back. In fact, he said he guaranteed it. Jason was such a kind person she should have known that he wouldn't have done anything to deliberately hurt her.

In retrospect, a lot had happened that weekend. The incident about the union still bothered Leah. But, the way things turned out, maybe it wouldn't matter. She might never see Jim again.

Two dealers from the Plaza ambled up to Leah's table. They each threw a twenty-dollar bill down on betting squares.

Leah won the hand and they cursed.

The more surly of the two pulled out another twenty from his pocket. "Here goes my child support," he grumbled to his friend.

Leah took that, too.

"Come on," his friend complained, "we'll be late for work."

"One more hand," the surly dealer insisted. He extracted a fifty-dollar bill and placed it on the betting square.

Leah didn't call out money plays because the pit boss was standing close by. She deliberately reshuffled the cards, even though there was no reason to do so.

The dealer grabbed his money back, cursing, and Leah smiled to herself with satisfaction. He and his friend stalked away. He had been counting on the law of averages. Leah took his advantage away by shuffling.

It was incidents such as these that hardened Leah to gamblers. Gambling away his child-support payment was unforgivable in her eyes.

It was a bad omen starting the day like this, Leah thought, and she didn't look forward to what else the day might bring.

Jim woke with a throbbing headache. He drank enough Scotch the night before to bathe in. He lifted the telephone and dialed eight and the number he wished to call.

"Give me Matthews' office," he demanded.

After a long pause, Matthews' voice boomed into the receiver. "Where the hell are you?"

"Where the hell do you think I am?"

"I thought you were flying back last night. Did you run into a problem?" His voice took on a cautious tone.

"You might say that. Have you been able to do anything about getting me out of this mess?"

"Look, man, I've tried, but you should know better than anyone, you can't buck the system. Hang in there a while longer. This will blow over and things will get back to normal. Are you getting anything that will help us?"

"It's not easy, especially when I was sent here so totally unprepared. Whoever the hell prepared that briefing should be shot! I've been forced to do some research on my own. Damn good thing—saved my ass this week. Look, Matthews, I'm doing my best, but let's face it, my credibility has been questioned. It's going to take longer because of that. Try to bear in mind, this is not my forté.

"The organization, in punishing me, didn't do themselves any favor. Look, just between you and me...this situation stinks. I sure as hell don't appreciate being put in a spot like this."

"It's all in the game. Do what's expected of you and your life will be a lot easier." Matthews hung up the telephone.

Hearing the finality of that click, Jim dropped the

phone from his ear, glared at it in disgust, then flung it into its cradle. Running his hands through his hair, he let out a deep sigh. The torments of duty versus personal conviction once again became a source of concern to him. In the past six years it had come up occasionally, but never to the degree that it did now. Was it because of Leah? His personal involvement with her was clouding his vision. But would his thinking be so different if it were not she who was the target?

He ordered coffee from room service, started the shower, and watched until it steamed up the bathroom before he entered. He let the fiery sprays of water beat against his back, slowly relieving the tension building there. He shampooed his hair and turned the water to cold. The change of temperature was an awakening shock to his system. All the while he towel dried, shaved, and brushed his teeth, he thought about the evening with Leah. He went over every word again and again.

A knock sounded on the door. He opened it to roomservice and directed the young man to leave the tray on a small round table, pushing paperwork and documents aside to make room for it, then signed the check, writing in a generous tip for the boy. He immediately took the cardboard cover off of the carafe and poured a cup of the steaming coffee. Sipping the hot dark liquid, Jim closed his eyes, savoring the pleasure that first cup always gave him. He leaned back in the chair beside the cluttered table, closed his eyes again and tried to evaluate his position.

His walking out on Leah had nothing to do with duty. But then, neither did his desire to bed her. In fact, he was the one complicating the situation. One thing was for sure, he wouldn't get anywhere letting false pride rule him. So what if she did have a live-in lover? His duty was still the same. And then there was still the possibility that she was telling the truth. But, he found it hard to believe that any man could live with her on a platonic basis. Above all else, his duty was clear in his mind.

Leah sat beside Jenny at the snack-bar.

"You haven't said a word, Leah. Didn't you get any sleep last night? Did you and Mr. Wonderful do the town?"

"Oh, Jenny, everything is such a mess."

"What's the matter? Whatever it is, we'll fix it."

"I know I asked for it—by not telling Jim about Jason."

"It had to happen. It was just a matter of time. How bad?"

"Really bad. I was in Jim's arms when Jason came bouncing in the door. It blew the whole evening. Jim left...just left."

"Didn't you try to explain?" Jenny asked incredulously.

"I was so shook up, I don't remember just what I did say. Whatever it was, it apparently wasn't convincing. I did get a little defensive, I guess. I won't be treated like an errant child. Who is he to give me the third degree?"

"Leah, is there anything I can do? Would you like me to call him? Try to explain?"

"No, Jenny. Maybe it was meant to be this way. I just wish we could have gotten to know one another a little better. He wouldn't have questioned me if he really knew me. We were so close..." Her eyes lowered and a tear escaped, falling down her cheek.

Leah's display of emotion shocked Jenny. She sat quietly for a moment. "Leah, are you in love with Jim?"

"In love with him? Don't be silly. I-I'm just disappointed. He was so good to the children. He was fun to be with. That's all. It's just that I feel...a loss."

"Leah, I think you'd better take a closer look." Jenny patted her on the back and got up to leave. "I have to make a phone call. Catch you next break."

Leah went over the evening in her mind. If only it could have turned out differently. If only they could have continued their embrace. If only they could have...

Leah felt a hand on her shoulder. It wasn't the light touch of Jenny's hand. She turned quickly to gaze up into Jim's eyes.

"Leah, I'm sorry." He spoke softly, his eyes reflecting the suffering she felt.

"Sit down, Jim." She motioned to the seat that Jenny had just vacated. "I thought you would be back in Reno by now," she said with contained emotion.

"I couldn't go back, not with things the way they are. Leah, I am sorry. I had no right to judge you. I wouldn't even listen to your explanation. That wasn't fair, I know it. And, I guess, I really don't have any right to expect loyalty from you. I—I just don't want it to end with us. Will you see me again?"

Leah was speechless, her emotions in turmoil. It sounded as if he still thought that there was something between her and Jason. She wanted to explain, then again, it angered her. She decided to withhold further explanation, not play the part of the desperate female trying to cling onto a relationship, explaining away his fears. She was too independent to grovel.

"I'm not the one that walked out. I don't have a problem with seeing you. Did you have something specific in mind?" Her voice was a controlled casual monotone.

"I have to catch the next flight out. I'll be back in town Friday. Why don't you think about what you'd like to do—dinner, a show, whatever you decide."

"Are you leaving right now?" Leah tried to disguise her disappointment.

"Yes, Love." Jim took her hand and squeezed it. "This week will be torture. I'll be thinking of you at every turn." As Jim spoke, he realized that he had never said truer words.

They parted with Leah's thoughts and emotions more confused than before.

The week was nothing more than a ticking off of days until Friday finally arrived.

Jim took an earlier flight than usual. He had done his homework and knew that he could more than likely catch Jason before Leah arrived home. He had to satisfy his own curiosity. It wasn't important to his assignment, but it was important to him personally. It had obsessed him all week. He visualized Leah living with Jason. He saw them as help mates to one another—as potential lovers, if not lovers already. His information told him otherwise, but he still found it hard to believe. Jason was a handsome man and Leah was a beautiful girl, how could it be otherwise?

He steered the rented car into the parking lot and turned off the engine. His eyes drifted up to Leah's apartment, focusing on the closed door. It was five o'clock. He knew that Leah wouldn't get off work until six. He had time to question Jason but, he would have to do it carefully in order not to invoke Leah's wrath. Taking a deep breath, he flung himself out of the car. Stepping spryly, he crossed the parking lot and climbed up the stairs. His knock was confident and determined as he steeled himself for what was to come.

The door opened. Jim's apprehension vanished as Carrie grabbed hold of his legs and squealed, "Jim! Jim!"

Sherry came running, too. She greeted him with an

equal amount of exuberance, but in a more refined way, in keeping with her prim personality.

Jason popped his head out of the kitchen. "Hey, Jim! Come on in."

Jim was taken aback by the warm greeting from Jason. He had half expected an unpleasant confrontation. He eased in the door, closing it behind him. Now that he was here he had second thoughts.

"I'm making hot chocolate for the girls. Do you want some? Or maybe a beer?"

"Uh...yeah, a beer," Jim answered, being thrown even more off guard as he sat down on the sofa, the twins scrambling for his attention. He settled them down beside him, one on each side, ruffling their hair and tweaking their cheeks. They giggled with delight. Now more interested in each other than him, Jim picked up a book of trivia from the side table and thumbed through it.

Jason entered with a tray, set it down on the coffee table and handed him an imported beer, no glass.

"All right you little monsters," Jason bellowed, "get over here and drink this hot chocolate and get off of Jim. He's not a rug!"

The girls ran to Jason, not in the slightest affected by his harsh booming voice.

"Thank you Uncle Jason," Carrie said.

"Thank you for the chocolate, Uncle Jason," Sherry echoed, adding, "Could we have a tea party with it in our room?"

"Sure, but be careful not to spill it." Jason sat down and glanced at Jim, who was holding the book of trivia.

"Did you know that the shortest man in the world is twenty-eight inches tall and earns his living as a farmer?" Jason's ludicrous question and lopsided grin put Jim at ease.

"Thanks for making this easier for me," Jim said. "I wanted to hear it from you. Is your relationship with Leah platonic, or do you have some kind of open relationship?"

Jason laughed effusively. "You don't know Leah very well. She's not the type to have any kind of open relationship, come to think of it, I'm not sure she's the kind to have a relationship." Jason became more sober. "I'm very fond of Leah. I care what happens to her. I love her children. She and I don't have anything going. She married my best friend. Well, he used to be my best friend. He got rich on an Oklahoma oil swindle—got my money, too. The son of a bitch got off scot-free." Jason brought himself back to the problem at hand. "That's not what you wanted to hear about. Leah was upset when you walked out. She went straight to her room and I couldn't talk to her that night. The next morning she chewed me out royally. It's been difficult, this living arrangement. But, it's beneficial to both of us. Enough so that we endure the consequences. I have to admit that I found it amusing—funny as hell, actually," Jason burst into a toothy smile. "She finally experienced some of the problems I've had all along. What the hell do you tell a girl when she wants to go to your place to get laid. Damn! I've spent more money on motels."

Jim couldn't help but like Jason. His outgoing ways were charming in an innocent way. He understood how Leah would be so taken with him. "Jason, you understand, I had to ask. I didn't want to get into any kind of flaky deal. Vegas...well...you never know."

"Yeah, I know, it can happen, but Leah isn't that type. I have a lot of respect for her, and you should have, too." Jason gave him a pointed look.

"I do, Jason. Believe me I do. If I didn't care about her, I wouldn't be here right now." Jim said those words with honest conviction.

Jason directed a powerfully scrutinizing gaze toward Jim. "Best not let Leah know that you questioned me. She's awfully independent—Gemini, you know. Never know what to expect."

Jim favored Jason with a genuine smile. "I know what you mean. Thanks. It means a lot to me."

The twins came giggling into the room. "Uncle Jason, my Teddy bear drank all the chocolate," Sherry said.

Jason smiled at her affectionately. "You should call him Piggy bear. It's time for Star Trek. Why don't you turn on the TV for us?"

Carrie ran in front of her sister to turn on the set.

Jason turned his attention to the television, and Carrie and Sherry climbed up on the loveseat next to him.

Carrie looked at Jim from across the room, apparently decided that he shouldn't be alone and bounded over to him. She sat beside him as lady-like as she could, with her back straight and hands in her lap.

Jim smiled as he put his arm around her. He watched Jason and Sherry entranced with Spock and an unknown alien. Carrie, too, had her attention fixed on the set. Jim felt at ease. More than that. He felt as if he had stumbled into a twilight of warm acceptance, of understanding and of love. He felt a strange desire to become a part of this. All of his fears had been put to rest. Now the ball was back in his court and that gave him some reason for discomfort. He had found a woman that, despite his dark purpose, had become an obsession with him. She was under his skin and in his blood. If he had any sense, or any control over the situation, he would run like hell. But he was a prisoner, forced into a situation that meant sure destruction for him, if he followed his heart. Could he betray her?

Leah opened the door to find a new Star Trek fan. Or so it appeared. "Jim!" Her surprise was so great that she couldn't say anything more than his name. She made a quick survey. All seemed to be in order. In fact, she felt that she was the intruder more so than Jim. The tranquil atmosphere was barely ruffled by her presence.

Jim rose and approached her. He spoke in soft tones so as not to disturb the TV viewers. "I got in a little early. I hope you don't mind my coming over here. I couldn't wait." He kissed her lightly on the lips.

"No, of course not," she said.

Her easy smile relaxed Jim.

"Don't let me disturb you," she said, gesturing to the TV with a nod, amusement in her voice, for she was no Star Trek fan.

"It is getting pretty interesting," Jim answered. "The Klingons have captured Captain Kirk. I've got to see him through this."

Leah wasn't sure whether he was serious or making fun of Jason. He did, however, sit back down and turn his attention back to the TV set. Leah sat down beside him and loosened her black kerchief. She pulled the red and white die down through the length of the tie and pulled it free.

Jim rested his hand on her knee. In hushed tones he whispered, "Did you miss me this week?"

Leah gave him a sideways glance, lifting one eyebrow.

Devilment flickered in his eyes as he chuckled playfully.

Star trek came to an end and the household sighed

with relief. Jim stretched out to his full length, his long legs stretched before him, his hands cupped behind his neck. "I feel like doing something totally different this weekend," Jim exclaimed. "Why don't we all go to Lake Mead tomorrow. You too, Jason."

"Count me out. I have a hot date tomorrow." Jason raised his eyebrows in a comic expression.

"Sounds good to me," Leah responded.

"That's one taker. How about it, girls? Do you want to go to Lake Mead? We can go swimming or boating. Do you want to take a boat tour? How about horseback riding...or all of the above?"

Jim had a captive audience after the first question. It wasn't necessary to entice them further. He was building excitement to a high pitch. Leah observed with irony how good he really was at that.

The children were getting out of control. They were all over Jim now.

Leah laughed with secretive pleasure. "Let's see how well you calm down what you stir up."

The secret meaning didn't pass by Jim's attuned senses. He whispered something in their ears and they immediately scampered off to their bedroom.

"Magic?" Leah asked in amazement.

"I'll let you be the judge of that, in good time," he smiled. A gentleness in his eyes reached out and touched Leah.

Jason, beginning to feel like the third wheel, pushed himself to a standing position. "I better get some shut-eye. I have to work tonight." With his John Wayne-walk, he swayed out of the room.

"Recognize that walk?" Leah whispered, laughing. "He practices it."

Jim laughed amiably. "If he were a little taller he'd

make a hell of a good John Wayne."

"I guess his efforts haven't been wasted. You recognized it."

"I did misjudge him." Jim said. "You can't help but like him."

"I'm glad you see it that way." Leah wondered why the sudden change of heart. "Have you been here long?"

"No," Jim lied. "Just a few minutes." Then he quickly changed the subject. "How about dinner tonight? Before you answer, I have to confess, I promised the girls—their choice."

"I hope you like McDonalds." Leah gave him a warning look.

"Don't worry. I'll talk them into Chinese," he said with an air of confidence.

"In that case, I'll change. Make yourself comfortable." She stood and unbuttoned the collar of her white shirt.

With an easy grace, Jim rose and closed the space between them. He pulled her hand away from her shirt. "Let me do that." A promise flickered from the depths of his eyes as he unfastened another button.

Leah's breath caught as his hand slid across her breast. She pulled away from him, pushing his hand away, but at the same time, sending him a message with her eyes. She, too, acknowledged the inevitability of their union.

They had a pleasant meal of Chinese cuisine. Jim tried to teach the children how to eat with chopsticks, but his efforts were more laughable than exact. Leah didn't bother. She let them play their games while she enjoyed her dinner with conventional utensils.

They went to the MGM gameroom afterwards. Jim

filled the girls' hands with quarters and they played the numerous arcade games that didn't require the skill of more than a five year old. Around ten o'clock they called it an evening. The twins could barely stay awake, their heads bobbing with sleep. Leah wondered if that wasn't Jim's plan.

As was inevitable, they fell asleep on the drive home.

"I hate to put them to bed without a bath," Leah lamented, as she and Jim left their bedroom after struggling to get them into pajamas.

"Let them be children, Leah. A little dirt won't hurt them."

"A little dirt! They have bubble-gum ice cream all over them."

Jim smiled that magnetically contagious smile of his and Leah found herself smiling, too. All of a sudden nothing mattered except being in the rainbow of his smile.

"Is Jason gone?" Jim asked.

"Yes, his door is open. He frequently leaves early."

"Then, we're alone?"

"As alone as I ever get." Leah laughed.

"The girls won't wake up. It's my perfect opportunity to take advantage of you." His resolve was offered in humor, but a determination filtered through.

His steady gaze on Leah was compelling. She laughed nervously. "How about some coffee?" She didn't wait for an answer.

While Leah was in the kitchen, Jim found a Nat King Cole tape and inserted it into the player, then turned down the lights. His opportunity would never be better, he thought, and fully intended to have his way with her tonight.

Leah brought the coffee in on a silver tray. With it she offered a pony glass of Anisette.

They sipped coffee and Anisette while music filled the room and assaulted their senses. Glowing magical feelings washed over Leah as she slipped out of her shoes and leaned luxuriously back against the sofa, her feet tucked up beside her. Her blonde hair shimmered in the faint streaks of light shooting across the room. Her filmy dress lay in scarlet flounces about her slender legs.

Jim watched her with growing passion. His eyes moved from her golden hair to the cleavage her low-cut dress exposed. Her eyes were closed and she seemed to swoon in the dawn of their solitude.

Being with Leah was as lovely as a spring morning, as exhilarating as a fresh sea breeze. Jim's senses were overwhelmed with the closeness of her as he touched her hand.

She opened her eyes slightly and eased closer to him. She felt so mellow. Yet, the closeness of him was working a magic all its own.

Jim slid his hand along the satiny finish of her dress. "So feminine," he whispered, almost to himself. "So lovely."

Leah's hand came up to stroke his face. He caught it in his and pressed a kiss in her palm.

The tender gesture transported Leah to a higher plane of sensitivity. Jim's worshipful gaze pleased her and sent rippling waves of desire through her limbs. Leah had fantasized about moments like this with Jim, and now it was finally a reality, soft music, low lights, and mellow feelings. Her eyes sparkled with pleasure as she appraised the man beside her. His masculinity was almost a visible aura about him. She could faintly smell the clean fragrance he always wore—a combination of musk and spice. His hair was almost platinum against his golden forehead. His tie was loosened and collar unbuttoned. He normally dressed more casually. Leah surmised that he had come straight from work.

Jim took her hands in his and gently pulled her to him. She felt his lips, whisper-soft against her brow. Slowly they descended. As soft velvet cradles a priceless gem, his lips covered hers. A touch so light, so warm, so moist, created an unbelievable intimacy. With feather-like softness, his fingertips touched her face, sliding back to her neck and down across her shoulders, easing her closer to him. His mouth moved against hers, developing her untapped passion to rivers of desire. Slowly and deliberately, his lips eased away from hers, marking a path of fire down the length of her regal neck. Leah felt his breath and moist lips hot against her bare flesh. She wrapped her hands around his neck, feeling the tension and strength there. His hands explored the tiny buttons at the bodice of her dress, but he couldn't master them.

"Help me, Leah," he implored in a raspy voice.

She obeyed his command with trembling fingers. If there was any doubt in his mind of her submission, it was dispelled now. But she didn't care. She didn't want to play games anymore. All she wanted was to be in his embrace, experiencing the ecstasy which filled her.

Jim's delight at finding her breasts bare beneath her dress manifested itself in a low moan of pleasure. His mouth closed over a taut nipple while his hands moved downward and around to the small of her back.

Leah's hands were lost in a mass of thick hair, as she held his head. The pleasure his mouth bestowed on her tender breasts was sweet agony. Her body writhed with impatient anticipation. Her hands slid between their bodies and she anxiously unbuttoned his shirt, pulling it away from his chest. Her hands slid from his waist up the front of his chest, savoring the silky sensation of fine hair against her fingertips. His muscles were firm and rigid against her touch. With one hand, Jim took hers and lowered it to his thigh. Following his encouragement, she found the expression of his manhood. A river of liquid fire flowed through her as the hardness of him made her gasp.

A tormented moan came from deep within Jim as his hard body slid over hers, pulling her beneath him. His hand slid under her dress and traveled up her thigh.

When he touched her an involuntary gasp mingled with a shuddering ecstasy enveloped her. Her senses reeled as she arched her body into his, demanding the satisfaction his touch promised. Her actions lit a fire in Jim and his hands rapidly went to her waist and expertly pulled her pantyhose down. She helped remove them from her feet. Barely a moment was lost and Jim's exploring hands worked magic on her ready body. He touched her magically, tenderly, expertly. Leah writhed against him impatiently.

He eased his body over hers. Unable to contain the raw passion that possessed him, Jim took her—not tenderly now, but with abandon. His control was gone and fiery passion took over, bringing out the oldest of animal instincts. He devoured her lips, hungrily drinking of her very essence. His hands slipped under her hips pulling her into him, giving a pleasure that caused involuntary cries of passion.

Jim crooned words of love against Leah's ear, incoherent and hoarse. The rhythm of their bodies was perfectly synchronized, rocking in unison to a cadence that exploded in a crescendo of release.

LAS VEGAS ILLUSION

Jim eased to his side, gazing down at Leah. Her eyes were brilliant with the afterglow of spent passion. "I never want to make love to any other woman," Jim whispered. His blue eyes had turned as dark as a raging sea, burning with determination. "I'll never let you go. Your passion is mine, for now and all time. Your body will be mine to pleasure and explore and possess." His lips came down on hers and lightly brushed against them. "I haven't begun with you yet. There's fire in you that's never been touched. I want it all, everything you have to give—and then some."

Leah was shocked by the new passion that burned inside her. His voice hypnotized her into response. Breathlessly, she eased up on one elbow. "Jim, I would like to take a shower, look at us, we're a mess." She managed a small laugh, but she was afraid he wouldn't let her go. Her thoughts were fragmented. She was, even though after the fact, embarrassed that they had so recklessly made love with their clothes still on.

Jim smiled down at her. "I love your proper ways," he teased. "I'll help you."

In the shower Jim lathered his hands with soap and smoothed them across her chest, around her breasts and down her stomach and thighs. It was more a priming than a cleansing shower. Leah abandoned her reserve and explored his hard muscular body with equal delight. The streaming sprays of hot water warmed their bodies to greater desires. Jim took hold of the spigot and turned it away from them, causing it to spray against a wall. He lowered his head to her waiting breast, taking the rose-hued nipple into his mouth. He nibbled with patient pleasure. His hands circled her waist as he lowered himself to his knees, then slid over her stomach and around her hips. He pulled her close to him as his mouth took her in a new and delightful way. Leah gasped with a pleasure so new it sent shudders of fiery sensations through her trembling body. Her reaction fired Jim to more demanding liberation.

Leah's deepest fantasies were being fulfilled and to a magnitude that she had not thought possible. Her body responded to his caress with a force of its own. Leah's hands dug into his shoulders and her body arched in a spasm of total rapture. A tormented cry of release escaped Leah's lips, coming from deep within her throat. Her chest heaved and she swayed, threatening to lose her balance.

Jim quickly rose and put both strong arms around her. "Steady." He laughed, kissing her on the neck and shoulder. "Let's go to your bed," he said huskily.

Leah touched his cheek lightly. "Only if we dry off first." She laughed softly.

Jim stepped out of the shower and got a towel, wrapped it around Leah gently, pressing it to her body, then pulled her close to him and kissed her lovingly. He held her a moment, then pulled the towel away and patted her body dry. Leah smiled. A heady feeling overpowered her. She glowed in the warmth of his attention. Pulling away, she took a fresh towel and dried him, marveling at his muscled body. The hardness of his shoulders and back, the strapping muscles in his legs, the sheer beauty of his body mesmerized her.

She wanted to pleasure him as he had her. She was unskilled, but natural instincts took over as she took him into her mouth. Jim moaned with pleasure, all the while moving and gently instructing her. Leah enjoyed being his protégé.

Satisfied with his student, Jim pulled her up and embraced her tenderly. "My God, Leah, you're so lovely."

You're so wonderful, I don't ever want to lose you." He lifted her into his arms and carried her into the bedroom, lowered her gently onto the bed, and eased in beside her. He stroked her damp hair and murmured words of love.

All through the night, Jim and Leah swayed in Love's embrace, experiencing one another anew. Leah had passed from consciousness into a twilight of ecstasy she never dreamed possible.

The next morning, Leah woke with an inner peace that she had not felt in a very long time. Jim had left her with a sated body and contented spirit. She stretched languidly and if she had been a cat, would have purred.

She could still smell his fragrance on her bed and body. The afterglow of love shone on Leah's face and made her eyes radiant.

She should have been exhausted, Jim having left only a few short hours ago. But she wasn't. She felt a new vitality and with a surge of adrenalin, vaulted out of bed and prepared for the day ahead.

Jim, Leah, and the twins drove to Lake Mead. It was a warm day but the lack of humidity kept it comfortable. They did all the fun things that Jim had promised. It seemed that since meeting him they were experiencing one new thing after another.

It felt good to Leah to get away from the clamor of the casino. The sounds of Vegas were unique unto themselves, the ever-ringing slot machines, the murmur of the "21" pit, the energy and excitement of the crap tables, the tension and mystique of the baccarat pit...the feel, the sounds, the smell...Las Vegas, an empire in the desert.

The people who lived in Vegas were special, too.

Friendships seemed stronger, acceptance of one another more automatic. Leah reflected on all of this from a rare distance.

The day with Jim was magical. Their eyes met in secret embraces and his tenderness extended to the twins in an intensified manner. Being with him in this way gave Leah thoughts of permanency—not planning thoughts, but curious thoughts. She became more interested in his life. She wanted to know about his friends, his hobbies, his likes and dislikes. As she mulled this over in her mind, it became more apparent to her just how closed-mouthed he had been. She knew so little about him, and now it had become even more important. He did love children and animals, that could only be to his benefit, and he kept in marvelous shape. He either worked-out or he participated in some out-of-doors sport. The latter seemed more likely, since he maintained a healthy tan. That thought provoked deeper consideration now that she was more knowledgeable. His tan was obtained while wearing a bathing suit—a skimpy one at that. She hesitated to start a dialogue that sounded like an inquisition but, all of a sudden everything about him was important.

In spite of heightened fascination with Jim, Leah couldn't put aside that old nagging feeling. She looked at the magnificent man at her side and wondered anew, who this man was that was inching his way into her heart. It was the most enjoyable day Leah could remember since coming to Vegas.

In the next few weeks, Leah's relationship with Jim intensified. He spent more time with her, finding new reasons to be in Vegas. Jim seemed to fit right in with Leah's friends. He was quick-witted, amusing, and complimentary. He fast became an accepted face around the Golden Nugget. He was frequently in town during the week and was often included in conversations about tokes, which was considered privileged information, particularly for the times.

Leah was pleased that friends and co-workers liked and trusted him and that was even more reason for her to be sure of Jim. She had brought him into the fold, that made her responsible.

There was something in Jim's manner that sometimes triggered a suspicion in Leah. The occasional tremor of his voice or hand when he spoke was an incongruity. His demeanor was otherwise extremely self-assured.

Leah, only through necessity, came to terms with her staunch upbringing and decided that not only for her own sake, but for the sake of all of the dealers who had become friends with Jim, she would call Harrah's. It was the only way her doubts could be dispelled, or verified.

CHAPTER FIVE

Leah's heart was in her throat. Her pulse raced and her hands trembled—all over a phone call.

She clapped away from the table and forced her footsteps toward the pay phone on the wall. She called information and got the number for Harrah's in Reno and, using her telephone credit card number, dialed direct.

"Hello, do you have a shift boss there by the name of Jim Henderson?"

"Yes, just one moment please," a feminine voice answered.

Oh, damn! What will I say to him. She quickly hung up the telephone. *Well...he is a shift boss! He does work at Harrah's. I guess he is on the level. I must be crazy! Why was I so suspicious of him?* Leah leaned back against the wall, letting out a deep sigh. A voice startled her.

"Leah, you look like a snowflake—before the pollution got to it. What are you up to? Who died?" Jenny asked.

"Oh, God! Jenny, I just called Harrah's to see if Jim really works there. He does!" she said incredulously.

"Damn, Leah, you act surprised if someone tells you the truth. You're such a cynic!" A smile slowly spread across Jenny's face. "I'm glad," she said softly.

"Me, too." Leah relaxed. I like having him around. I didn't think I could ever care for another man, but I think I'm in love with him. Maybe true love is the kind that grows, slowly but surely."

Leah went back to her game feeling a relief that almost defied gravity.

Jenny had suggested a cook-out that weekend as a sort of private celebration between the two of them. Everyone would be there, but only she and Jenny would know the true reason for it.

Leah was on auto-pilot, her deft hands a blur as she dealt to the three players in front of her.

Out of the corner of her eye Leah caught sight of a threesome strolling down the aisle toward her. They epitomized the "High Roller" image—two heavy-set Italian men flanking a beautiful blonde. All were expensively dressed and sporting pounds of gold jewelry—chains, bracelets, rings. They scrutinized each table and dealer as they passed.

They settled at Leah's table. She wondered what it was about her that drew their attention. The standard reason for players to choose a particular table was if it looked like the dealer was losing. Many thought this was indicated by the amount of chips in front of the players. Of course this didn't always prove true.

Two of her players left immediately upon hearing the newcomers call for markers. Leah was grateful for that, as one of the two was such a slow counter that she was practically playing his hand for him. She couldn't get away with that if there was any big action at her game. Leah called the pit boss and he took care of the markers, arranging for the chips to be delivered from the cage. He handed each man a voucher to sign and the cocktail waitress was summoned with the Cricket-Clicker.

The men were playing blacks. Hundred-dollar chips weren't handled any differently than one-dollar chips. It only became complicated when several color chips were being played at the same time.

Leah watched the blonde. She was magnificent with long platinum blonde hair, perfect white teeth, and a classic nose. There wasn't a feature on her face that didn't emulate perfection. Her bosom swelled out of a low-cut, but sophisticated, white dress. She wasn't thin, but what one might call voluptuous. Her demeanor was not haughty as Leah had expected. She seemed genteel and her attitude, pleasant.

The Italian man on her left occasionally shoved a stack of chips to her. She never played more than one chip at a time and he frequently instructed her on how to play her hand. If the probability was that she would take his card, he would have her pass, even if it meant staying on less than ten.

The shift boss was in the pit now and the game was being closely monitored.

Leah puzzled over the blonde. She was watching every move Leah made. She also had an unusual interest in the pit boss and observed the other tables and dealers, as well.

The three were playing conventionally, which took the pressure off Leah. If they had been fluctuating the size of their bets drastically, it would indicate that they were counters.

Leah saw the casino manager's long strides bringing him down the outside aisle. He reached the table and greeted the men warmly, clapping them on the back. "It's nice to see you again. Is Leah being good to you?" he asked good-naturedly. His glance toward Leah gave his words a different meaning.

"Not bad. Not bad." The man smoking the wrinkled cigar put one arm around the voluptuous blonde and said, "Murrey, I would like you to meet Johanna. She's from Reno. Just moved here. She's a hell of a good blackjack dealer."

Nothing more needed to be said. Murrey got the message. He gave the girl a quick appraising glance. "Let's see what she can do. Leah, let Johanna take over for a few hands."

Leah took the deck from her left hand and clamped it over the cards in the discard rack and brought them all out and spread them on the table. Her heart went out to the blonde. Panic was written all over Johanna's face as she awkwardly removed herself from the chair.

Murrey unsnapped the velvet rope sectioning the pit off from the rest of the casino and let her pass through.

Leah stepped to the side and watched the blonde approach.

She wiped her palms on her dress and gave Leah a desperate glance.

Leah spoke in hushed tones so that only Johanna could hear. "You'll be all right. Just relax. Go slow."

Johanna looked grateful and with trembling hands scooped the deck up and started shuffling.

Leah wished there was something she could do to help, but there wasn't. She kept her position beside Johanna, as was customary when a dealer auditioned. They frequently made mistakes in their high state of anxiety and it was Leah's job to make sure that didn't happen on her table.

Leah's audition at the Nugget stood out vividly in

her mind, even now, and she shuddered to remember her recent audition at the Flamingo Hotel on the strip—a disaster of the highest degree. She hadn't been aware that their discard racks weren't fastened to the table as they were at the Nugget. She had dealt one hand and with exaggerated force, due to tension, slammed the discards into the rack, causing it to fly across the pit. Cards scattered in every direction and, to make it worse, Leah left the table to pick them up, leaving the money rack unprotected. She was so flustered that she left the pit, giving the game back to the dealer. She never called back to see if she got the job. She knew she didn't.

Johanna was not a smooth dealer, but she knew the basics, which only indicated that she wasn't experienced.

Murrey had seated himself at the table and after a few hands he said, "Johanna, report tomorrow morning at ten o'clock, ready to work."

He said a few words in parting to the men and strolled off.

Johanna looked at Leah, confused. Murrey hadn't said that the audition was over but for all practical purposes, it was.

Leah smiled at Johanna. "I'll take it from here and, congratulations."

Johanna *handed* the deck to Leah.

Leah felt awkward in the transaction for it was not the thing to do—but knew that Johanna, in her excitement and relief, had simply forgotten the rules.

Leah glanced at the pit boss to see if he had witnessed the exchange. He was shaking his head in disbelief, but at the same time an amused smirk covered his face. He, too, remembered what it was like to audition for a dealing job. It was an experience that one never forgot. He unwrapped a new deck of cards and was checking them before replacing Leah's deck. Decks were replaced periodically throughout the day so as to always keep the cards fresh, but especially necessary after a nervous dealer auditioned. They inevitably bent the cards, not to mention the effect of sweaty hands. Tomorrow would be an important day for Johanna.

Johanna's presence at the Nugget was not readily accepted. There was jealousy among the girls. One thing that went against her was the way she procured her job—flaunting her juice. Things like that were generally handled in a more discreet way.

Leah befriended Johanna and, with Jenny's help, did her best to make her feel welcome.

Friday morning, Johanna joined Leah and Jenny for breakfast.

"Johanna," Jenny asked, "didn't you say that you were from Reno?"

"Yes, I did. I have to confess...I wasn't a dealer there. I never dealt anywhere before. I did go to Dealers' School, that's how I learned." She lowered her eyes, displaying perfectly applied black lashes. Slowly, she raised them, fixing a gaze on Leah. "You knew it, didn't you?"

Leah laughed. "Not at first, but, when you *handed* me the deck of cards, I was strongly suspicious."

Johanna put her hands over her eyes as a rush of crimson spread over her cheeks. "Oh, I know! I could just die. I can't believe I did that."

Jenny interrupted, "What did you do in Reno?"

"I was a cocktail waitress at Harrah's."

"Ah ha! Jackpot! I never met anyone from Reno that didn't work at Harrah's."

Johanna looked puzzled.

"Did you know a shift boss by the name of Jim Henderson?" Jenny asked.

"Sure, I knew Jim. Tall, good-looking guy. Kind of quiet, kept to himself. Dressed real conservatively, except for those outrageous ties. He never paid attention to what was in style. He would have a real wide one on one day and a skinny one the next. He was a little strange."

Leah took it all in. Until the last revelation, she had been pleased. But this didn't sound like the Jim she knew. He was the epitome of style.

"Johanna, was Jim about six foot two or three, blond hair, blue eyes, square jaw?" Leah asked.

"No. Jim is not a blond. He has brown hair and brown eyes. About that tall, though."

Leah and Jenny looked at one another, their eyes locked in a moment of shared revelation.

Leah's eyes grew wide and an expression of near panic covered her face.

Jenny, too, looked panic stricken.

Johanna watched the two of them. "Is something wrong?"

"Not anything we can't handle," Jenny recovered. Her voice took on a determined tone and fire virtually shot from her green eyes. "Leah, don't even think about canceling dinner tonight. I'll come up with something. There's got to be a way to get to the bottom of this."

Jenny went on to her game. Leah and Johanna stayed for another cup of coffee. They were relief dealers today and didn't go on until 10:15.

Johanna spoke softly. "Leah, if there's anything I can do to help...well, you were there for me and I want you to know that I'm grateful for that. If there's anything at all..."

"Thanks Johanna. I don't think there's anything anyone can do. I've been seeing a guy for a few months now and it seems that we're about to find out that he's...someone else."

"Someone else?"

"Yeah, someone else. His name is Jim Henderson. He's blond-haired and blue-eyed—a shift boss at Harrah's in Reno."

Johanna stared at Leah, her eyebrows furrowed together. "I can't believe it. There's only one Jim Henderson at Harrah's...oh, Leah. What are you going to do?"

"For the moment, I'm going to forget it and put in a good day's work. After that, I might slit my wrists." Leah's voice never changed.

They got up to leave and Johanna put her arm around Leah. "No man's worth it, Honey. I can tell you that for a fact. I had my whole face redone for a man and then he walked out on me."

Leah looked at Johanna in amazement. "You mean, plastic surgery?"

Johanna laughed. "No one is born with a nose like this." She pulled her hair away from her face to give Leah a profile view. "Chin extended, deep creases in my forehead filled in, full face lift, nose job, of course, and all my teeth are capped. I mean every one."

Leah's mouth was agape. Finally she said, "It's none of my business but how old are you? I mean, if you've had a total face lift."

"Don't let it get around but, I'm pushing fifty." Johanna smiled proudly.

Leah couldn't believe her ears. "My God, Johanna. That's incredible. You look twenty-five, and your face is perfect. That guy did you a favor if this is the result."

"Well, maybe he did," she said. A sadness crept into her

voice. "See you later."

Leah was determined not to let the conversation of the morning disturb her. In her heart she felt that there was a logical explanation. She wasn't at all convinced that the two Jims were one and the same.

The day went by swiftly and her only opportunity to speak to Jenny again was on the way to the parking lot.

"How are you doing, Babe?" Jenny asked, keeping stride with Leah.

"I'm doing fine," Leah answered, a brave smile on her face.

"I have an idea. Tonight when you and Jim get to the house, pull into the driveway. I'll have my car in the garage."

"Jenny, you never put your car in the garage. What's the deal?"

"We don't have time to go into it now. I'll explain tonight. Don't worry about a thing. Just be cool. Don't let Jim know that we're on to him. Okay?"

"Okay, Jenny. I'm not so sure Johanna knew what she was talking about. It sounds too bizarre."

They walked by the cage and had their parking tickets stamped and took the elevator up to the Plaza parking garage.

"Later," Jenny said, as she took off in the opposite direction from Leah.

Leah got in her car and cautiously descended the gray coil of cement until finally reaching the street. The drive home was spent convincing herself that Jim was indeed truthful and trustworthy.

Leah arrived home to find Jim and the children anxiously awaiting her.

"Mommy! Mommy, Jim has a surprise for you!" the

twins excitedly reported in unison.

Jim modestly confirmed their report. "Now, just sit down and relax. Here goes." Jim gave the twins a secretive look as they sat, one on each side of him, on the sofa.

The children's electric organ was on the coffee table in front of them. Jim pushed his sleeves up and with a grand gesture, planted his fingers on the keyboard. He pecked out the melody of *Two Loves*. The twins on occasion had a part, too. They were all so proud when they had finished.

Tears filled Leah's eyes. "That was lovely. Just lovely. What a nice surprise."

"We worked on it all day, Mommy," Carrie confessed.

Leah kissed the children and turned to Jim. "You're crazy," she said smiling. "Wonderfully crazy."

Jim took Leah in his arms and held her close.

Leah pulled away abruptly. "I almost forgot, we're having a cook-out at Jenny's tonight. I hope that meets with your approval, T-bone steaks, twice-baked potatoes, corn-on-the-cob. Doesn't that just make your mouth water?"

"All of a sudden I'm starving! What can we take?"

"Let's stop and get some red wine on the way."

They stopped at a *Skaggs-Albertson's* on the way and Jim went in for the wine. It seemed forever before he came out. When he finally did, he was all smiles, his arms loaded down with the wine and a huge bouquet of fresh-cut flowers.

"What in the world took you so long?" Leah asked.

Jim seemed extremely pleased with himself. "I've got something for the girls." He smiled and pulled out a half-gallon size paper bucket.

Leah recognized it immediately as one of the paper buckets used at the slot machines.

"I can't believe it, these are Eisenhower silver dollars!"

"I won the jackpot," he said with satisfaction. "There are fifty in all, twenty-five for each of the girls." He turned to the back seat. "You kids save these, because someday they'll be worth a lot of money."

"Thank you! Thank you!" they squealed, as they ran their fingers through the silver dollars in the bucket. Anything Jim did for them was extraordinary in their minds. They adored him. It meant nothing to them, of course, that the gift was Eisenhower silver dollars. To them it was simply money—money that they couldn't spend.

They arrived at Jenny's house and Jim bowed and presented Jenny with the vivid spring bouquet. "For our beautiful hostess."

"What did you go and do that for?" Jenny demanded, with mock disapproval.

"I was hopeful that this would get me out of cooking," he teased.

"Well, it didn't work." She handed him a tray of steaks. "You can get these started any time." Standing nearer to him she whispered, "You know Drake burns them every time!"

Jim started the grill and Leah poured the wine. Drake was already well on his way to oblivion.

"Jenny, what can I do to help?" Leah asked.

"I just need to fix this salad and we'll be ready to eat. Here, you can score and slice this cucumber."

"Jenny, I don't understand why you put up with Drake, he's such a lush. You deserve better than that.

You didn't say anything to him about Jim, did you?"

"I didn't say a word about Jim. I didn't think it was any of his concern. Besides, we couldn't trust him worth a flip and he'd probably rally to Jim's aid to boot."

"Probably so. I have to hand it to you, you sure handle that chauvinistic bull shit better than I could." Leah rolled her eyes.

"That's no problem, I just ignore him. He throws a lot of it around but when it comes right down to it, he's damn lucky to have me and he knows it." She flipped her long red hair in an arrogant gesture.

"You're too much, Jenny." Leah laughed. "Hand me some salad plates and I'll get this dished out."

"Steaks are ready," Jim announced, as he entered the kitchen.

"Good, your timing is perfect." Jenny handed him a tray. "I'll pour more wine and we're all set."

Jenny had arranged the cut flowers into a low centerpiece for the table.

"This steak is absolutely melting in my mouth. You have really out-done yourself," Leah praised.

"Thank you." Jenny and Jim responded in unison.

"What do you mean, 'thank you'? I'm the one who cooked them," Jim spouted.

"How good do you think you would look if I had bought tough steaks?"

"If you two don't stop there will be no dessert for you," Leah admonished. She watched them affectionately, thinking how lucky she was to have such wonderful friends. Her lover, her best friend, all the children—so happy together. She felt happier and more complete than she had in a very long time. Then, suddenly, she remembered. How good she had become at blocking out bad things. *Oh, God, don't let it be true.* She had been so wrapped up in her contentment that she forgot Johanna's revelation. She forgot Jenny's undisclosed plans for the evening. A tightness gripped her chest.

"Leah, why so serious? I have the distinct impression that you're not really with us," Jim cajoled her.

Leah started. She laughed nervously in an effort to camouflage her thoughts. "Just drifting. What do you say we go into the living room and get comfortable?"

"Let's do," Jenny joined in.

They were all sprawled out in the living room, relaxing and letting their dinner settle, when Jenny exploded, "I have got to have some ice cream! Pralines and cream. Doesn't that sound good?"

Jim and Drake both groaned.

"Jenny, does this mean you want someone to go to *Baskin Robbins* to get it?" Drake asked suspiciously.

"No, it certainly does not." Jenny jumped to her feet. "Leah and I will get it. Won't we?" She gave Leah a meaningful look.

"Sure," Leah laughed, pulling herself up from the sofa reluctantly.

"Oh, I forgot, I put my car in the garage and you're parked behind me." Jenny turned toward Jim. "I guess we'll have to take your car. Is that all right?"

Jim resisted only slightly. "Yeah...sure."

Leah walked into the kitchen to find where she had abandoned her purse. "Okay, I'm ready," she announced as she entered the living room, just in time to see Jim extract one key from his key ring and hand it to Jenny. Leah was immediately struck by the gesture as she sensed Jenny was. They both walked out of the door in silence.

Once outside, with the door closed behind them,

they stopped in the middle of the sidewalk and looked at each other—a multitude of unspoken words passed between them. Jenny handed Leah the key. Leah continued to the car, opened the door, got in and started the engine. Jenny slowly followed. They drove in silence the short distance to the ice cream store. Leah pulled to a stop in the parking lot, just short of the bright lights surrounding the store. She turned the engine off and stared straight ahead.

"Leah," Jenny said softly, "you know what this looks like, don't you? I was hoping for your sake that I was wrong. Jim played right into our hands."

"It was a strange thing to do. It looks like he doesn't trust us with his keys. Why wouldn't he trust us? What keys did he have on that ring that were so important?"

Jenny reached for the glove box and pushed the button. It didn't move. "The key to the glove box, for one," Jenny said angrily, slamming her hand against it. "Do you remember what I told you about Jim not carrying a billfold?" Jenny asked.

"Yes, I do. You said it wasn't uncommon for men to leave it in the glove box of their car. Is that what you're thinking?"

"Yes, that's what I'm thinking. But I didn't count on Jim extracting the ignition key." She looked strangely malicious as she tried to wedge her fingers into the slight opening on either side of the lock.

"Jenny, my God, what are you doing? You'll break it. This is a rented car!"

Jenny pulled viciously and suddenly a loud, "Crack!" sounded out as the panel of the glove box split, half of it falling to the floor.

"My God! My God! Jenny, what have you done?"

Jenny swiftly reached through the opening and extracted

a brown leather billfold and a small yellow legal pad.

Leah watched, awe-struck as Jenny opened the billfold. The look on her face sent chills down Leah's spine.

"Jenny, what is it?" Leah asked, her voice barely a whisper, her heart nearly stopped.

Jenny's face was pale and she didn't move her eyes from their fixed state.

Leah reached over and took the billfold out of Jenny's hand. There was an identification card. *United States Government, Department of the Treasury, Douglas Lourdes.*

"Department of the Treasury!" Leah looked puzzled.

"IRS, Honey," Jenny said, with the utmost disgust, as she leafed through the legal pad in her hand.

"IRS!" Leah gasped. "Whose billfold is this?" she said fearfully, not fully grasping what was happening.

"Leah, look at this." Jenny handed her the legal pad.

Leah grew pale as she read out loud: "Leah Aston, thirty-two years old. Address, Desert Inn Road. Married twice: First husband, Tom Jennings, deceased—father of twin daughters, Carrie and Sherry, age five; second husband..." Leah read on and on as her life lay sprawled out in front of her on yellow paper.

"How did he get all this information?" Leah asked weakly. "What does he want from me?"

"I'll tell you the truth, Honey, I don't know. He's probably known for a long time now how much we're making in tokes. Damn! When I think, he's actually been in the Dealer's Lounge with us when tokes were being counted...we've really been taken for a ride. I guess your initial instincts were right. I'll never question them again."

"You know," Leah mused, "his hands sometimes

shook, just a little when he talked. No wonder he was nervous, living a lie—a double life. How much more is there, I wonder? What kind of trouble am I in?"

"Let me see that billfold, maybe there's more to discover right here." Jenny started going through the billfold, not missing a scrap of paper. "Ah-ha! Here's a business card!" She read out loud. "Douglas Lourdes, United States Government, Attorney-at-Law, San Francisco, California. Office phone, home phone...Leah, here's a home telephone number!"

"Jenny, do you think he stole that wallet?" Leah asked in desperation.

"Not likely." She flipped through the credit cards until she came to a picture of Jim, kneeling with his Saint Bernard sitting in front of him, Jim's chin resting on the dog's head.

Leah touched the picture affectionately. "Flower," she said softly, tears in her eyes.

Jenny looked at her with awakening concern.

"Flower, that's his name...the Saint Bernard." Leah smiled.

"Leah," Jenny shook her. "Pull yourself together. We've got to figure out what to do next." She thought for a moment. "First, I'll go get the ice cream. You stay here."

Jenny got out of the car and was soon back with the ice cream. She opened the door to Leah's side of the car. "Get over," she instructed. "We've been gone too long. We need to get back. Give me one of those business cards."

Leah obeyed and moved over to the passenger's side, allowing Jenny to drive. She removed one of Jim's cards from the wallet and handed it to her.

"Now, let's put everything back like it was," Jenny barked.

"Like it was!" Leah screamed. "The god damn glove box is broken. My heart is broken. My life is in shambles. The IRS is after me!" Tears ran down her cheeks.

Jenny knew that Leah needed her help now more than ever before if she were to get through this.

"Leah, do I have to slap you?" Jenny said calmly.

Leah looked shocked, then slowly a smile spread across her face. "No," she sighed. "My dear friend, what would I do without you?"

Jenny sloughed off the compliment. "Leah, hand me that broken piece, let's see if we can push it back into place."

"Jenny, how will we get home tonight without Jim noticing that this is broken?"

"Put one of the girls on your lap, or slouch in the seat with your knees against the dash, if you have to."

"Jenny, I'm so scared."

"I know, Babe. I know. There's just one thing to do now, take it one step at a time. Try to act like nothing happened. Let's go home, eat ice cream, and make a telephone call."

"I'm not sure I want to know more," Leah said, sighing heavily.

"You can't run away from the truth, no matter how much it hurts. Leah, I wish I could say something to ease the pain. Maybe, just maybe, it's not as bad as it looks." Jenny spoke the words but even she didn't believe them. How could she expect Leah to. She knew how Leah felt—as if something had been taken away from her, a private part of herself, her life. She had exposed her children to a man who now proved to be a fraud. The guilt again...did it ever end for a single mother? As Jenny drove home she stole a glance at Leah. She was trying to pull herself together, swiping at the tears that didn't want to stop. Jenny pulled into the driveway and turned off the engine. She patted Leah on the hand. "You look a mess. Don't get too close to anyone until you get a chance to wash your face and get some powder on. Chin up, now." She gave Leah a reassuring smile.

"Where have you been?" Drake demanded, as they walked in the door.

"We couldn't decide on a flavor." Jenny kissed him on the nose. "We finally decided on the flavor we went for." She laughed as lightheartedly as she could manage and dished out ice cream for everyone.

"Come on," she whispered to Leah, and they headed for the bedroom. Jenny reached into her pocket, pulled out the card and dialed the home phone number. "Hello, may I speak to Jim Henderson?"

"Jim Henderson?" A woman's voice seemed puzzled on the other end. "This is not his number. He lives in Reno, you can get his number through information. Are you sure it's not Douglas Lourdes with whom you want to speak?"

Jenny didn't know what to say. She stammered, "I...I don't know...may I ask who this is?" Jenny held her breath. She knew she was pushing it.

"This is Mrs. Lourdes," she answered. "I don't understand why you would be calling Jim at this number."

"I'm so sorry. I just have the wrong number. Thank you for your trouble." Jenny hung up quickly before the woman could ask more questions. She let out a deep breath and then drew in another.

"What is it?" Leah asked.

"There is a Mrs. Lourdes," she said gently.

"Maybe it's his mother," Leah rationalized.

"I don't think so, Leah. She was too curious about this call. It's interesting that she apparently knows, or knows of, Jim Henderson. This is getting more confusing all the time."

"So then, we can assume that Jim is not only a fraud, but a married fraud. What else can happen?" Leah sighed defeatedly.

"Nothing, I hope," Jenny retorted. "Just get the kids home safely. You might not want to even mention this to him. It would be safer. Just get him out of the house and forget it."

"Forget it? Forget the man I love. I can't believe this is happening. I've been used in some bizarre bureaucratic game. I just can't believe this has all happened." Leah was totally distraught and even more frightened. She composed herself to the best of her ability and they returned to the living room.

"Jim, let's call it a night," Leah suggested, without a trace of deception in her voice. Concealing emotion was a big part of her daytime life and now it served her well.

They drove home in silence. Jim could not see the glove box from where he sat behind the steering wheel. Leah was holding Carrie in her lap as the child slept. Sherry was asleep in the back seat. Leah was wondering what she would say to Jim when they got home. She knew she would have to confront him. She couldn't possibly hold this inside.

Jim pulled into the parking lot, parked the car and yawned as he turned the engine off. "I'm exhausted," he said, "but not so much as to pass up a brandy with my best girl." He smiled widely, showing perfectly matched white teeth.

Leah's heart ached, but she tried not to show her feelings. "Let's get the girls to bed first," she said, as she opened the car door. Jim picked Sherry up from the back seat and carried her. Leah took Carrie, had the key ready in her hand, and opened the door. She quickly tucked the girls in their beds. Jim had a brandy waiting for her in the living room.

"Leah, you're stunning, even after a long day." He smiled. "Have I told you that I'm crazy about you?"

Leah raised one eyebrow and fixed a mute gaze on him. "You wouldn't lie to me, would you Jim? Or should I say...Douglas?" Leah's knees felt weak. She moved slowly from the hallway entrance where she stood, to the loveseat across the room from him.

Jim stiffened. He didn't say a word, but seemed to be wildly searching for an escape route out of his dilemma.

"Just tell me, is it true? Are you Douglas Lourdes?" she demanded.

Jim fidgeted uncomfortably. "Yes, I am. Let me explain, Leah. It..."

"And Mrs. Lourdes? Your wife?"

Jim showed renewed shock. It appeared that he might deny it, but on second thought, "Yes, Leah, but it's not like it seems. Please let me explain."

Leah slowly rose, her face showing no emotion as she opened the door and waited for him to leave.

"Leah, you're in shock, you need time to think. There is an explanation," he insisted.

She didn't answer, just stood holding the door open.

Jim walked over to her. Standing very close, his blue eyes misty, he said, "Leah, I've never said it in just so many words, but, I love you. I love you more than life itself. I know this looks bad...but honestly, I can explain."

Leah didn't think he believed what he was saying himself. He seemed scared.

"Good night, Douglas." The name felt strange on her lips.

He silently walked out of the door, a defeated look in his eyes.

Douglas Lourdes heard the door close behind him. He took the steps one at a time, shoulders slumped, hands in his pockets. He cursed over and over to himself, and at himself. How could he have expected it to end any other way? But, end it wouldn't. If it took the rest of his life he would make it right with Leah. He hadn't been honest with her. But even now, he still couldn't be totally honest. There was so much more at stake here; not just the IRS. That was only a small part of the picture. One thing for sure, he would have to turn his report in on the Golden Nugget. He had prepared it over six weeks ago. It would probably hurt Leah, but then, he had warned her. If necessary, he would help her. But would she let him help? Douglas opened the door to his rented car. He slid in and leaned back in the seat, his hands cupped behind his head. He closed his eyes and mentally transported himself to his own special utopia. He was piloting the Catalina Express around Clear Lake. The salt air was whipping at his hair and stinging his skin. No one ever found him when he stole off to Seabrook, Texas. It was a secret that gave him tremendous delight. Just he and his little Chris-Craft Cruiser...funny, he lived a stone's throw away from San Francisco Bay, but that wasn't the same, somehow. Jim's gaze fell across the glove box and his eyebrows furrowed. Suddenly, he broke into a laughter filled with surprise and admiration. So, that's how they found out, he thought. Crazy Las Vegas women!

Jim pulled himself upright and with a new determination, turned the key in the ignition. He knew that somehow, somehow, he would win Leah back. There were a lot of obstacles, some of which he hadn't resolved yet, but he would. Suddenly, his thoughts turned to Samantha Lourdes. His eyes lost their sparkle. That was another story.

CHAPTER SIX

The night was endless as Leah paced the floor. Opening the patio doors, she took a deep breath of clean night air. It was a balmy evening in Las Vegas. The days were becoming increasingly warm but after sundown it was glorious. Her patio overlooked the pool and the sight was as lovely as any postcard. Its glistening rivers of aqua mesmerized her. The deep green of palm trees was acutely accented by the muted black of wrought iron fencing.

Leah was in a trance-like state. She relived the evening over and over in her mind. What hurt the most was the fact that Douglas was married. Their whole relationship had been a lie. She wondered if he had children, too. There were so many questions and no answers. Yet, if she had let him explain, could she believe him even then? In her deepest heart of hearts she wanted him to explain and convince her that it was all a wild mistake, that he loved only her and would never leave her.

Leah watched the sun rise. There was no sleep for her tonight. In a few short hours the twins would be up. Leah heard a key turn in the door. Jason's body stiffened in surprise.

"Leah, what are you doing up so early on a Sunday?"

Jason's eyes narrowed, concern filtering through.

"It's a long story, Jason. A horror story at that."

"I'll make us a cup of tea and you can tell me all about it."

Leah unraveled the events of the evening to him as he sat in stunned silence.

"That Jenny has guts, I'll give her that," he finally said.

"And our Jim, or I should say Douglas, I guess we could say he has guts, too, couldn't we?" she said bitterly.

"He's a hell of a nice guy, or so I thought. I really think you should at least give him a shot at explaining."

"He's married, Jason. What is there to explain about that? I just can't fathom what he could say to me that would justify all the deception."

"Give him a chance, Leah. Do it for yourself if not for him. You deserve an explanation."

"No, Jason. I won't. I don't ever want to see him again. Jason, I trusted him. I trusted him with my children. I trusted him with my friends. I may have jeopardized the entire Golden Nugget through him. He's an IRS agent. What does that suggest to you? With this litigation going on, it can mean only one thing."

"But, Leah, the litigation has nothing to do with how much in tokes the dealers make. It has to do with whether or not *any* amount of tokes are taxable. If it comes down that tokes are not taxable, it won't matter how much. On the other hand, if the IRS is confident that they will win...then they're just up to their old tricks—finding out how much. They're not stupid! The dealers claim something like ten percent of actual tokes per day. Waitresses and waiters do the same thing but it doesn't take a lot of intelligence to figure out that it's a conspiracy. Tell me, when you first started at the Nugget, weren't you told by more than one dealer roughly how much to claim? I know I was, at the Horseshoe."

"That's true, I was. If only one dealer claimed the true amount, it would mean curtains for all the rest. I didn't want to be that one dealer. Jason, I'm not sure I agree with this deception. In a way, I feel like we're cheating the government. Other people have to pay taxes on all their income. Why should we be different?"

"You're getting into ethics, now. I'm not interested in debating that. We're just one on a team of players. I'm damn sorry that Douglas has to be on the other side. Regardless of how it looks, give him a chance to explain."

Leah sipped her tea. She didn't answer Jason.

"Leah, there's something that I probably should tell you. I hate to bring it up in view of everything that's happened. It's about Jenny."

"Jenny. What about her?" Leah sat at attention.

"Well, maybe I should say Drake. I don't know quite how to put this, or even if I should."

"Jason, stop beating around the bush and tell me."

Jason sat on the edge of the sofa looking down at his feet. He laboriously lifted his gaze to meet Leah's. "I might as well just say it the way it is. Drake is a pusher, a dealer, and I don't mean cards. I don't mean the small stuff either, like grass and whites, he's into the heavy stuff. He's seeing a girl at the Horseshoe. I recognized him and asked her about him after he'd gone."

Leah bit her lower lip in dismay. *Poor Jenny.* "I'm glad you told me, Jason. Jenny is my best friend. If she's having trouble, I want to be there to help her. I had a feeling something was wrong, but Jenny didn't confide in me. I wonder if she knows, or suspects."

"I don't know," Jason sighed. "Jenny is independent as hell. Cute, too. I hate to see her get involved with someone like that. Sooner or later he'll get busted and she could find herself in the middle of it. I don't know, hell, maybe she knows about it. Maybe she uses it, too."

"Jason, don't be ridiculous. Jenny? She's as straight as I am."

"Leah, you just take for granted that everyone's a good guy. You really are naïve. How do you know that? Maybe she was using him. Maybe Drake isn't the bad guy in this at all. We can't make a judgement until we know the facts. I was just trying to give you the facts, as I observed them. The same with Douglas. You don't know all the facts. So, how can you make a judgement?"

Leah sat dumbfounded. Jason was not one to get on a soapbox.

"I don't know," Jason sighed. "Life gets awfully complicated sometimes. I'm beat. I've got to get some shut-eye. I had a bunch of loud-mouthed Texans at my game all night. They worked my ass off. Took it home with them, too."

"Does that bother you, Jason? I mean the losing."

"I wish I could say it didn't. Unfortunately, it's built into the system. In any job we do, we want to excel. For us, winning is excelling. Winning puts us in favor with management. It wouldn't be natural not to feel inadequate when we lose the House's money. In that respect, we must be strong. I guess there's no such thing as a perfect job."

"Perfection is a hard thing to come by in any area. It's not very smart to look for it, is it?" Leah's voice trailed off, and she was no longer really talking to Jason, nor was she thinking of dealing.

Jason rose and took his cup to the kitchen.

"I've kept you up long enough. Get some sleep now," Leah said.

"All right, Mother," he grinned as he lumbered off to bed.

Alone again, Leah thought of Jenny, so vivacious, so fun-loving, so tough. She couldn't really determine how strong Jenny's feelings for Drake were, because Jenny didn't talk a great deal about him. Her relationships with men never lasted very long, so chances were it wouldn't break her heart. But then, she couldn't be sure of it. Jenny was one who needed someone all the time. Leah suspected that she was actually looking for a husband. Now Leah was faced with the problem of what to do with the information she had just obtained. Her thoughts were interrupted by the ringing of the telephone. She quickly picked it up, not wanting to wake the girls.

"Leah, this is Douglas."

"I'm sorry, I don't know any Douglas," she said coldly, and she hung up the telephone with a thud.

Leah spent the rest of the day at the pool with the twins, cherishing them more than ever. They were the one stable thing in her life and they loved her unconditionally, as she did them.

"Jenny! Do you know who that was playing third base on your table?" Leah asked breathlessly.

"Yes, isn't he divine? He asked me out," she said dreamily.

"And..." Leah waited.

"I'm ready for something new."

"What about Drake?"

"The last time I saw that son of a bitch he was in

Caesars Palace fountain."

"In the fountain?"

"Yeah, stark naked! I decided right then that it was time for a change."

"I can't say that I'm sorry to hear it. He wasn't good enough for you. But, Jenny, going out with that guy really spells trouble."

"Who, Hank? That gorgeous hunk of a man?" She grinned.

"Jenny, don't go off the deep end on me now! Granted, he takes one's breath away, but he's a politician and involved in every dirty deal in town. Besides that, he's married."

Jenny eyed her suspiciously. "How do you know that?"

"It doesn't matter how. I know it for a fact."

Jenny flipped her long red locks across her shoulder, a gesture that had become familiar to Leah as one of defiance. "So what. I'm not looking for a husband."

"What are you looking for, Jenny?" Leah looked her pointedly in the eye.

"A good time, Babe." Jenny threw fifty cents on the counter as she got up to leave. "I'm tired of playing it straight and getting dumped on. From now on I'm going to do whatever the hell I feel like, and whenever I feel like it." She snapped the small black apron around her full hips and sauntered back to the pit, every ounce of her being screaming defiance.

Leah took a last sip of coffee and hurriedly followed her friend. She felt strange seeing Hank again. He still evoked anger in her. It was more than anger, she hated to admit. It was almost as if there was an unresolved situation between them—a mystery unsolved. She had met him while working at the Hilton as a keno runner.

For weeks they had a romance of sorts going. Leah had so looked forward to seeing him. He took a long time asking her out, and when he did, it was always for the afternoon. It was difficult if not impossible for Leah to go on an afternoon date. She refused him numerous times. During one phone conversation, the last one actually, Leah asked why he always suggested afternoon dates. She offered that she would be free that evening. She heard only silence on the other end of the phone. Then it dawned on her and she said, "You're not married, are you?"

He answered in the affirmative. Leah simply made one comment: "I don't date married men." Then she hung up on him. That hurt. That really hurt. He never called her again. And he must have stopped going to the Hilton, too, because Leah never saw him again.

Back on her game again, Leah felt depleted. The day had barely begun. She felt as if she had the weight of the world on her shoulders. She had been running hot, so consequently was still on the five-dollar minimum table. At the Nugget there were roughly thirty tables, twenty-eight were one-dollar minimums, and two were five-dollar minimum games. Leah was lost in thought when she suddenly noticed the casino manager escorting a man to her table.

"This will be your dealer, Leah," he said to the man. "Leah, this is Mr. Ames. Jack," he beckoned to the pit boss, "give Mr. Ames a five-thousand dollar marker and make this a one hundred-dollar minimum game."

Leah braced herself as the pit boss spread a new deck of cards on the green felt and placed a $100 minimum placard on her table.

Leah had dealt for thirty minutes before she felt a relief tap her on the shoulder. Thank God, she thought, she must have lost thirty thousand dollars already. She backed away from the table and looked at her watch; she had fifteen minutes before her break.

"Go to Table 6," Jack said coldly.

They had pulled the dealer off of Table 6 and inserted a pit boss to deal until the exchange could be made.

"Bad news in Silver City?" He smiled as Leah relieved him from the game.

Leah gave him a weary smile in answer. He was one of the nicest pit bosses at the Nugget. It was hard to determine his age. He had silver hair and the most angelic face. He had seen many, many years at the Golden Nugget. So unlike some of the young cocky pit bosses, he knew the win and lose of it all. He knew the odds and the emotions. He had told Leah many stories about the early Vegas and the archaic superstitions. He told her about the shift boss who had an aversion to red socks. If a dealer showed up wearing red socks, he was sent home. Then there were the salt shakers that were kept at every podium. It was believed that when a dealer was running cold, if you threw salt over his shoulder it would change his luck. Funny place, Las Vegas, she thought, and still the superstitions, only to a lesser degree.

Leah's relief dealer finally showed up and she left the game feeling low and dejected. She slowly walked to the snack-bar. She was trying to remember Jason's words from the night before. It was all so true. I can't always win, she told herself, but it sure felt like hell to lose.

"You really blew it over there, didn't you?" Jenny teased.

"Stuff it," Leah retorted miserably.

"It'll be the Shoe for you tomorrow, you know," Jenny said.

"I'm almost relieved, Jenny," Leah sighed. "You could be a moron and deal out of a Shoe. That's just what I need right now. I'll shuffle my five decks, put them in the Shoe and go to sleep."

"Don't knock it, Leah, that plastic box has smoothed me out many a time when the pressures of the single deck got to me. Feel like something to eat?" Jenny changed the subject.

"Not really, these ten-minute lunches are giving me an ulcer. Why can't we have a regular lunch break like people with real jobs?" she moaned.

"Ours is not to question why, besides, this is not the real world. This is an illusion created for the tourists—those big-shots that go to the cage and establish credit. How many of them stop to think that those markers they call for will come due? Just like a charge account, due upon receipt."

"You're right, Jenny. I feel sorry for some of them. They go crazy out here. They forget about their responsibilities at home: the mortgage, the kids, the car payment."

"Before we get too sympathetic, let us not forget, if it weren't for them, we wouldn't have this high-paying job," Jenny warned.

They found two empty seats at the end of the snackbar and ordered coffee.

"Oh, no!" Jenny gasped, in a muffled voice. "Look who's here."

Leah looked up just in time to face Douglas, standing beside her.

"Leah, I must talk to you," Douglas demanded.

"Douglas, I would have thought you were back in San Francisco by now," Leah said, ice dripping from her words.

"I'm not going back until you listen to what I have to say," his voice soared in determination.

"Douglas, for God's sake, people are beginning to stare. This is not the time or place to discuss this." Leah glanced around her, noticing the other dealers beginning to watch.

"May I see you after work?"

"Not here, Douglas. Meet me at my place at seven o'clock." She got up and walked back to the pit. Her heart ached from the pain of deception. At the same time, she hungered to be in his arms.

Across from the pit, on the lounge stage, auditions were being conducted. It was a nice change. Leah's table faced the stage so she had a good view. The lounge show never started until after six p.m., when the day shift had already left.

Why did she agree to see him? Leah wondered. Hadn't he caused her enough anguish?

The day seemed to drag endlessly. Finally it was six o'clock.

"Leah," Jenny caught her coming out of the pit. "Do you want me to come over and get the twins tonight? I could come right now. That way they won't be there when Douglas arrives."

"Thanks, Jenny, that's a good idea. I don't want them to know anything is wrong."

"I'll just keep them for the night and bring them back in the morning."

"Jenny, you're a good friend. What would I do without you?" Leah walked out of the casino and down Fremont Street to the Plaza Hotel to retrieve her car. The ritual seemed never ending.

Driving home, she felt breathless and apprehensive. Suddenly, in her rear-view mirror, Leah noticed a flash-ing-red light. Oh, damn, she thought, not a ticket!

She pulled over and the police car pulled in behind her. The policeman was so tall he had to stoop to his knees to look in her window.

"May I see your driver's license, please?" he asked in a professional manner.

Leah pulled the license out of her wallet and handed it to him, her eyes on the brim of tears.

"This is all I need," she wailed. "This has been a miserable day and now you're going to give me a ticket." Tears fell freely down her cheeks and her mouth quivered.

The policeman let his head fall to one side, giving her an exasperated look. His eyelids fell and he muttered, more to himself than to her, "Damn, why do I have to get the ones that cry?" Slowly he let his gaze rise to meet hers. "Look, it's been a hard day for me, too. I don't really need to write another ticket. So stop crying. I won't give you a ticket, but damn, lady you were going fifty in a thirty-mile zone. Slow down, will ya?"

Leah stopped crying and looked into his eyes. They were soft brown, the same color as his hair. Something about the uniform and good looks suddenly struck her.

"You're a nice man. Go ahead and give me a ticket, I deserve it, and after all, that's your job," Leah offered.

"This just isn't my day! Go on lady, just be careful."

"What's your name?" Leah smiled.

"Eric, and if you don't get going right now, I might change my mind," he warned with a smile.

"Thanks." Leah started the engine and out of the corner of her eye she noticed him looking at her Golden Nugget name tag. Okay, she thought, now he knows where I work. He'll probably be laying for me.

Jenny was in the parking lot waiting for Leah. Together they got the twins ready to spend the night. Leah carried the tote to the car as Jenny held each twin by the hand.

"I'll see you in the morning, darlings. Be good for Aunt Jenny." Leah kissed them both on the cheek. "Ciao, Kid." She waved as she watched Jenny drive away.

Leah pulled off her white shirt and black slacks and jumped into the shower.

She hurriedly slipped into a coral jumpsuit, pulled up the front zipper and tied the self-belt. She selected a pair of white satin slippers, then, hastily checked her appearance in the mirror, sliding her hand over the sensuous coral silk. She smiled to herself as she thought of the handsome policeman. She couldn't believe she actually got out of that ticket. Letting out a sigh, she searched the cupboard for something to sooth her nerves. She found two bottles of Pinot Noir. Douglas had left them at one time or another. He did have good taste in wine. She was wishing there had been some white wine, though, as the doorbell rang out.

Her heart seemed to stop as she took a deep breath and moved toward the object of her anxiety.

Opening the door, she found her wish fulfilled, for Douglas stood holding a bottle of her favorite Chardonnay. In the other hand was a large bag which turned out to have smoked salmon and cream cheese canapés, stuffed eggs nantua, and sautéed shrimp.

"I don't know about you, but I'm starved," he said lightly, trying to retain an air of normalcy. He walked to the kitchen and got the glasses as if nothing had changed.

"Jim, I mean Douglas," she corrected herself, "it's so hard for me to think of you as Douglas...there is a Jim Henderson, isn't there?" she asked.

"Yes," he said softly, pouring the wine. "He's a good friend of mine. A shift boss at Harrah's."

"My guess would be that Jim Henderson is something more than a shift boss at Harrah's," Leah said. Her eyebrows elevated just a fraction, and she watched for a reaction.

"Leah, it may seem to you that we're on different sides of the fence, but things are not always as they appear to be. One fact remains, I love you. I could give you a million reasons why I did what I did. Basically, it was my job. I can't deny that. I'm an attorney, more specifically referred to as a special agent, and normally, this sort of thing is left up to people in the field, but, there were reasons why I was chosen." Douglas let his head fall into his hands. "I'm not doing a very good job of this, am I?"

A faint smile crossed Leah's lips. "No, you're not. I'll put this food on a tray." Leah walked into the kitchen. Douglas was using a lot of words but saying nothing, it seemed to her. She arranged the hors d'oeuvres on a tray and carried them back into the living room.

"Thanks, Leah. I knew you wouldn't let me starve." He shot her a devastating smile. It only created a pain this time. Leah wasn't hearing what she had hoped for. She wanted to give him the opportunity to say what he intended to, but if she didn't get the answers she wanted, she would ask the right questions.

"Leah, I tried to warn you. You're up against a power bigger than you know. The IRS isn't going to let this revenue get away from them. Do you realize that some dealers on the strip make as much as four hundred dollars a day in tokes? If it weren't me, it would have been someone else. I had the information that I needed weeks ago. I didn't have to stick around. And furthermore, I didn't get the information I needed, from you."

"You didn't?" Leah's eyes flew open.

Douglas held her gaze, but didn't answer her.

Leah wondered how he did get the information. Was he seeing another girl? Or did the IRS have other methods for getting information other than exploiting women?

"Why did you have my life history written on that legal pad? Was that part of your job?"

"That was personal, I'm afraid. I wanted to know. I had to know. You see...Internal Affairs keeps a close eye on all of us. We have to be careful who we see on a personal level. When I realized that my interest in you was more than job-related...well, you get the picture."

"Douglas, I—I'm at a loss for words. I feel like I'm in the *Twilight Zone*. I keep learning things about our government that shock and awe me. I've led a sheltered life. It's never been more apparent to me than now. My God, what different worlds we live in." Leah rose and walked in a tight circle. "You came here under the auspice of explaining, but, all I'm hearing is that you were simply doing your job. If you'll try to look at it from my point of view, maybe you could understand how I feel. Suppose I could accept the fact that you are a special agent on assignment. Isn't there more to it than that? Are you a married man out for a fling, as well? And, how does Big Brother feel about infidelity in marriage?"

Douglas' eyes didn't waver, but a sadness developed there. He clasped his hands together, elbows on his knees. He lowered his eyes momentarily. "It's difficult for me to explain."

"Why don't you try?" Leah's voice was not tender.

"Six months ago, Samantha and I decided to go our separate ways. Our marriage had been a charade for years. It was to be a simple divorce. We had worked out a property settlement. It was to be a simple, uncontested divorce. We made an appointment with our attorney, and on the specified day, met in his outer office. Samantha was in the process of moving out, had an apartment in town, and was returning to work as an interior decorator. It was her profession before we married. Anyway, while we were discussing the terms of the divorce, Samantha collapsed."

Leah sat up straighter, weighing every inflection in his voice.

"An ambulance was called. After eight days of intensive tests, it was discovered that she had a brain tumor. An operation could be done but her chances would be less than fifty-fifty. In the end, she decided against it. Had we continued with the divorce, she would not have been able to work, she would no longer have the benefits of my insurance, and basically, she could not have taken care of herself. I did the only thing I could. I had her move back in and waived the divorce proceedings."

Leah sat in stunned silence. What a story, she thought. But, was it only a story? Could she really believe this?"

"Leah, I didn't want to burden you. I had hoped that it wouldn't come to this. And I damn sure don't want any sympathy. I'm just telling you the facts. Samantha won't live another three months if she doesn't have the surgery. And if she does have the surgery, it might kill her anyway. I can't influence her in this decision. It must be hers alone. All I can do is stand by her until...until the end."

The pain in his eyes was plain. Leah wanted to reach out to him, but something held her back. The thought of Samantha, perhaps. She rose from the sofa, walked to the patio doors, and gazed toward the mountain tops in the far distance. The sun was low in the sky and an orange haze blanketed the horizon. She felt a stinging sensation in her eyes as the tears surfaced. It all seemed so unfair. Could her happiness possibly depend on the death of another human being? How could she live with something like that? She admired Douglas for taking Samantha back. Like he said, he did the only thing he could. The noble thing. Leah knew there were men in the world who wouldn't have. She was glad Douglas wasn't one of them. As much as she loved Douglas, she couldn't keep seeing him, not as long as Samantha was his wife and needed him for her very existence.

From behind, Leah felt Douglas' strong hands grip her shoulders. She leaned back against his chest, closing her eyes tightly, tears spilling down her cheeks.

The silence was deafening.

With his hands still on her shoulders, he gently turned her to face him. His eyes were misty and had turned a midnight-blue. He pulled a silk handkerchief from his jacket pocket and dabbed away the tears from Leah's face. He soon discovered that the effort was in vain, the tears kept flowing. He pulled her close to him and rocked her in his arms, blinking profusely in an effort to contain his own tears of agony.

No words were spoken, yet a communication was taking place. Douglas understood what Leah's silence meant. He knew that she couldn't accept the relationship under these circumstances. He should have known it all along. His loyalty to Samantha was out of pity, not love. But he knew that wouldn't make a difference to Leah.

Slowly, she pulled an arm's length away from him. She made no effort to hide the tears that still fell freely from her now reddened eyes. "Douglas," she started falteringly, "we all have our time in the sun. For us, for you and me, there is no sun. We would forever be living in Samantha's shadow."

Douglas dropped his hands from Leah's shoulders. His lackluster eyes told the story of defeat. He knew she was right. But he knew, too, that time would solve the problem.

"One can be altruistic to a fault," he offered, knowing full well that the remark wouldn't have an effect.

"To be noble is an admirable quality. I'm glad that I had an opportunity to see both sides of you. I'm glad that I didn't have to remember you, solely, as a ruthless, dispassionate, revenue agent." Leah's gentle voice turned bitter. "Oh, I know your training conditions you to be detached. The Service comes first, doesn't it? Above all else. Right? Your responsibility to the National Treasury supersedes any small affair..." Leah broke down, sobbing pathetically against his chest. Futility and despair gripped her.

Leah's words stung Douglas. What she said had been true of him for many years. His loyalty to the Service had been paramount in his life. He believed that there was only one law, the IRS' law. But times had changed. He was no longer the innocent, just out of law school. His mind was no longer a sponge. It would have pleased Leah to know of his special project, but he couldn't take a chance on telling her, or anyone else, for that matter.

"Leah, your scenario of the average IRS agent is correct. I'm just sorry that you put me on the top of the list. There are a few things that I must tell you, not as an agent, but as a friend and someone who wants to help you. First of all, the dealers won't win this case. If the IRS loses the case again, they'll simply take it to another court district until they get the ruling they want. There's no way you will win. No one, and I mean no one, ever beats the IRS. They play with a loaded deck.

"There is a high probability that you will be audited. And you, as a taxpayer, in the eyes of the IRS, are guilty until proven innocent. The burden of proof is yours."

"Do you really think I'll be audited?" Leah's eyes grew wide.

"As it stands now, the chances are good. The tax accountants you've all been using and being advised by are on the 'problem list'. Because of this, you are automatically audited. The IRS is all-powerful. They can get to your safe-deposit box, pull out records of your checking and savings accounts—wipe them out, in fact—confiscate your automobile, and garnishee your paycheck. There's no limit to what they can do. You all have taken this so lightly. You're like a bunch of naïve children."

"I thought this was America! The home of the brave and the land of the free. It sounds to me like our own government is the enemy!" Leah wailed.

"Forgive me if I can't entirely sympathize! It's not like you're innocent."

"Douglas, what am I going to do?" Leah slumped onto the sofa, feeling as if there were no answers. No redemption for her sins.

"It may not be as bad as you anticipate." Douglas walked the floor, his hands in his pockets. "The IRS is not anxious to get into criminal litigation. Once a case goes to court the situation changes. Then, the burden of proof is theirs. Not that there would be much of a problem there. We have it very well documented what tokes are, all over town. The problem is, you all have actually willfully hidden income from the government. That constitutes fraud, and fraud is a criminal act. My guess would be that because of the magnitude of this—I mean we're talking about the entire state of Nevada—the IRS will simply recalculate your taxes and add penalty plus interest. They can't take every dealer in Nevada to court and try to prosecute. It's not economically feasible."

"What are you saying then, that maybe I won't be audited?" Leah asked.

"I can't say for sure, Leah. I just don't know yet. The important thing is that you're not charged with fraud. Damn, you could go to jail! I will try to stay apprised of the situation. I won't be directly involved so I'll have to rely on someone from the District Office to keep me posted. Don't worry, Leah. I'll help you all I can."

"No, Douglas. I got myself into this and I'll get myself out. You have your hands full with...other things."

"Don't be that way, Leah, I never wanted to hurt you. Please, at least let me help."

Leah covered her face with her hands and sobbed openly.

Douglas went to her, easing down beside her on the sofa. He sat close to the edge, holding her slender hands in his. He studied them for a long moment. Dealers worked hard to keep their hands beautiful, but the callouses from the constant shuffling couldn't be hidden from the touch. They made him love her more. She was not only beautiful, but ambitious, independent, and brave. What rare qualities in a woman, he thought. And with all this, she could still make a man feel needed. She could still appear to be vulnerable. Slowly he lifted his head and fixed a smoky gaze on her.

"Leah, I would like to console you the only way I know...by holding you, and loving you—caressing you, and making the pain go away."

Leah looked away from him, unwilling to be comforted.

Douglas rose slowly, releasing her hands. "I'm going to go now, but, it's not good-bye. We will have our time in the sun."

Leah watched him cross the living room and open the door. He hesitated a moment, then turned to face her. He smiled a brilliant white smile and said, "Like MacArthur, I will return."

His humor was lost on Leah. She started as the door closed with a thud. Tears flowed anew, racking sobs engulfing her whole body. "The sun will never shine for us, Douglas."

CHAPTER SEVEN

The casino grew silent as the loudspeaker announced the death of Howard Hughes. A minute of silence was observed. It was bizarre to experience the uncommon silence. All action came to a stop for one full minute.

Douglas stood across from the oversized mahogany desk that was too neat to belong to a man who actually did much more than finger-point.

"I want the Hughes' case, Matthews."

"You and everyone else! Hell, man, this is the hottest thing since Hoffa's disappearance!" Matthews leaned back in his huge leather chair and swiveled around to gaze out his office window facing Golden Gate Park. A smile spread across his face. "This is going to be a big one. We'll get everything he's got." He swung his chair around again to face Douglas. "Won't that fatten up the coffers?" His milky white skin showed beads of sweat and his jowls shook with an evil laugh.

Douglas watched him with veiled disgust. "I heard on the news today that another will has surfaced."

"Yeah, and it probably isn't the last." He sat upright in his chair with a herculean thud, then took a cigar out of the box on his desk and lit it, deliberately blowing smoke toward Douglas. "So you want in on the Hughes' case." The rotund man fixed a steady gaze on Douglas, seemingly evaluating his worthiness. "We just got notice from the National Office to send someone out to Vegas to investigate his activities there. From what I understand, it's more extensive than anyone imagined. Never been there myself, don't know what the attraction is."

"Why not send me? I'm familiar with Vegas. I just spent nearly two months out there." Douglas was trying to be persistent without letting the old man know just how badly he wanted to go. It seemed like a year since he'd seen Leah, but in actuality it had been only six weeks.

"Hell, we've got lots of agents out there already. We're auditing half the town. What makes you think you could do a better job?"

The old man was playing his favorite game of cat and mouse. Douglas had the strongest urge to punch him in his arrogant face. He maintained his cool manner however, and casually, with hands in his pockets, said, "Would you send a boy to do a man's job?"

The old man laughed heartily, then, as if abruptly removing a mask, his face turned sober and he returned to a small, neat stack of papers on his desk. With the cigar clenched in his teeth, he said in a voice of dismissal, "I'll think about it."

Leah descended the narrow stairway from the Dealer's Lounge. She opened the bulging small brown envelope and pulled out a wad of twenties. Tokes had tripled in recent weeks. Conventions were spilling over from the Strip and to make things look even brighter, there had been a rumor that the Nugget was going to build a hotel. She tucked the envelope in her purse and hurried to the casino restaurant.

She slid in the booth beside Jenny. "Hi! Wow, what do you think about tokes?"

"I think they'd better get even stronger. In a hurry!" Jenny handed her a long brown envelope.

"Oh, Damn! They've actually done it."

"The way I hear it, half the dealers in town have received letters. You haven't gotten one yet?"

"No," Leah answered. "The IRS didn't waste any time. Douglas was right, we didn't have a chance."

"Maybe your connections kept you out of the barrel. After all, Douglas is in love with you. Maybe he just pulled your name out of the pot, or however they do it."

"Don't be ridiculous! If anything, he probably tried to put me at the top of the list. I suppose I'll get one yet. What do you have to do?"

"It's easy enough. I either pay what they say I owe, or I go in for an audit and prove differently. I don't imagine they'll consider my little black book sufficient evidence. They've already made up their minds. We can't do a thing about it. They have us making twice what we actually did. The sons of bitches! But, what can we do? I think it's just their way of letting us know who's boss. Maybe we ought to consider moving to Australia!"

"Do you have the money?"

"What? To move to Australia?"

"No, damn it! To pay the IRS."

"Six thousand dollars? Get serious. Of course I don't have the money."

"Jenny, what are you going to do? This is serious business. You can't just slough this off!"

"I have one thing in my favor, nobody else has the money either. What will the IRS do if they can't get payment from any of us, huh?"

"Oh, Jenny, I don't know. It scares me. You didn't hear Douglas talk about the IRS the way I did."

"Hi Kids!" Johanna slid in beside Leah and Jenny. "I see you've joined the Brown Letter Club, Jenny. How about you, Leah, a member yet?"

Leah shook her head.

"Don't act so smug," Jenny piped in, "just because you haven't been here long enough yet."

"Oh, I'll get mine," Johanna said. "I hear they've gotten the waitresses at Harrah's. Unless they've lost track of me, knock on wood."

"Not much chance of that, Johanna. We have a computerized government, didn't you know?" Leah said.

"So we do." She hailed the waitress and ordered a large country breakfast. "Some of the dealers are talking of quitting and escaping to parts unknown."

"A lot of good that will do," Leah said.

"I don't know," Jenny offered. "Maybe it's worth considering. We could change our names and social security numbers."

"Jenny, for God's sake! Get serious!"

"Well, it was just a thought. Gee, don't come unglued." Jenny laughed.

Leah opened her game and stood patiently waiting for her first players. She liked the short lull in the mornings before the players started filling the casino. It gave her time to collect her thoughts and psych up for the competition.

She wondered how long it would be before she, too,

would become a member of the Brown Letter Club. How could Douglas have betrayed them? It didn't matter where he got his information, or how. The fact remained that he sold them out.

She had heard from Douglas several times by letter and he had sent a delicate bouquet of tiny pink roses. But he had not called or shown up in person. She assumed that he had gone back to San Francisco and resumed his life there, his Las Vegas assignment over. Leah wanted to cry or strike out, or both. How could she have let herself get involved with him in the first place? All her caution thrown to the wind. It saddened her to have to lie to the twins about him. She told them that he was out of town on business. She hoped that in time they would forget him. She knew the best way would be to replace him with someone else, but that was out of the question. He would remain the last man in her life. She had sworn off completely, convinced that she had no talent for choosing men. Leah's heart ached and a sad melancholy shrouded her as the memories flooded back. Oh, the longing was so bittersweet. She was beginning to realize how much she had loved him. His letters were brief, but always decried how much he loved her. There was never a mention of when he might return to Vegas. She wondered if she would ever see him again. And then, she wondered if she really wanted to. As long as Samantha was in the picture...oh, if only she would have the surgery—successfully. It would be their only chance for happiness.

Leah had thought it all out. If Samantha died, and Douglas came back to her, it would never work. She would never escape the reality that her happiness had been at the expense of another's life.

A heavy-set man fell onto a chair and laid a twenty-dollar bill on the table. Leah pulled it to the middle of the table. She withdrew ten silver dollars and two five-dollar chips, laid them beside the twenty, then pulled the twenty back and dropped it into the drop-box. The man placed three silver dollars on a betting square. He glanced apprehensively over his shoulder.

Leah dealt several hands, curious about the man's preoccupation with the south end of the casino. Suddenly he sat bolt upright, his eyes taking on the urgency of a trapped animal.

"Shit! The old lady found me!"

Sensing the exigency, Leah quickly finished the hand. The man grabbed his money and shot under the red velvet ropes, across the pit and under the ropes on the other side. The intrusion immediately summoned the pit boss.

"What the hell was he doing?"

"Hiding from his wife," Leah snickered. Just then a fierce woman of tremendous stature stalked down the aisle, her eyes searching menacingly. Leah hoped she wouldn't stop and ask questions. She hated to lie, but wouldn't dare tell where the man went. Fortunately the woman continued past her table.

Leah smiled to herself. People were funny, really funny. There was fun in her job. In spite of the pressures, the magic still touched Leah.

She stood, again waiting. She watched as the elderly couple ambled down the aisle. They were there every day, for all the world looking like a grand couple out of the twenties. The woman wore an elegant hat today, as she did every day. Her dress flared slightly at the hips before streamlining to the floor, barely baring her ankles. The padded shoulders gave the woman the appearance of having more flesh on her bones than was evident anywhere else.

The man was just as thin as she was. He walked proudly, his pinstriped double-breasted suit with oversized lapels looked almost appropriate with the wide tie. They held their heads so high. He crooked his arm for her and she proudly hung on to it. Her bearing was regal. Tears filled Leah's eyes. They were so obviously in love; so proud of each other, though stuck in time, probably a time that was prosperous and memorable for them. Leah yearned to know their story, but knew that she never would. They were just part of the *colorful Locals*. Stories that never got told—like Cracker.

There was but one man who could speak of the Nugget as it had been at its inception. He was called Cracker. No one knew why. When Leah met him he was a frail old man, small of frame with a concave appearance. The snow white hair on his head was sparse. But, one could always hear a good word from him. Leah could still visualize him in his red checkered western shirt and black kerchief held tightly in place with a red Nugget die which had been drilled out for that purpose. The Nugget had since gone to white shirts, to the delight of most dealers. Cracker had been a dynamite dealer in his prime but had been exiled to the Big-6— Wheel of Fortune, due to his advanced age. He had become a legend in his own time. When he became ill the Golden Nugget continued his salary. Leah doubted that anyone would ever again enjoy the benefits of a *pension* from a casino. When Cracker died, a large part of the history of the Golden Nugget went with him. It was a sad day, but for those who knew him, a day of gratitude, as well, for they realized how their lives had been touched and enriched by this remarkable man.

Leah watched the couple as they faded from sight. She couldn't help wondering whose arm she would hold in her twilight years. At the rate she was going, none. Leah didn't often think of the future, but at times like these, she couldn't help but speculate. What would it be like to be old and alone, helpless and maybe penniless, unloved? No. That wouldn't happen to her, she wouldn't let it.

A young couple sat down, tittering and flamboyantly affectionate. "Hi! We're on our honeymoon!" the young man grinned.

Leah smiled at them but didn't say anything. She picked up the cards and shuffled while they scrambled for some money. Finally the young man produced two twenties.

"We're allowing ourselves twenty dollars a day, each, for gambling. When we lose that, that's it. No more," the young man said.

Leah leaned forward and said in hushed tones, "That's a good idea." She wouldn't dare let the pit boss hear her say that, after all, the object was for people to spend money.

The newlyweds grabbed the cards as Leah pitched them. They sat holding the cards as if they were playing Canasta.

"I'll take one," the young man said.

Leah explained to him how to call for a card by scratching them on the table. He blushed and awkwardly scratched the cards on the table.

Leah grimaced as she saw the cards bend. Nothing was harder on cards than an amateur. She gave him a card and he immediately added it to the cards he held in his hand in front of his face.

Leah cringed again. She hated to have to tell him that he made another mistake, he was so embarrassed by the first one, and she was sure he didn't want to look like a fool in front of his new bride. She had no choice. She could have been brusque with him but decided to try and help him save face.

"Sir, perhaps you haven't played at the Nugget before, but we have rules here that may seem strange to you. I'll explain to you as we go along." Leah smiled at him and his wide-eyed bride. "To begin with, you may not pick up the hit cards. They must remain just as I have placed them."

The couple looked at her with puzzled expressions. Leah thought back to what she had just said, trying to figure out where she lost them. Then it dawned on her.

"The hit cards are the cards that you ask for—by scratching on the table with your cards." She was sure to reiterate the way a card was called for, just in case they forgot. It always took two or three tellings, sometimes more, before a player got it stuck in their mind.

They grinned at one another while making an immense effort to keep their cards out of Leah's view. They bent the cards in a circle. Leah almost laughed, and would have if the urge to cry wasn't as strong. Well, she might as well give them the whole lesson, she thought. She began to explain that it didn't matter if the dealer saw a player's hand, because a dealer played to a certain set of rules. The pit boss was behind her now; she knew he would be. Any conversation would be monitored, but she didn't care. Someone had to educate the public. Besides, she would go crazy if they continued to play the way they were.

"A dealer must stay on a hard seventeen, and hit a soft seventeen or less. It doesn't matter what you have in your hand. I must always play by the same set of rules. In fact, in some casinos, the game is dealt face up, and you, as a player, never touch the cards. You simply scratch your index finger on the table if you want a hit, and wave your hand over your cards if you don't." End of lesson. Maybe she was giving them too much too soon.

Leah dealt to the couple for an excruciating half hour before her break. As she backed away from the table she heard her relief dealer request a new deck. A lot of good that will do, she thought with a smile. In five minutes they will have it in shambles again.

Leah stopped at the mall on her way home. The *Broadway* was her favorite place to shop. She wasn't looking for anything in particular but, sometimes it helped her spirits just to browse. She found herself in the lingerie department, surrounded with billowing chiffon and lace and delicate organdy. She caressed a sea blue gown with her fingertips.

"That's just your color. Why don't you try it on?"

Leah looked at the salesclerk with skepticism. Then in a moment of abandon, agreed. She followed the salesclerk to a dressing room where she was left alone. She peeled off all of her clothes and let the gown fall over her head to the floor. The bodice clung tightly to her bosom, then flared outward. Yards and yards of fabric hung in elegant flounces about her slender body. She turned one way and then another, admiring the inviting gown. Her thoughts immediately sprang to Douglas. How would he like it? Blue was his favorite color on her. Yes. Yes, she would buy it. Douglas would love it.

She stopped by the book store and to her surprise found that Boston Potter had a new book out. She immediately purchased it for the twins.

On the drive home she laughed out loud. Had she

actually paid ninety dollars for a nightgown? I may never see Douglas again, she thought. That's okay. I'll wear it anyway. She sometimes did that. An elegant gown and a cup of hot tea in her good china cup—in a way it was like playing house. It reminded Leah of her youth, the days when she couldn't wait to grow up so that she could do "anything she wanted to do."

Later that night, after dinner and baths, Leah tucked the twins in bed. She had saved the surprise until then.

"Guess what? I have a new story book for you." The twins bounced out of the covers, undoing Leah's careful tucking. She laughed and began to read the new book.

"Racy Raccoon looked into the lake and beheld a beautiful sight!"

"Mommy, we've heard this story, said Carrie.

"No you haven't. This is a brand new book," Leah said, with patience. "Perhaps you've heard one like it."

"We have heard it, Mommy," Sherry said.

Her patience was wearing thin. "Do you want to hear the rest of this story or not?"

The twins exchanged a perspicuous look and settled back into their beds. "Yes, Mommy," they said in unison.

Leah folded the book closed. She eased out of the room and switched off the light. Now it was time for her. She filled the tub and soaked for half an hour. Then, she donned the new blue gown. She slipped into white satin slippers and made a pot of Sassafras tea. The apartment was quiet. She put on a Diana Ross tape and dimmed the lights. What a waste, she thought, sweeping the folds of blue chiffon in a circle around her. But then, it was lovely. She needed to remind herself that happiness comes from within, and this atmosphere did make her happy. But somehow it was lacking tonight. She couldn't help thinking how much nicer it would be if Douglas were there to share it with her.

She sat down on the loveseat and sipped her tea. The music filtered through the room and created a magical mood.

The doorbell rang out and the sound jolted Leah. She went to the door and tried to look through the peephole as she warily asked, "Who is it?"

"Douglas."

Her breath caught as she opened the door to find Douglas' tall frame filling the doorway. Such a feeling of exhilaration filled her that she almost swayed. He was as handsome as she had ever seen him, his deep tan contrasting against platinum hair, casually askew.

His eyes held hers, and almost without wavering, he entered, closing the door behind him. They stood facing each other without speaking. No amount or quality of words could have expressed their feelings for one another at that moment.

Leah's heart raced. She was held captive by his sensuous, smoldering blue eyes, her feet frozen in place.

Douglas reached for her and she fell into his arms. They embraced silently. Finally Douglas released her, tipped her chin upward and frantically placed kisses all over her face and neck.

She laughed and cried and clung to him as if her life depended on it. "Douglas...Douglas, I didn't think I would ever see you again. How...Why..."

"Don't ask any questions, just let me hold you."

"I love you, Douglas. I love you so much."

"Oh, Honey, tell me again. Tell me again. I wondered if you would ever say the words."

Tears fell down Leah's cheeks. "I love you, I love you."

Douglas lifted her into his arms and carried her to the sofa, where he eased her gently down. He cupped her face in his hands and placed gentle kisses on her mouth. "I've missed you so much. I've missed the ivory smoothness of your skin against mine. I've missed the sweet scent of your body and hair." His hands began a ceremony of adulation on her body, tentative at first, then with her full approval, more arduous and pressing. The pent up passion that had been growing in him for weeks was given full reign and Douglas was almost savage in his desire for Leah.

Leah watched him unbutton his shirt and didn't resist when he lowered the thin straps that held the filmy blue gown over her shoulders. It was all he could do to keep himself from taking her violently. He pulled her close to him, their bare skin touching in an almost electric contact. Leah began trembling from sheer anticipation, her body virtually throbbing with desire for him.

Douglas couldn't contain himself, Leah's short raspy warm breath on his neck and her searching hands finding his loins taut was more than he could bear and with a wanton lust that defied bounds, Douglas tore at the blue gown and succeeded in removing it enough to thrust hard and unrelenting into her waiting pool of liquid fire. The universe exploded, lava pouring over mounds of warm flesh.

Douglas slept late the next morning. Leah closed the door so the twins wouldn't know he was there. After they had breakfast she sent them out to play.

"Wake up, sleepy-head!" Leah held a tray of steaming hotcakes, sausage, and eggs. There was also orange juice and coffee.

Douglas sat up enthusiastically. "Umm, I'm starved! That looks wonderful. Did I do something special to deserve this?" He smiled so seductively that Leah was tempted to pre-empt the breakfast. "What time is it? It's light out," he continued.

"It's past ten. Don't worry," she smiled, "the twins are outside. I closed the bedroom door so they don't know you're here."

Douglas looked disappointed. "Oh. Would it be so bad..."

"Yes, it would."

"Leah, I think of those girls as my own. I love them, too."

Leah placed the breakfast tray on his lap and sat down on the bed beside him. "I know, but I have to think of their future. I don't want them hurt."

"I'm thinking of their future, too. I want to marry you, Leah. I want to be their father."

"Douglas, how can you talk like that, with Samantha..." Leah turned away from him.

"Do I seem callous to you? How much must I sacrifice? Must I mourn Samantha, too. I don't love her, she doesn't love me. Why can't you understand that? Why can't you accept me and love me as I do you, without reservation?"

"Oh, Douglas, I wish I could. I wish I could forget about her, but I can't. I do love you."

"Then show me. Accept me as I am. Trust me."

"Did Samantha trust you?" Leah wanted to take back the words as soon as she had spoken them, but it was too late.

Douglas' eyes narrowed and his lips thinned. When he spoke his voice was fierce. "Samantha never trusted anyone! All she cared about in life was self! Her happiness, her material benefits, her social standing, her women's clubs! Don't lay a guilt trip on me! I don't need this!" His voice level lowered, the rage subsided. "Oh, Leah, there's so much you don't understand. And I can't tell you everything. You must trust me."

Leah stroked his head. She did love him so, but conscience wouldn't free her to love him unconditionally. There was still so much she didn't understand and pride prevented her from pressing him for answers. The man had a world of secrets. Did Samantha know about her? How had he handled that? What was he involved in that he couldn't share with her? What was the special project that he had hinted at? Why couldn't he trust her?

Douglas spent the better part of the weekend with Leah and the twins. His assignment would be a lengthy one by the looks of it. He checked in periodically with Samantha, who rarely had a kind word for him. He was beginning to feel that he was in a no-win situation. He had tried to persuade Samantha to have the surgery, but she was despondent. She had no desire to go on living. How had she come to that conclusion? They had drifted so far apart in the last few years that he hardly knew her anymore. They no longer had mutual friends. Their lives had become totally separate. If only he could persuade her to take the only chance she had left in life. Time was growing short. There was still one option, a long shot, but he began to consider it more seriously now.

It was Monday again and Leah was grateful for the return to routine—the traditional breakfast of eggs, hashbrowns, and toast, in the casino restaurant, that in later years she would refer to as a "Vegas breakfast". But she was preoccupied this morning, rotating her butter knife in a small circle on the table.

"Why aren't you eating?" Jenny asked.

"I'm not in the mood for breakfast."

"Then why did you order it?"

"Habit, I guess. We do a lot of things out of habit, don't we?" Leah said absently.

Jenny watched Leah. "What's eating you this morning?"

Leah looked at her. Her first inclination was to say nothing. But Jenny would find out sooner or later. It wouldn't serve any good purpose to deceive her. "Douglas is back. I've been with him all weekend."

"Is that bad news?"

"I don't know. Nothing has changed. I still can't live with the situation the way it is, but yet, I welcome him to my bed. I just don't know what the hell I'm doing."

"All right, let's look at this logically. What set of circumstances could you live with?" Jenny asked.

"Well, if Samantha had surgery, at least gave herself a chance to live..."

"And what if the surgery isn't successful?"

"Oh, God, Jenny, I don't know. I'm so confused."

"Why not do something about it?"

"Like what?" Leah asked, surprised.

"Maybe, like talking to her." Jenny approached it cautiously.

"Talk to her? Could I do that?" Leah asked incredulously. "Do you think it would do any good? She would probably hate me. How could I explain who I am? I don't know. I don't know if Douglas has told her about me; I couldn't bring myself to ask."

"It seems to me that it's your only option. Tricky, but I think you should do it, Leah," Jenny said with new conviction.

"I'll think about it. Would you help me? Help me figure out a way?"

"You know I will, Leah." Jenny continued eating her breakfast.

"What about you?" Leah asked.

"What about me?"

"What's happening in the field of romance?"

Jenny smiled coyly. "I thought you'd never ask. You were right about Hank. He is married, and as much as I wanted to...well, you know, I didn't. You didn't tell me that you knew him. He asked questions about you."

"I hope you didn't tell him anything," Leah said.

"I didn't. But you weren't entirely honest with me, you know."

"I'm sorry."

"It doesn't matter," Jenny said with a shrug. "What I really want to tell you about is Clint. I met him Friday. He's a Texan, your typical tall, dark, and handsome. He sat down at my table and lost a couple hundred dollars, then looked me straight in the eye and asked if I wanted to fool around."

Leah laughed. "What did you say?"

"Well, I looked him straight in the eye and said, 'Sure, why not'." Jenny laughed excitedly. "You should have seen the other players. Their mouths dropped open; I'm sure they were thinking, 'Wow, it must be true what they say about dealers'."

"Jenny, you're completely loony! I'll bet you loved the shock value."

"Of course I did," she said smugly. Then a wide smile spread across her face. "Leah, he's so wonderful, you can't imagine. I think I'm in love!"

"I suppose he has oil wells and all that good stuff."

"As a matter of fact, he does. He doesn't brag about it, but it comes up in conversation. When he's not talking about golf, that is. To tell you the truth, I'm a little bored with the golf talk, but it's a small price to pay."

"This sounds serious. Tell me more."

"We went to see the Bill Cosby show at the Hilton. Clint was marvelous. We got the best seats; he knows all the tricks. He slipped the Maître d' a twenty. He's been out here plenty—knows the ropes."

"That always helps."

Jenny laughed excitedly. "If there is such a thing as love at first sight, I've got it."

"Like the flu. Just be careful. Hell, I don't have to tell you that. Never mind me, I'm just down on love today."

"That's all right, I understand. We'll work that out, too. Come on, it's time to go."

"Let's stop by the ladies' room first," Leah said.

They rounded the corner and entered the lavish sitting room adjacent to the lavatories. Huge mirrors covered the walls from ceiling to floor. Pale blue velvet, French Provincial sofas lined two walls, and the attendant stood, starched and waiting to serve. Carmen was standing in front of one full-length mirror, hands on her hips, turning first to one side and then the other, preening and bending in a self-appreciating manner.

Jenny winked at Leah. "Carmen, you're lovely," she said laughingly.

"So I am," she said haughtily, but a blush was evident under her heavy makeup. She sashayed out of the room.

"I heard...you're not going to believe this, Leah, but

I heard that she's a stripper at night at the Palomino Club."

"You're kidding! Do you really think that's true?"

"Hell, she could be."

"You know, Jenny, it's dealers like her that give us all a bad name."

"I think you're too sensitive about the reputation of dealers. We can't really be categorized. We're all so different. There's good and bad in all things. We can only be responsible for our own actions. Remember, *To thine own self be true.*

"Yes, and that can be a full time job." Leah sighed.

They proceeded to their assigned tables, Leah taking a short-cut under the ropes. The pit boss unlocked the cover of her rack and removed it, then stood beside her while he finished checking the new deck. He spread the cards in front of her in a quick, short motion and moved on to the next table.

Leah picked up the deck and began the standard shuffle. As she was completing the process and getting ready to spread the cards in wait for her first player, she was startled to see a uniformed policeman standing in front of her with a studied expression on his face.

"I thought I recognized you, you're Lee, aren't you?"

"Close. It's Lee-ah" She smiled at the handsome man in blue. Of course she remembered him, with the soft brown eyes and soft brown hair and...from the look of him, that was probably as far as soft went. "You're Eric. I remember you well. If you had given me that ticket, I'm sure you would have been wiped out of my memory completely. But good deeds are worth remembering. What are you doing here?"

Eric hesitated. "Just passing through. When I saw

you...I just thought I'd stop a minute and say hello."

"Well, Hello." Leah smiled. What else could she say, she wondered.

Two gentlemen walked up to her table and after a cursory glance in Eric's direction, each took a seat. Leah scooped up the deck of cards and began once again to shuffle the virgin deck of cards. When she next looked up, Eric was gone. She wondered if he would have asked her out if they had not been interrupted. Did he consider that, at least, his due. Was there always a price to pay, she wondered.

It was late that evening before Leah saw Douglas again. He appeared at her door, haggard, tie askew.

"You look like you've had a rough day. How about a drink to unwind?" Leah asked.

"You read my mind." Douglas sank to the sofa and dropped his briefcase beside it.

Leah poured a Scotch on the rocks and handed it to him. She sat close beside him and swept a tendril of blond hair from his forehead back to blend with the rest.

"Douglas, you haven't said how you happen to be in Vegas again. Is this a top secret mission, or can you let me in on it?"

"It's no secret. I'm investigating the Howard Hughes estate. It's going to be a real killer. You've probably read about it in the papers. He apparently didn't leave a will. Now, they're popping up all over the place. My bet is that none of them are legitimate. This could take years to settle." He grinned. "I hope so, if it means I can stay close to you."

"I hope so too." Leah tried not to think of Samantha, but somehow she was always there, lurking in the shadows of her mind. "Have you eaten? I have some roast."

"No, thanks. I had a late lunch, and then a very late meeting. I hope this isn't an example of how it's going to be. I'm finding it hard to get people to talk."

"Why should it be easy? You're a representative of the infamous IRS. Do you expect people to greet you with open arms? Your presence indicates only one thing, that you're there to take something from them."

"Is that how you feel?" Douglas regarded her poignantly.

Leah lowered her eyes. "No. Not any more." She lifted her head and gazed into a love light that blinded her reason.

"Am I such a bad guy? Can you love me as I am?"

"Can you, love you?" Leah asked.

"Yes, I can. But then, I know more about me than you do." A smile washed over his face and he lifted Leah's chin and planted a gentle kiss on her lips.

Leah smiled, a little perturbed. "Then, tell me about you. Tell me everything about you. I really know so little. I know that you have a sister, a sister who knows Boston Potter, but, what about your family? Your mother and father?"

"My sister is the only family I have. My parents were killed in an auto accident many years ago. I was in college at the time."

"I'm sorry, Douglas."

"That's okay, it was a long time ago. What about your parents? You never mention them."

"My father was killed in the war, toward the very end of it. I never saw him, of course. My mother didn't remarry. She has a small dress shop in Michigan. Actually, not so small anymore," Leah laughed. "Anyway, that's all there is, just her and I, no brothers or sisters."

"It must have been lonely for you."

"Oh, I don't know. It's the only life I knew. I did miss having a father. I swore that I'd never let my children grow up without one. I guess I didn't do a very good job."

"Don't blame yourself for that, Leah. Sometimes it just works out that way. I know you did the best you could. Besides, it's no longer a problem. They're still young, and now they have me."

"Douglas, I love you. I wish that it were all that simple."

"Don't think about it, Darling. It will all work out. Trust me."

Douglas took her in his arms. His beguiling smile and unflappable optimism eased her fears. Secure in the warmth of his embrace she could easily imagine that none of these complexities existed.

Unfortunately, she couldn't hide there forever. A new day always seemed to compel Leah to face the quandaries in her life.

She closed her eyes tightly. Douglas pulled her closer to him, his hand sliding up the back of her neck, pressing her face against his chest.

"Our greatest joys can be in the here and now. Right now." His voice faltered.

Leah felt the tempo of his heartbeat quicken. Her arms were around him, ferreting his shirt from his trousers. She slowly unbuttoned it, savoring the eclipse of masculinity that emboldened her.

"You're an incorrigible temptress," Douglas crooned, a satisfied smile on his lips.

"It's your fault, I read your mind." Leah pulled the upper part of her body back away from him and looked into his eyes with a sultry, erotic, sensual expression that captured him instantly.

The percussion of their union excelled credence. The more impossible their relationship seemed, the greater passion developed. The bond between them became more profoundly fused. Their need for each other was becoming consumptive.

Leah knew that something had to be done. She wasn't going to give Douglas up. Not now. It had gone too far. Absolution of the guilt she felt could only come through Samantha. It was inevitable from the beginning that they would meet. But Leah didn't know that.

CHAPTER EIGHT

Samantha Lourdes lay curled up on the 18th-century French bed that was part of the immense wealth of furnishings bestowed upon her when her mother returned to France. She was painfully aware of the sacrifice that her mother had made by returning to the States with her diplomat husband—Samantha's father. Never really being content living in the United States, but feeling it a nuptial requirement, Samantha's mother lived her life in quiet dignity, dutifully entertaining her husband's colleagues and hosting the many diplomatic parties that were requisite of her political position. Samantha was her only confidante, and it was upon her that she poured out her discontent.

When Samantha's father fell ill, it was with malevolent anticipation that his wife looked on. She dutifully nursed him but, Samantha could see beneath the facade. It was no surprise that upon his death, her mother booked passage on the first ship to France. Within a year, her mother married a duke, once again a member of the aristocracy to which she was born.

Samantha's hand went to her head. It ached this morning. She slowly sat up in bed, her long auburn hair cascading over her shoulders and into her face. Bright sunlight shot through the sheerly draped windows, causing her to wince.

She stretched languidly, forcibly putting thoughts of her mother out of her mind. It seemed to get harder lately. It was like a recurring nightmare, thoughts of her mother. Perhaps it was the imminent union with her father that provoked these memories. She was actually looking forward to it. At long last he would be hers alone. She wouldn't have to share him with her mother, ever again.

Samantha was as small and delicate as her mother was buxom. She favored her father in every way. He was a gentle man, small of stature but in Samantha's eyes, a giant. Not like Douglas, who reminded her more of her mother.

She swung her frail legs over the side of the bed and scooted forward, forcing her feet down toward the floor. It felt cold on her bare flesh. She had often thought of laying a small rug beside the bed but it would create an imbalance in the decor. The room was perfect just as it was—cream-painted furniture covered with pink-flowered cotton fabrics, derived from the French Louis XVI tradition.

She stumbled out of bed and walked over to her writing desk where a vase of vivid red roses sat. They were just beginning to open, the fragrance delicate and the hue intense. She looked at the bouquet with sudden disgust, lifted the imperiled roses from the vase, and threw them into a trash can, then turned swiftly at the sound of footsteps. "I told you to have fresh flowers in my room every morning!" she lashed out at the nurse.

"Yes, Madame. The florist has not yet arrived this morning. Are you ready for your breakfast?"

"No! I'll ring for you when I'm ready."

Samantha was accustomed to the things money could buy, yet, had no conception of the drain her luxuries had on Douglas' income, nor would she have cared.

When her father died, he left everything to Samantha's mother. She hated him for that. It should have been hers, but he was a weak man when it came to her mother, and she forgave him that, but she wouldn't forgive her mother.

Samantha was surrounded with wealth. She had the finest collection of Louis XVI furniture in the country. Her home was full of notable French paintings, bronze statuary, silver, Continental porcelain, French Aubusson carpets, and a private collection of French art glass that would, in itself, bring a small fortune. She ignored the fact that her mother gave all of this to her. She simply refused to acknowledge it.

"Mrs. Lourdes, there is a gentleman here from the embassy to see you," the nurse announced with unusual aplomb.

"I'm not receiving anyone," she snipped.

"Madame, he insists."

Amarillo Slim caught everyone's eye as he walked into the casino restaurant.

"Who is he?" Leah asked.

"That's Amarillo Slim! He's here for the Poker Tournament. Clint says he's quite a celebrity in Texas."

"He does cut a dashing figure. I wonder if all Texans dress like that?"

Jenny laughed. "The day I met Clint he was wearing a Panama hat and baby-blue, denim jeans with no pockets. They don't come any more Texan than him. I suspect that he has a closet full of boots, though."

"Is he planning on coming back soon?"

"He called last night, wants me to come to Texas."

"For a visit, or for good?" Leah asked.

"Not for good," Jenny smiled. "For as long as I can

get away. I don't know how I could manage more than a weekend."

"Even a weekend could be nice. It would give you an insight into his lifestyle. You could meet some of his friends. I don't think I'd pass up that opportunity, Jenny. Not if you're serious about him."

"Then I guess it's settled. I am serious about him."

"Is there any way I can help? Keep the children for you, perhaps."

"That won't be necessary. Clint offered to pay for someone to stay. And he's sending the airline ticket. Money doesn't seem to be an object with him."

"Jenny, of all people to land a rich Texan, you would be the one. You're the one person who couldn't care less. It's laughable when you think of all the girls here who are holding out for just that."

"That's probably why they're not finding it, insincerity is not easily hidden."

"I never thought of it that way. So many of us are supporting children and I know what a struggle that is. I can't blame them, but I don't really think they would marry just for money. My mother used to tell me that it was just as easy to love a rich man as it was a poor man. I'm sure that they're simply choosing whom they prefer to love."

"Leah, you are so naïve! You really believe that, don't you? I'll bet you believe in the Golden Rule, too."

"Yes, damn it! I do. I don't see any reason why we can't all live by it."

"I'm surprised that living in Vegas hasn't taught you what life is really all about. Every day you witness greed and degradation; you see men cheating on their wives with hookers or chip hustlers and don't tell me you haven't seen the little wives slipping out the side door while their husbands are at the crap tables. You've got to be exposed to the very worst in people here. Vegas brings it out."

"Jenny, you see in people what you're looking for. If you're looking for the worst, that's what you'll find. Just once, try to look for the good. It might surprise you."

"I can never win with you, Leah. Somehow, you always seem to bring me around to your way of thinking."

"Jenny, it's not just my way of thinking. You just fall off the deep end sometimes and get cynical on me. We must have some similar thinking in common or we wouldn't remain such good friends. Now, tell me, when are you leaving for Texas?"

"I hadn't made a decision when I last talked with Clint. When he calls again, I guess I'll give him the go-ahead."

Leah smiled. She hoped that Clint was all that Jenny thought he was. She was quick to get involved and didn't always look at things realistically. With dealers or Locals, it was usually a short-lived affair. This was a different matter. When a dealer got involved with a tourist, they either got hurt or married. The former, mostly. Tourists would say anything to get what they wanted. The dealers all knew that. But sometimes, they were good enough to get away with it. Jenny was sharp. Leah didn't think she would fall into a trap like that. She hoped not.

Douglas hailed a taxi and, throwing his briefcase in, quickly followed. The Reno airport faded into the distance behind him. He squeezed into the corner of the cab and quickly glanced out the side window and then the rear. Letting out a deep breath, he instructed the driver to take him to a remote section of the city. It was a long drive and Douglas couldn't escape the feeling that he was being followed. Several blocks from his destination, he told the driver to stop, paid him and ducked into the nearest building, which turned out to be a rather seedy gay bar. He ordered a Scotch and downed it, then headed for the men's room. But that wasn't what he was really looking for. He found the rear exit and hiked to his real destination.

It was another dark bar, but apparently of a somewhat higher caliber. Candles burned on all the tables, grapes and wine bottles hung from the ceiling and the smell of oregano filled his nostrils. Douglas became aware that it was actually an Italian restaurant. Along the walls of the dimly lit room were private alcoves with heavy tapestry curtains. From an obscure corner, Jim Henderson stepped forward and clamped a large hand over his arm. He didn't speak, but motioned with his eyes to a closed curtain and the two men quickly stepped in. Behind the curtain was a large booth with a huge antipasto centered on the table. Jim motioned for Douglas to sit down and as he complied, noticed at his elbow, two drinks. Douglas quickly downed one. It didn't surprise him that it was Scotch. Jim knew him well.

"We can talk here," Jim said. "You weren't followed?"

"I don't think so. No one knew I was leaving Vegas, not even Leah."

"Ah, the tortoise who caught the hare. How is she?"

Douglas smiled. "Fantastic."

"Yeah, I know that. I mean how is she?"

Douglas' smile faded. "She's okay. No one has hassled her."

"You realize the position you're putting her in. This could be dangerous as hell, for both of you. And what about Samantha?"

"I think that problem is about to be resolved, not that it's necessary, she doesn't know anything."

"How about your itinerary? Even that could be damaging."

"Jim, she doesn't know anything. Neither does Leah. Okay? Did you get the file?"

Jim opened his suit coat, unbuttoned his shirt and unbuckled a strap that held fast to his chest a manila envelope, then handed it to Douglas. Their eyes held in a mutual covenant.

Douglas lifted the second glass to his lips and threw his head back, disposing of the cool amber liquid.

In bold red letters across the envelope was printed, TOP SECRET. Douglas scanned the contents quickly, then put it in his briefcase. "How long do I have?"

"A dummy file has been substituted, but that doesn't get us off the hook. It just depends on who pulls it. It might be detected, and it might not. The sooner you can get it back to me the better."

"Jim, what are you going to do when this all blows up?"

"Douglas, old friend, I've been planning this for a long time. Don't worry about me, I'll be well out of the reach of Big Brother." Jim's lopsided smile was deceiving in its boyishness. There was nothing boyish or innocent about him. He was playing the biggest high-stakes game in the nation.

The two men clasped hands over the table, their eyes meeting in joint resolution.

"There's a taxi waiting at the back door. It'll take you to the airport. Will you be going back to Vegas?"

"I'll go back to Vegas first." Douglas was silent for a moment. "I'll be going south, soon." Douglas rose and slipped from behind the curtain, along the darkened wall, and out the back door to the waiting taxicab.

Leah came home to find, instead of the warm greeting she had expected, a note from Douglas. Her heart sank when she read the words. *Darling, I've been called to duty. Don't know how long I'll be gone. Don't worry. Be back before you know it. Love you, Douglas.*

What did that mean, *called to duty?* She thought he was already on duty—the Hughes case. Isn't that what he told her? She didn't like his disappearing act, it brought out the acquired mistrust she felt for all men. Maybe it had to do with the things that he couldn't tell her about. But then, did that mean he was lying to her, again? The ambiguous terminology, *called to duty*, could mean anything.

A cold chill shot through Leah. A sudden fear gripped her. She didn't know why, but something frightened her. Was the fear she felt, for Douglas, or herself.

The door burst open and the twins clamored to get her attention.

Leah folded the note and tucked it under a porcelain figurine. They stayed in that evening and Leah cooked dinner for the twins. It was one of the nights that they usually ate out, but Leah was strangely fearful. She made sure the doors were locked, something she frequently neglected of late. Since Jason had come to live with them, she seldom felt so vulnerable. Tonight was different. They bathed early and got into pajamas, piled on the sofa and watched television until the twins fell asleep.

Leah carried them to her bed. She didn't want to sleep alone tonight, nor did she want them to be far from her side. She walked back into the living room and curled up on the sofa. She wasn't sleepy.

Hours passed, and Leah had finally dozed off. The television produced a fuzzy screen and a shrill hum. Suddenly, Leah sat bolt upright. Something had awakened her. What was it? Someone was turning the doorknob. A scream escaped her throat. Then suddenly there was a fierce pounding on the door. "Leah! Leah! Are you all right? Open the door!"

Leah was dazed with fear, not fully awake or sure she wasn't dreaming. Abruptly, the door burst open and Douglas came charging into the room. He ran to her.

"Leah, I heard you scream. What happened?"

She stared at him in disbelief. Relief washed over her, but it was quickly replaced with anger. "What happened?" she mimicked in a shrill voice. "You nearly scare the life out of me, break my door down and fly in here like *Peter Pan*, and ask *me* what happened!"

Douglas burst into laughter. He laughed so long and hard that Leah got caught up in it to. They embraced and fell onto the sofa holding their stomachs, tears filling their eyes.

Douglas regained his composure first and quickly closed the forgotten door. The lock would have to be repaired and he made a mental note to do that first thing in the morning. He would install a dead-bolt lock as well. If he could break in so easily, so could someone else.

"Douglas, why didn't you ring the doorbell? You scared me half to death. Woke me out of a dead sleep."

"Honey, I'm sorry. I wasn't going to wake you. I thought I'd try the door and if it was unlocked, I'd just come in. I thought sure you'd be in bed by now."

"I would have been, but...I...I felt frightened tonight. That sounds silly, I know."

A strange sensation shot through Douglas as he heard her words. He had intended to be gone for several days and it wasn't until Jim asked about his plans that he decided to come back to Vegas tonight. It was a spur of the moment decision. Wasn't it strange that she felt fearful for no good reason, and at the same time, he felt compelled to come back? Perhaps this was some kind of telepathic experience. Or was it that they both rightly perceived an outside danger?

"You're safe now. I don't want you to ever leave that door unlocked again, day or night. Do you hear me?"

Leah was stunned by the intensity of his demand. Something in his voice frightened her, and she now knew that her fears were founded in reality. He was afraid too. But of what? Afraid just for her, or for them both? She shook her head in obedience, fearful to say anything.

Douglas took her in his arms. "You've become so much a part of me that I think I feel your fears and pleasures. I think I sense when you need me. I hadn't planned to come back tonight; but, somehow I felt I must."

Leah pulled an arm's length away from him, looking sharply into his eyes. "I was afraid for you, Douglas. You were in some kind of danger, I know it. I feel things like that. You must tell me the truth."

Douglas laughed lightly, pulled her close to him and rocked her back and forth. "Leah, Leah, you're watching too much television. I wasn't in any danger. I was just doing my boring, routine job. No danger, believe me."

Douglas' heart was racing. Could she be clairvoyant? If so, it could put her in more danger than he anticipated. He must throw her off the track. The less she knows the better off she will be if something goes wrong, he thought.

"I get strange feelings sometimes," Leah said. "Maybe it's all in my head. My mother used to tell me it was honestly inherited ESP."

Douglas listened with increasing concern. He didn't want to believe this, and he didn't think it would be in Leah's best interest to encourage her own belief in it. "We all have situations at some time or another that support that belief. The sixth sense, you know. Someday there will be studies, serious studies into this phenomenon. I, for one, don't put much stock in it." Douglas wanted to change the mood. Leah was looking much too serious. "How about some hot chocolate? It'll help us sleep."

"Good idea, I'll make it." Leah bounced off to the kitchen. She was just as anxious to change the tone of this conversation.

Douglas took a kitchen chair and propped it under the doorknob, creating a barricade. He planned on being up before Jason came in.

"Douglas, what are you doing?"

He assumed a sinister expression. "You never know what evil lurks in the mind of man."

"Douglas, don't! You're scaring me," Leah protested.

He laughed. "I'm just protecting you against drunks who might try to put their key in the wrong door. I'll fix your lock tomorrow, after all, I'm the villain who knocked it down."

Leah started giggling. "I had no idea you were so chivalrous."

"I'll show you chivalry," he said with a slow grin.

Leah saw him coming and quickly turned the fire off under the milk. The hot chocolate was soon to be forgotten.

The next few weeks were spent in quiet harmony. Douglas seemed to be with Leah every moment. He was there when she woke and there when she returned home. He seemed to match his work schedule to hers.

Leah's life began to revolve around him. They ate most of their meals at home; Douglas loved to cook and, more often than not, had dinner prepared when she arrived home. She was being put higher on a pedestal than ever before in her life, and the children seemed happier and better adjusted than ever before. They were in pre-school now and full of vigor and excitement when they returned each day. Douglas would sit and patiently listen to their tales of woe or accomplishment. He helped them with home projects and encouraged them when they were dispirited.

Leah found it hard to believe that one man could be possessed of so much perfection. Yet, there were still subjects, taboo. Samantha, for one. And the evening he broke the door down, they didn't speak of again. Nor did they discuss his work.

It was a shock to Leah when Douglas announced that he had to leave.

"I wouldn't go if it wasn't imperative. I have a job to do and I'll be gone for as long as it takes. I don't know how long that will be. I'll give you a number where I can be reached in an emergency. I want you to take this." He handed her a piece of paper with a long list of numbers written on the back. "Hide it somewhere safe. You should be able to reach me at the number on top of the list, but if there's no answer, try the next one, and so on."

Leah took the list. She didn't ask any questions, but the fear she once felt overwhelmed her anew.

They didn't linger over good-byes. Douglas drove

quickly out of sight. Leah didn't know where he went. She didn't know how long he would be gone. She knew just one thing, that she loved him more than she had ever loved any man. She loved him beyond reason. She loved him enough to wait for him.

Jenny Graham stumbled out of the airplane in Abilene, Texas. She turned around and looked again at the abomination that had transported her from the terminal in Dallas. Chaparral Airlines had the only carrier out of, or into, Abilene. It was called a commuter line. No smoking, no drinks or food served, and no bathroom. The plane was only large enough for about a dozen people. The pilot and co-pilot were separated from the passengers by a half-open curtain. The seats were narrow and cramped. The ride was uncomfortable, even for someone as small as Jenny. Her ears rang and she was convinced that one of her eardrums had ruptured.

She waited for her luggage at the miniature terminal but none arrived, and after filling out the necessary forms for lost luggage, stepped outside. A long sleek limousine was parked just outside the door. The driver immediately walked up to her.

"Are you Miss Jenny Graham?" he asked, tipping his cap.

"Yes, I am," she answered, puzzled.

"Mr. Clint Sheffield instructed me to deliver you to him at the Fairway Oaks Country Club. Do you have luggage, Miss?"

"I did have, but now I don't," she said sharply.

The chauffeur smiled. "Don't worry, it happens all the time. It'll come in on a later flight." He held the door open for her.

The limousine was the most elegant thing Jenny had ever seen. It was plush royal blue throughout. She felt as if she were sitting in a living room instead of an automobile.

It would take half an hour to arrive at her destination. The terrain looked like wilderness to her with its parched lands and brown grass and the ugliest trees that she had ever seen. They were grotesque, gnarled, and barren. She later learned that they were called Mesquite, and Texans were quite proud of them.

Her trip had been a horror thus far. Jenny was enraged that Clint hadn't picked her up at the airport, and infuriated that her luggage had been detained, and wasn't convinced that she would get it at all. More than anything right now, she wanted half a dozen margaritas and a hot bath. She was wearing a pale yellow linen suit and it was wrinkled beyond recognition. She began to wonder if this whole idea hadn't been a gargantuan mistake.

They seemed to have arrived. The driver instructed her to remain in the car and briskly walked through the entrance door.

Jenny was seething. But, within moments, Clint came running out of the entrance and immediately opened the door, smiling in at her like a Cheshire cat.

He was gorgeous! Jenny's breath caught and she managed somehow, to smile back at him. He was wearing green polka-dot slacks with a white knit shirt and his skin was so golden it glowed. He wore his dark hair shorter than men in Vegas and somehow it gave him a completely different persona than she was accustomed to.

He held his hand out to her. She gave him hers and he virtually lifted her out of the limousine. Then he took her in his arms and held her for a long time. He didn't speak but she could feel his heart beating. Oh, she was glad she came.

It was deadly silent in the Aston household. The twins had just been put to bed. Leah put a pot of water on the stove to warm for tea. She felt so desolate without Douglas or Jenny. Even Jason would have been a welcome reprieve, but he had been enchanted of late with a new flame, consequently she was seeing little of him. Jenny had extended her trip to Texas and Douglas had been mysteriously silent. Leah felt that she had been deserted by all of those she held dear.

But, of course Douglas was the one she missed the most. She had almost come to take him for granted. She missed him in bed with her at night, missed reaching over in the morning and feeling him beside her. She couldn't understand his absence. Why couldn't he call? Surely he could drop a note, but nothing, only silence. Could it be possible that he wasn't coming back? Maybe he went back to Samantha. Maybe this had just been a short-term romance for him. Had she been a fool for not demanding answers—given him too much respect?

The telephone rang and she quickly answered, hope springing to life, but her heart sank when she heard a woman's voice—a deeply accented voice.

"Leah Aston?"

"Yes?"

"This is Madame...this is Mrs. Bouvia. I am Samantha Lourdes' mother."

Leah sat down on the sofa and gripped the receiver tighter in her hand, her pulse racing. Was this an irate mother trying to eradicate a wrong done her daughter?

"Leah, are you there?" the voice asked.

"Yes, Mrs. Bouvia."

"You'll excuse me if I seem awkward, but this is a rather...difficult call. I need your help."

Leah's eyebrows furrowed. "How could I possibly help you, Mrs. Bouvia?"

"I'll come right to the point. I want you to see Samantha. I've spoken with Douglas and he told me all about you. I want to take Samantha back to France with me. We have the best doctors in the world; I'm convinced that she can be helped. The problem is, she won't go. Oh, I could drag her, and I might have to yet, but I would prefer to use more civilized measures. I think it would help if she could talk with a contemporary. I am surely not that. And these braggadocios that she considers friends are nothing more than leeches in my opinion! I realize this is a strange request under the circumstances but, knowing what I do of you, I think you will come."

"Mrs. Bouvia, you said you spoke with Douglas. Was it recently?"

There was a long silence. "I spoke with Douglas a few weeks ago. Has he been in contact with you?"

"No, but I do have a number where he can be reached in an emergency," Leah offered.

"This is not an emergency, you mustn't disturb him!"

Leah was puzzled by the intensity of that directive. Could it be that Mrs. Bouvia knew more about what Douglas was up to than she did?

Leah took a deep breath and said, "To tell you the truth, I had entertained the thought of speaking to Samantha. Can I assume that she knows about me? I wasn't sure..."

"Leah, she does not know about you."

"Then, I'm more puzzled than ever. Are you asking me to spring it on her? And what are your feelings in this? I'm sorry, I simply don't understand what you expect of me."

"Perhaps I've been ambiguous. And for a fact, I'm putting a big responsibility on you. I will make myself as clear as possible. Samantha is a spoiled, undeserving child, but she is my only daughter and I love her. She has robbed Douglas of happiness for too many years. You see, I love Douglas, too. He is like a son to me. I want happiness for him as much as I do for Samantha. Douglas will be happy with you. Samantha will need a firmer hand. I have no doubt that the doctors in France can make her well again, and I have big plans for her. She should travel in the circles that befit her desires. Leah, the problem is, she has no desire. She doesn't remember what it's like to be in love. Maybe she never was. I must give her a reason to live. I say I...but I really mean you. I tried and failed. I know that you care. Douglas told me of your...reservations, because of her."

Leah's heart went out to her. The sheer determination in her voice tugged at Leah's heart strings.

"I think you and Douglas must be very good friends."

"You will come, then. There is a ticket waiting at the airport for you. I will, of course, compensate you for any loss of revenue."

Leah smiled. This was a woman who was accustomed to having her own way. "When shall I come, Mrs. Bouvia?"

"Immediately."

Leah boarded the plane to San Francisco. She found her assigned area, put her coat in the overhead storage compartment and settled into the window seat. She fastened her seatbelt and released the lever to lower her backward. She knew she had only a few minutes before takeoff and would just have to put it upright again but she was so keyed up she had to stretch out. The "No Smoking" light was on. She needed a cigarette. She needed a drink. She needed a lobotomy! What was she doing on this plane? Her anxiety was increasing by the minute. What would she say to Samantha? How could she make a difference? Samantha would hate her, how could she not? *The woman who stole her husband.* Well, not really, but isn't that how Samantha would view it?

The stewardess approached, readying for takeoff, and Leah returned her seat upright, already in the process of talking to herself now, using a form of self-hypnosis she occasionally relied upon in especially tough situations.

The "No Smoking" light went out and Leah reached for a cigarette and ordered a drink from the first stewardess that came near.

It was what she wanted, she reminded herself. She did want to talk to Samantha. She closed her eyes and concentrated on Samantha, imagining a lovely frail girl with shining auburn hair. She was curled up in a large bed with her knees tucked under her. It reminded Leah of the way the twins sometimes fell asleep when they were little. Samantha was in pain. She was unhappy. She wanted to be with her father. And yes, there was something else...the figure of a tall, dark-haired man with a mustache kept fading in and out. Leah tried to picture him more clearly, but couldn't.

"Miss, we're preparing to land, please bring your seat to an upright position," the stewardess said.

Leah was shocked at the lapse of time. She couldn't believe they had already arrived. The images Leah had seen on the blank movie screen she concentrated on in her mind's eye had been so sharp, so incredibly clear, yet she knew full well that imagination could create this scene as easily as not. She had been successful in using this technique in the past, but it was successful only in highly charged situations. This situation was that, to the highest degree, but this was not a science one could count on, and in truth, Leah very rarely even tried it. Yet...there were times in the past that it had been one hundred percent accurate.

Leah disembarked and found the limousine that Mrs. Bouvia had sent for her. It was late afternoon and already there was a chill in the air. They were driving through a very grandiose part of town. The houses seemed to grow more luxurious as they progressed. Leah was calm now, her sense of purpose more defined.

The limousine pulled up in front of a charming old-world Victorian home. The grounds were remarkably lush. Leah caught a glimpse of the courtyard to the side of the house which extended to what appeared to be a pool house, and beyond that, a smaller building that looked like a miniature of the main house.

Could this be where Douglas lived! An attorney for the IRS? He couldn't possibly make enough money to afford all this grandeur.

Leah was admitted by the duchess herself. She was the most elegant woman Leah had ever set eyes on. She wore a long white caftan with intricate gold threads woven throughout. Her hair was pure white, but beautifully styled in a high chignon with gold braiding woven into it.

The grandame escorted Leah into a sitting room where they briefly exchanged pleasantries. Madame Bouvia told Leah of her estate in the South of France where she planned to take Samantha to recover. She seemed to be a gracious lady with a benign nature.

The house was chaotic with servants scurrying around packing boxes, covering furniture, and taking pictures off the wall.

"As you can see, Leah, I have made up my mind. Samantha will come with me, she has no choice in the matter; however, it would be better if she thought she had. I am having her personal belongings and those pieces of art that I know she is especially fond of, shipped to France. I doubt very much that she will be returning to the States. Since she is in no condition to make intelligent decisions for herself at the moment, I am forced to make them for her."

"Where is Samantha?" Leah asked.

"She has cloistered herself in her boudoir. I'm afraid that she will have to receive you there. I hope you don't mind."

"Not at all, Madame. May I ask, is there anything particular that you would like me to say to her?"

"As you know, she and Douglas had begun divorce proceedings. It was a mistake, in my opinion, to recede them. It really wasn't fair to Douglas. I want you to let Samantha know who you are. Will that be a problem for you?"

Leah sat silently for a moment, her hands clasped in her lap. "I don't think so. Madame, you must realize that I came here, not so much for you, but for myself. And, I hope, for Samantha. I'm not a callous woman, nor am I a home-wrecker. I would like to say that had I known of Samantha's existence..."

"Leah, you needn't go into detail. I know the nature of Douglas' work for his government and I place no blame on you or Douglas. Believe me, I have your interest at heart. I want my children to be happy. Douglas is a marvel. He deserves a woman who will love him and who will give him children. Samantha would never bear a child for him, she doesn't have that kind of love to give. But, there are men who are looking for a woman just like Samantha, particularly men of the aristocracy in France. I have no doubt that she will find her place there, with me to aid her."

Leah thought it sad that this genteel woman all but ignored Samantha's illness. It was a mother's determination and love and faith that sustained and urged her on, Leah was sure of that.

"I have just one question before I see Samantha. About her father..."

The woman's features turned stern for the first time since Leah had entered the house.

"Her father is dead."

"I'm ready to see her now."

CHAPTER NINE

Leah ascended the circular staircase with deliberate hesitancy, giving her perceptual vantage point time to strengthen. She was relying heavily on her senses.

A calm washed over her again, shrouding her with an inpenetrative efflorescence.

Leah found Samantha's bedroom door open. She was standing before her cheval glass, a picture of elegance from the past.

Samantha held an alabaster brush in her hand, meticulously stroking through her long auburn hair, then, catching Leah's reflection, slowly turned to face her.

There was a serenity in her voice as she spoke. "I've been expecting you. I don't know who you are, but I felt that you were coming." Samantha crossed the room, her dressing gown shimmering streaks of golden-hued copper. She extended her hand to Leah.

Leah accepted it in greeting, all the while getting more of a sense of camaraderie.

It was a curious scene. Two women, adversaries in fact, but strangely drawn to one another, each knowing inwardly that in some bizarre way their future was intertwined.

Samantha directed Leah to the winged chair directly

beside her favorite chaise lounge, where she sat down, leaned back, and straightened her legs out in front of her. She watched Leah expectantly, then reached for a buzzer beside the table. In moments, a white-clad woman appeared.

"We will have tea now," Samantha said to the wary servant.

Leah heard excited whispering and anxious footsteps scurrying outside the bedroom door. There was a tension in this house that defied description, a tension that stopped like a visible wall at the entrance to this room.

"My name is Leah Aston. I've come because I wanted to know you." Leah was hesitant in her beginning, not knowing how Samantha would receive her, but the attractive woman sitting across from her seemed to accept the visit without question.

Leah continued, "Sometimes we tend to lose perspective in our lives, defeats and unfulfilled expectations can become overwhelming, until they reach unrealistic proportions." Leah stopped talking. She wondered if Samantha was really hearing what she said. She decided to take a more direct approach.

"Why have you given up, Samantha?"

Samantha didn't answer, yet this incredibly serene expression remained on her face.

"Why do you want to join your father? Do you think you deserve to be punished? Who is the tall, dark man with the mustache, and why have you refused to see him?" If only one perception was correct, Leah thought, it could strike a cord and create the opening she needed to draw Samantha out.

Samantha's color had changed. The emotions in her face evolved from surprise, to rage, to acceptance.

"Who are you?" Samantha said with awe in her voice.

"I told you," Leah answered.

Samantha studied her.

Leah could see her eyes begin to brim with tears. She wanted to reach out to her, but consoling wasn't what Samantha needed now. She needed to be forced out of her shell, her self-absorption.

Samantha began to talk. She talked about her father and, as she did, she walked to the chiffonier and picked up a picture and held it close to her breast. The frame was elaborately gold-leafed. She approached Leah and offered it to her, much as a child would a secret to share.

Leah took the picture carefully from her. "Do you think your father wants you with him?" Leah asked. Then quickly added, "Or would he want you to be happy and living a full life?"

"He wasn't pleased with me," she wailed. "I failed him. I failed him miserably."

"Why, Samantha? What did you do that was so terrible?"

"I betrayed a sacred trust. My marriage vows. Papa never forgave me that. And the child...Papa said I was inhuman. I deprived him of his only grandchild. I wanted to have an abortion, but in the end, I didn't. I went away to Paris. I had the baby and gave him up for adoption. But, Papa had betrayed *me*. He helped Antonio, and now he has our son."

Leah's head was swimming. "Is Antonio the father?"

"Yes," Samantha said dryly.

A soft knock sounded on the door. Leah quickly answered it, not wanting to break the spell. She took the silver tray from the maid and carried it to a small table beside Samantha, and silently poured, not regarding the reversal of roles she was initiating.

"And what about your son, Samantha? Have you ever seen him?"

"No." Her voice sounded strange, unreadable.

"How does Douglas feel about that?"

Samantha's eyes grew wide and she said with a gasp, "Douglas doesn't know!"

Now it was Leah's turn to be surprised. She looked at Samantha incredulously. "You mean you had a baby and Douglas didn't know about it? How is that possible? Weren't you living together at the time?"

"Sounds incredible, I know, but it really wasn't difficult. I didn't even start showing until the sixth month. I only gained a total of fifteen pounds throughout the entire pregnancy. Douglas had gone south at the beginning of the fifth month. He was gone for two months, and when he returned he found that I had just left for Paris. There was nothing even remotely suspicious about it. I was in the habit of going to France with my father on extended trips. Douglas didn't even give it a second thought." There was a far away look in Samantha's eyes. "We've always led such separate lives. Our interests seem to lie in different areas. If he found out about the baby...I hate to think what he might do. You know, Douglas and I were getting a divorce—before I became ill." Suddenly, Samantha had a look of revelation in her eyes. "Do you know Douglas?"

"Yes, I do." Leah's words became softer. "I'm in love with him." It occurred to Leah that perhaps she had been mistaken for a psychologist. It seemed likely that perhaps on occasions one had been called in the past.

Samantha's expression didn't change. Then, slowly her eyes opened wider and a rare smile crossed her face, a smile that changed this small, solemn creature into a dazzling beauty. She blinked and looked quizzically at Leah. "You're in love with Douglas?"

For the first time since entering Samantha's rooms, Leah was nervous. She gathered her courage and said, "Yes, Samantha, I'm in love with Douglas. I have been for a long time."

"And he loves you?"

"Yes, I think he does." Leah sensed that in some inexplicable way she was freeing Samantha.

"It's strange," Samantha said, "even during the divorce negotiations I felt so guilty. I know I haven't been a good wife, but Papa said, 'Once married, always married.' I thought I would be forever imprisoned. Oh, I must have loved Douglas at one time, but he was away so much, and then Antonio came into my life. He was tall and dark and handsome, had a dashing mustache and that air of mystery that Europeans have."

Samantha was caught up in the memory of Antonio. The rapture in which she spoke revealed to Leah that she was still in love with him.

"When did you see him last, Samantha?"

"That's strange you should ask, he was here only a week ago, after all this time he showed up." Samantha gazed off into the far distance, seemingly trying to put the pieces together.

It wasn't as difficult for Leah. She knew the mastermind behind all of it, the one responsible for her being there.

"Does Antonio live in France?" Leah knew the answer before she asked it. Madame Bouvia was thorough in her plan.

"Yes, Antonio is the Spanish Ambassador to France." She giggled. "It must have been difficult for a man in his position to adopt a newborn child."

"Samantha, in light of what we've talked about, don't you think it's time for you to get on with your life?"

A sadness veiled Samantha's eyes. "I wish I could, but surely you must know that I'm terminal."

"That's not true. Your mother has found a doctor in France who thinks he can help you. Isn't it time you put your differences aside?"

"I want none of my mother's help!"

"Yes, you do. It's time to forgive past sins. You've shared in a hardship and it should bring you closer, not tear you apart. You don't have to take sides. You can love your mother without forsaking your father. She loves you, Samantha, and has gone to a great deal of trouble for you. She is responsible for my being here, and you must realize that Antonio wasn't just in the neighborhood. She is trying with every ounce of energy she has, to save your life. Why can't you accept her love, Samantha?"

Tears came to Samantha's eyes. She rose and walked over to Leah.

Leah held her arms out and they embraced. Slowly, they left the room. Not a word more was spoken. Servants stopped their duties and a hushed silence fell over the house. Hours had passed since Leah first arrived. She hadn't realized the impact of her visit until she read it on the faces of the inhabitants of this house.

Madame Bouvia stood at the foot of the stairs. Her eyes held Samantha's as she descended. Samantha reached out to her and the old woman embraced her daughter, tears streaming down her face.

Samantha cried openly.

The duchess lifted her red-rimmed eyes and nodded to Leah.

That look of gratitude was all the thanks that Leah needed. Mother and daughter reunited. Leah slipped out the front door unnoticed. She found the limousine waiting and instructed the driver to take her to the airport.

The director of the Central Intelligence Agency swung around a straight-backed chair and straddled it. It could have been a horse, and had he been given a choice, it would have been. He was a tall, lanky, mosquito of a man, hollow-eyed and intense. He spoke in a slow drawl as he addressed the commissioner of the IRS. "You all have been getting a lot of bad press lately. I always believed that where there's smoke, there's fire."

"What business is this of the CIA? We take care of our own problems."

"Well, Hitch," the director drawled out, "let's just say it's been made our business."

The commissioner understood what that meant and an arrow of fear shot through him. "Now, Edgar, just a damned minute, you can't believe what those sniveling TP's say. You know they're all crooks; if we don't get 'em, they'll get us."

The director's eyes narrowed. He knew in that moment that he had a psycho on his hands. He personally detested having taxpayers referred to as TP's. He wondered how many people had suffered at the hands of this man. He would have to talk to the President immediately. Now, to the task of correcting the problem and covering it over—if the press got wind of this it would mean no less than a revolution. There was no doubt in his mind that the sporadic stories the press had been picking up about individual taxpayers being tricked, lied to, and coerced, had been true. In one case a man had actually been beaten by an agent. The President would be in a rage.

Edgar Monahan was set apart from his counterparts by one thing: He had a conscience. The CIA was already in deep trouble over the MK/ULTRA project. All records concerning the experimental drug program had been destroyed, but in spite of that precaution, word had leaked out that at least two of the unwitting subjects who had been used for testing, had died. The program had been initiated in response to U.S. concerns over foreign brainwashing techniques.

Now, after all this time, a public research group had filed a request, under the Freedom of Information Act, for names of researchers and any other information associated with the drug program.

The CIA had denied the request, leaning on a provision of National Security Law authorizing them to protect intelligence sources.

Edgar was nervous about it. The experimental drug testing program was one which had been full of horrors.

And now, an internal problem. He wondered how wide-spread it was. It was no secret the CIA, FBI, and IRS had their power plays, but all within bounds.

His men would enjoy investigating the IRS. He could see it now—a gleam in their eyes, palms rubbed together with the glorious anticipation of nailing their asses to the wall. He grinned unconsciously, not aware of the gleam in his own eyes.

Douglas was anchored in the middle of Clear Lake. The Catalina Express rocked lazily as a motorboat went by. It was Monday, and the lake was nearly deserted. On weekends, boaters would come down from Houston and the lake transformed into a crowded freeway. Douglas didn't go out on weekends.

He pecked away on his manual typewriter, sheets and sheets of discarded white paper strewn around him. He had decided to call his exposé, "Fight Back America", and in addition, had accomplished the formidable task of finding a publishing house that wasn't afraid to handle it. Subject matter like this was dynamite—in the truest sense of the word: dangerous, explosive, destructive.

Douglas had taken a leave of absence from the IRS—not that he intended to go back. Had he suddenly quit, there would have been raised curiosity. Doing it in this way bought him time—so he hoped.

Some of the hundreds of documents which had been smuggled out of the system over the past year had been lost in transit, and sooner or later someone would recognize the substituted files as dummies.

A small network of men, headed up by Douglas, had been systematically documenting the cases of brutality and deception by IRS agents. The list went on forever, each story more heartbreaking than the next. The IRS had become too powerful. The taxpayers literally had no recourse against it.

There had been a culling of agents going on over the past two years. Those who didn't fit into the new way of doing things were demoted to paper pushers, and if they still proved troublesome, were pushed out the door, being put on the audit-every-year list.

The majority of agents had fallen into line easily, enjoying the new power they were given. Most of them were megalomaniacs in the extreme. They thought of themselves as generals, passing out retribution as they saw fit.

Douglas had been naïve in the beginning, only gradually becoming aware of the changing attitudes of his superiors and co-workers. Even then he rationalized that it was the thinking of his immediate superiors, but soon came to suspect that it flowed from much higher sources, filtering poison through the system, out every channel of the complex IRS network. Nothing short of a public explosion could rectify the problem; a total and complete public awakening.

Douglas had started his little investigation from a newspaper clipping which had a strange ring of truth to it. He pulled the file and studied the case. The IRS had triple-taxed a taxpayer. Then, when she couldn't pay, they confiscated her home and sold it at auction, bringing only a small fraction of the true market value. The woman was an 80 year old widow. Shortly after Douglas had pulled that file, a brief article appeared in the newspaper describing the woman as a bag lady—she had been found dead in an alley, her skull crushed, apparently the victim of a mugging.

Douglas had arranged and paid for the burial. No family came. The woman was utterly alone in the world.

It was shortly after this incident that Jim Henderson had contacted him. He was a member of a small group that had been gathering data for years. Jim, it seemed, had been a high government official who split ranks for the same reasons, summed up: injustice. They needed Douglas because he had the special talent and visibility to attract media attention. His probing and sympathies had not gone unnoticed by Jim's group, and they rightly felt that they had finally found their perfect tool for change.

Not long after the burial of the widow, with the injustice still raging in his mind, Douglas had been given a similar case. She was a gentle woman with kind myopic eyes.

"Call me Rose," she said. Rose had lived with and nursed an elderly man for the past ten years. Rose was herself, seventy. Her charge died at ninety-eight.

Her understanding with him was that upon his death she would inherit his home, since he could not afford to pay her a salary. The IRS had several ways to interpret this situation. Should there simply be inheritance tax? Or did the agreement constitute a retroactive salary which should be pro-rated back ten years and taxed as regular income.

Douglas saw it one way, his superiors saw it another. With accumulated penalty and interest, the woman would have had to sell the house to pay the tax debt. She would virtually have ended up with nothing, had he done it the way he was instructed.

His punishment for that decision had been the Vegas assignment.

"Squeeze them dry!" his boss had said.

Now, Douglas had a clearer picture. The question screaming to be answered was, how high up did these directives come from? Did it stop at the commissioner? He didn't know and couldn't take a chance. That's why it had to be made public.

Leah was drained from her trip to San Francisco. She wondered now, how she had the strength to do such a thing. Where had the words come from? Where had the perceptions come from? And how would Douglas feel about her trip to see Samantha?

A week had passed. Leah regained her strength, but was still filled with apprehension over what she had done. She wondered what the outcome had been. Jenny was due back today and that made the morning sail swiftly by. Leah dropped the twins off at school and decided to go directly to the Nugget. She would arrive much too early, but today, somehow, she wanted to get away from the house.

She walked into the casino restaurant and took her usual place at the booth. The dealers' area was nearly vacant.

The smiling waitress greeted her with a cup of coffee and took her order. Leah drew leisurely on a cigarette and leaned back against the booth. Surprised, she saw Jenny approach. She was hollow-eyed and haggard.

"My God, Jenny, what's happened to you!"

She looked at Leah, empty-eyed. "My house has been stripped. They even took canned goods."

"You were robbed?" Leah asked incredulously.

"That depends on who's looking at it. It was the IRS. They told my sitter that the things would be sold at auction to satisfy my tax debt."

"I can't believe this! I've never heard of such a thing!"

"Believe it. If my car hadn't been at the airport they would have it, too. Mrs. Collins took the children to stay at her house after it happened. I wondered why I couldn't reach them by telephone. Something terrible is happening to this country."

"I thought the IRS gave you time to pay the debt, or contest it."

"I contacted them and said that I didn't have the money. They wouldn't discuss terms with me. An obnoxious man on the other end of the phone accused me of lying. Then he said that if I couldn't find the money, he could. I guess this is what he meant."

Leah was thoughtful for a moment. She wondered again why she had not even received a letter from the IRS, when everyone else at the Nugget had. She knew that Douglas had to have something to do with it. "Jenny, I want you and your children to move in with me until you get things straightened out."

"I couldn't, Leah. That would be too much of a strain on all of us. You really don't have the room to spare. I've decided to simply replace the household goods. I'll have to charge it but what choice do I have?"

"I think if I were you, I'd move first. And don't give the Nugget a change of address. Don't leave one at the post office, either."

"I've already thought of that. I'm looking for a place today. I'll talk to Murrey and arrange to extend my vacation a few days. I only came in today to talk to you. I tried to call the house but you had already gone."

"This is a terrible thing to come home to. How was your trip?"

"It had the same impact as my homecoming. I'm wild about Clint, but, oh, his friends! They're really something else. Texas must be the most conservative state in the union. Talk about narrow-minded. I felt like a freak. And preconceived ideas? They originated them."

"What now?" Leah asked.

"I don't know. I really don't know."

"Vegas is our home," Leah said. "We build a life here and somehow, if we try to leave, it backfires. Look at Carmen, and Virginia. Lisa, too. They all left and married, and now they're back. Our world is so different, so unlike the outside that we don't fit there anymore."

"I won't accept that. I can make it."

"Then you're not giving up on Clint?"

Jenny smiled. "I wish I could. I know myself better than that. I don't want to give him up. I'm just not sure I could marry him."

"Has marriage come up?" Leah asked.

"He's been hinting at it. We even looked at houses. Such beautiful houses, you wouldn't believe. Abilene has at least three major colleges; I could continue my education."

"It sounds like you're trying to convince yourself," Leah said.

"Well, like I said, I really don't know. I'm trying to weigh the merits. I'm trying not to overlook the problems. In the end I suppose I'll do what my heart dictates." Jenny smiled sadly as she bid Leah farewell.

Leah sensed how troubled Jenny was. There was a deep sadness in her eyes that couldn't be hidden. They knew each other too well.

Leah's spirit had fallen into a sadness of its own. It seemed that her life was put on hold. She longed to hear from Douglas, but no word arrived and the doubts sprang up again. She wondered if it was over.

Another day had come to a close. Leah drove the route home automatically. She parked the car and walked up the flight of stairs. On the door was a note from Jason telling her that he had taken the twins out. She inserted her key in the door but before she could turn it, the door pushed inward. Her mouth dropped open and her eyes widened in shocked horror. The apartment had been ransacked. Not stripped as Jenny's had, but turned upside down. Leah's eyes darted from one end of the room to the other, assessing the damage in route. She ran to the kitchen, then the bedroom, fearful of what horror she might find. Her relief was bittersweet. She returned to the living room, turned a chair upright and slumped into it. She sat for a long while, surveying the damage around her. Nothing seemed to be missing. She suddenly remembered her jewelry lying loosely on the dresser and ran to her bedroom again. It was still there. Money which she kept in a large vase had been dumped out, but remained.

The intruder was looking for something, and apparently so unconcerned about detection that he didn't even bother to make it look like a robbery. But what? Then she remembered the phone numbers that Douglas had given her. Of all her possessions, that piece of paper was the most important. If she lost that, she might lose contact with him forever. She ran back into the living room. The porcelain figurine was not in its usual place, and the paper with the numbers written on it that had been hidden there was gone. Her heart sank. Papers were strewn everywhere.

Leah was in a dilemma. She wondered if she should call the police. What if the culprit came back? But what did she have to report? Not a burglary. After long deliberation, Leah decided to call Eric, the kind policeman who had almost given her a speeding ticket, the policeman who had made an effort to come to her table at the Nugget to say hello. She would ask his advice.

Eric was in the station when Leah called. He was just going on duty. "I'll be there in twenty minutes. Don't touch anything."

Leah waited for Eric. She wanted to start cleaning up the mess before the children and Jason came home. No use in upsetting the children, she thought. She looked at her watch again, wishing the time to vanish.

Eric was ten minutes late. He was alone and even more handsome than Leah remembered.

Standing in the doorway, surveying the damage,

Eric said, "Nice place you have." A smile softened the hard lines around his mouth.

Leah laughed, in spite of the dire circumstances. "I appreciate you coming. I didn't know if you would remember me. I wasn't sure how to handle this...situation."

Eric closed the door behind him. "You say nothing is missing?" His voice showed no surprise.

"Not that I can tell. There was cash and jewelry on my bedroom dresser that wasn't touched."

"Is anything *else* missing?"

Leah's eyebrows furrowed. "Like what, I don't understand. I don't own anything valuable like silver or coin collections."

"What about the company you keep? Any shady characters?"

Leah thought about that. Could Douglas be a shady character? Jason? Jenny? Her circle of friends was small, except for the people with which she worked. "What are you getting at?" Leah asked.

"Is the coffee pot handy?" Eric smiled warmly.

Leah was taken off guard. "Well, yes, I guess..." Then she realized that what he wanted was a cup of coffee. She wondered if this was his usual way of handling a case. She stumbled through the kitchen and put on a pot of coffee. Dishes had been taken out of the cupboards and food goods were strewn about. Someone had wanted something very badly. What was it? Leah wondered.

Eric was placing the cushions back on the sofa and had replaced the lamp which had been turned upside down on the floor. He sat down and lit a cigarette, his long legs crossed in front of him.

Leah served his coffee and took a cup for herself. She sat down beside him, placing her cup on the table in front of her.

She faced him squarely and asked, "Aren't you going to dust for fingerprints?"

"There won't be any fingerprints." Eric seemed to be studying her. "I don't think you know what's going on, do you?"

"Of course I don't know what's going on! What are you talking about?"

"This is my beat. Nothing goes on that I don't know about. The Feds have been staking this place out for weeks. Last night they searched your car. That's the first I knew who they were watching. You're in some kind of big trouble, girl."

Leah carefully measured her words before she spoke. "Then there's nothing you can do?"

"Honey, the department wouldn't touch it with a ten foot pole."

"Eric," Leah said, fighting back the tears, "I really don't know what they want from me. I'm not involved in anything. I just go to work and mind my own business. I can't imagine what they were looking for."

"If it's not you, then it's something you're involved with, or someone. How about that tall blond fellow you were seeing. What happened to him?"

Leah's eyebrows raised. She wondered if he knew as much about everyone on his beat. She decided not to answer his question. "How about some cookies to go with that coffee?"

Eric smiled. "Would you keep secrets from your protector?"

Leah walked to the kitchen and procured a dish of chocolate-chip cookies. She offered Eric the plate and he accepted two.

"Mmm, good, did you bake these?"

"Yes," Leah answered. "Now, tell me why you think I need a protector, and why you?"

"I have an idea," Eric said slowly. "If the Feds are after you because of a former love interest, the best way to throw them off the track would be to have a new love interest. Namely, me."

Leah thought about that for a moment. "What makes you so sure it's because of my friend?"

"I guess it's confession time. A few days after I stopped you, I noticed you driving into this apartment complex. I parked the squad car and watched for a while. I wanted to come in and...uh, ask if you wanted to go out sometime. Just then, I got a call and had to run on it. I came back later that night, just in time to see this blond fellow ring your doorbell. Off and on I noticed his coming and going. It didn't take much to put it together. So, I just figured you were taken. But, he wasn't just any guy. He usually drove a rented car. And on a few occasions he had a car with government plates. He also did some suspicious things. For one, he always watched that he wasn't followed. Another was the silver case he always took from the front seat and put in the trunk. He was a man with problems, I'd guess, or maybe enemies. Anyway, after a while, I noticed that he wasn't around anymore. You'll notice that I'm not questioning you," Eric said kindly. "This is not an official visit."

"You don't seem to miss much," Leah said. "What are you suggesting?"

"It wouldn't hurt for you to have a new boyfriend. A policeman, even better."

"But surely I couldn't be in any danger from Federal Officers."

"Would you expect Federal Officers to do this?" Eric waved his hand around the room.

"No, I really wouldn't. What makes you so sure they're the ones that did it?"

"It's not the first time this sort of thing has followed

their presence. I'm afraid our government has a nasty element of late."

Leah sighed and leaned back against the sofa. "Why are you doing this for me, Eric?"

He reached for her hand and took it in his, then he patted it with his other. "I like you. It's as simple as that." Eric got up from the sofa and started straightening the furniture. "Let's get things straightened up before the kids get home."

Leah looked at him, astonished.

Eric smiled. "The note on the door."

Leah realized that he must also know about Jason. She wondered how closely he had watched her, and why.

Together they did the major straightening. Leah got a laundry basket and threw all the papers in it. She thought she'd go through it and put them in their proper place later. She was anxious to look for Douglas' list of numbers, but didn't want Eric to know about that. She deduced that if her own government couldn't be trusted, maybe the Las Vegas Police Department couldn't either.

It was interesting that Jason's room hadn't been touched.

Eric finally left, saying that he would be back later that evening, *for appearance sake.*

The children and Jason returned. Leah said nothing of what had happened. Jason went to bed, which was his normal habit, having to work the graveyard shift. Leah took the twins to the neighborhood deli for dinner.

When they returned, Leah had the children bathe and dress for bed early. She read to them from *Nine Witch Tales: "Double, double, toil and trouble, fire burn and cauldron bubble. Round about the cauldron go! In the poisoned entrails throw: Filet of fenny snake, In the cauldron boil and bake,"* that's what she felt like. Like she were in the cauldron, round and round. *"Eye of newt and toe of frog,"* her heart really wasn't in it.

She got through *Shakespeare's Witches Chant* and tucked the twins in their beds. They weren't aware that it was an hour early for their bedtime. She wanted to find Douglas' phone number. Just as she was about to get the basket of papers, the doorbell rang. She looked through the peephole, then quickly opened the door.

Eric stood proud and erect in front of her. He reached for her and pressed a smoldering kiss on her lips. She started to struggle, but as she did he pulled his mouth away from hers and whispered in her ear. "Play the game for the nice gentlemen in the dark sedan below."

Leah's breath caught, and as she turned, Eric's body turning with her, she saw it. In the shadow of a palm tree, the dark car sat in silence, two shadows lurking within.

"Oh, Eric, I'm so scared." Leah pressed herself against him, clinging to him.

"Let's go in now. I'll stay for fifteen minutes and then go. I'm on a coffee break."

They went inside and Leah made coffee.

"Eric, what am I going to do?"

"Be patient, Leah. It'll take a while to get them off your case. Unless of course there is indeed something you have that they want. Don't you have any idea what it might be?"

"I swear, I don't!"

"How much did you know about Golden Boy?"

Leah smiled at the reference to Douglas. *"Golden Boy* was very much a mystery to me. He works for the IRS. A special agent, he said. He was working on the Howard Hughes' estate the last time he was here."

"Holy shit! That's strong stuff. If it wasn't for the government plates on that sedan down there, I'd consider other sources as well."

Leah didn't like the way Eric always referred to Douglas in the past tense. It wasn't as if he were gone, never to return. It was just a matter of time before he came back to her. She wondered where he was now and if he was in some kind of terrible trouble.

"I have to get back to work. Do you have an extra key?"

Leah looked at him incredulously. "What in the world do you have in mind?"

"A lover should probably spend the night." Eric grinned, his charm at its best.

"Not on your life!"

"Okay, whatever you say. It'll take longer to get the message across, and that's okay with me, too. Keep your doors and windows locked. Here's a number." Eric scribbled a number on the back of a scrap of paper and handed it to Leah. "At the slightest sign of trouble, call me. Tell the dispatcher it's an emergency."

"Thanks, Eric. It's good of you to do this for me. Just don't get any ideas." Leah smiled. "I have a deadbolt lock on the door and I don't think anyone will try a second-story job on the windows. I'll be fine."

"I'll make sure of it," Eric smiled, menacingly.

CHAPTER TEN

Eric became Leah's shadow. He showed up everywhere, at the Nugget, at the grocery store, at her apartment, and even at Jenny's place. Leah scolded him at first but to no avail and she soon became accustomed to his presence. He worked a rotating shift for the police department. She never knew if he was working days, four to twelve, or midnights. She had two numbers to call in case of emergencies now. No emergencies had occurred however, but the surveillance of her apartment had continued.

Leah lived in constant fear. She sensed that Douglas was in trouble, too. She had not heard from him in over a month. No more letters arrived. She wondered if he was aware of her danger.

The numbers Douglas had given her disappeared when her apartment had been searched. It was her only contact and now that was gone.

It had been another grueling day at thc Nuggct. Grueling for Leah because the thrill of adventure and excitement of winning had been replaced with a numbing fear, an exasperating helplessness.

Leah pulled into the parking lot and got out of the car. She found her mailbox key and held it in readiness until reaching the maze of metal boxes neatly rowed in a brick wall. In her box, along with the normal junk mail, was a notice that a parcel had been left at the manager's office. She hoped with all her might that it was something from Douglas, anything to let her know that he was all right.

Leah retrieved the package and walked up the stairs to her apartment. Once inside she anxiously tore the brown paper off. She had to get a knife to cut through the strapping tape that bound the huge box together. Finally, elbow-deep in styrofoam packing, she found the contents and carefully withdrew it. Leah gasped in shock. It was an 18th century Japanese porcelain vase decorated in gold. The domed lid was inverted and wrapped in paper. Leah searched the box and wrappings but found nothing more, no indication of from whom the gift was sent. The vase was extraordinarily expensive, she knew that much from art appreciation classes. But who sent it? She examined the exterior of the box once again. There was no name, but there was a return address. She examined it carefully and determined that it had come from France. Madame Bouvia came at once to mind.

She examined the vase once again. When she removed the lid, she found a long envelope stuffed inside. With trembling fingers she tore it open. Inside was a cashier's check for ten thousand dollars, made out to Leah Aston. Leah couldn't believe her eyes. A brief letter accompanied it. Madame Bouvia explained that Samantha's surgery had been a success and that she would be forever grateful to Leah for her help. The check was a *token* of her appreciation. No mention was made of the expensive and rare vase. It couldn't be said that Madame Bouvia didn't have flair.

Leah's first reaction was not to keep the money, but

reading the duchess as she had, determined that it would be in poor taste to return it. She had learned that it's just as important to be able to receive, as it is to give.

In spite of the generous gift, Leah was sorely disappointed. She had hoped for some word of Douglas. Suddenly an idea came to her. She would cable Madame Bouvia. She remembered her perceptions that the duchess was very much aware of Douglas' activities. She hoped that it was true.

Leah rewrapped the vase and put the box in her bedroom closet. Something warned her not to let Eric see it. As for the money, something equally covert would have to be done with it.

The next day, Leah opened a savings account in her maiden name. She would have preferred a better investment, but with things the way they were, that money could be a godsend. She might decide to move suddenly and needed to keep it liquid. It felt wonderful to have options. It gave her a heady feeling.

Las Vegas had turned cold. Not the bitter cold that Leah remembered from the Great Lakes region, only a mild discomfort. Christmas was nearing. From Leah's balcony she could still sunbathe in the strong afternoon sun, that is, if the chill wind wasn't blowing. The desert was a strange place to Leah, with sunbathing as late as January and freak snows in June.

It was Sunday and Leah and the children were making popcorn balls. Eric had the day off and it wasn't unusual to find him at the door, smiling generously.

"I love coming here when you're doing such fun things. It reminds me of home," Eric said.

Leah had learned a lot about Eric. He came from a

farming community in Illinois. He had been assigned to Nellis Air Force Base while in the service and had decided to remain and settle in Las Vegas. He had been married for a short time, then divorced. He had no children. Leah guessed that he wasn't currently interested in anyone of the opposite sex. It would have been impossible, given the time he spent with her. He had been a gentleman with her at all times, not to say that he didn't try occasionally to get close to her.

"Eric, come in and join us. You can help," Leah said.

"I'd love to." And he pitched in, buttered his hands, and pressed the popcorn together in large balls.

"Eric, I haven't seen that sedan down there in quite a while. Are they still watching my apartment?"

"They're changing cars. You can be sure they're not giving up. It must be something really important to sustain such a lengthy stake out. One thing we know, they haven't found what they're looking for. I have a theory. I think they're looking for your friend, and hoping that eventually he'll come back here."

"I think he will. When the time is right."

Eric turned away from her. He didn't respond to her statement. He walked over to the patio doors and gazed out. "I think I should stay tonight. I'll sleep on the sofa. Just to make a better appearance. What do you think?"

"Do you really think it would make a difference? They see you coming and going all the time. Surely they must think we're involved already."

"I'm not convinced they wouldn't make a move if they were pressured. Maybe they're waiting for the right time. Maybe they're waiting for an okay from someone higher up. It couldn't hurt if they thought that I might be here at any given time, day or night. I know they don't watch this place in the daytime. For some reason they must be convinced that your friend will come under cover of darkness, if in fact that synopsis is correct."

"Eric, I trust you. You've become a good friend. If you think it would help, then stay."

Eric did stay. Leah put the children to bed and made a make-shift bed for Eric on the sofa.

"I feel like I'm camping out," Eric said. "I wish we had a fireplace, then we could roast marshmallows and tell ghost stories." Eric's personality was stimulating even at its worst. But tonight was an achievement for him, and he was indeed at his best.

"I hope you brought PJ's. I don't want you sleeping in the raw, in case the girls get up in the night and investigate who's sleeping on their sofa."

"Leah, I had no way of knowing that you'd agree. Now, wouldn't that have been presumptuous of me?" he said with a wicked smile.

"I'll get you a pair of Jason's. They might be high-waters, but you're about the same around the waist." Leah went off to Jason's room.

When she returned with the pajamas, Eric was stretched out comfortably, the *TV Guide* in his hand. "There's an old Jimmy Stewart movie on tonight, want to watch it with me?"

"I don't feel very sleepy, maybe I will. I'm going to get ready for bed first." Leah hesitated. "You do promise to behave, don't you?"

Eric laughed irresistibly. "I won't touch a hair on your head. I promise."

Leah showered and put on a lounging robe. She returned to the living room and offered Eric the use of her shower. He gratefully accepted and disappeared.

When he returned, Leah burst into laughter. Jason's pajamas came to his mid-calf and the sleeves were several inches too short.

Leah stopped laughing, suddenly overcome with the intimacy of the situation.

"Maybe, maybe I should go to bed," she stammered.

"No, Leah, please don't." His voice was serious. Then, as if an inner sense warned him, he laughed lightly and said, "Be a sport. I don't want to sit up alone tonight. I do that all the time. I thought it might be fun to have TV company for a change."

Leah watched him and immediately felt guilty for her suspicious thoughts. He was such a kind person, doing so much for her, sacrificing so much of his time.

"All right Officer, a deal is a deal." Leah laughed sincerely.

They watched the late movie and then the late, late movie. When Leah saw that he wasn't going to make a pass at her, she relaxed. He lay sprawled out on the sofa and she leaned against it from the floor. They had a half-empty plate of popcorn balls between them.

Eric reached down and let Leah's hair slide through his fingers. "I wish you belonged to me," he said. "I would take care of you and keep you from harm."

Leah turned and looked into his soft brown eyes. "You are taking care of me, Eric. You're keeping me from harm, and I don't belong to you. Why are you doing it?"

Eric touched her brow, then looked away. He was silent for a long time. When he spoke there was bitterness in his voice. "If I didn't do it, someone else would have."

Leah's eyebrows knit together. "What are you talking about?"

"I don't think you really want to know, but I'm going to do myself a favor and tell you. I've been working for the Feds."

Leah listened to him in horror. "You son of bitch!"

"I did you a favor, lady. I don't give a damn if you have something they want or not. I took the job so that no one else would!"

Leah's anger subsided as she absorbed the meaning of his words. "I see. Then I owe you my thanks—I think."

Eric was sitting on the edge of the sofa now. He ran his fingers through his hair. "Come here."

Leah got up from the floor and sat beside him.

Eric took her in his arms and held her tightly. "How did you get mixed up in this mess?" he asked. A question asked in such a way didn't require an answer. Eric pushed her an arm's-length away. "Do you know anything about what's going on?"

"It occurred to me that you might know more than I do. What did they tell you they're looking for?"

"They want Douglas. They say that he has stolen Top Secret documents. They thought he might have stashed them here. I'm supposed to be searching your apartment while you're sleeping."

"They've already searched my apartment."

"I know. But they're convinced that you're an accomplice."

"That's crazy. What gave them such an idea?"

"You've been wiped out of the computer—IRS and FBI. If you remember, when you started to deal here you had to be fingerprinted when you got your Sheriff's Card."

"Yes, for my work permit at the Hilton and then later when I registered as a gaming employee."

"As far as the government is concerned, you no longer exist. I suspect that your friend, Douglas, did that little trick. It makes you look very guilty."

Leah understood now. That must have been why she never received a letter from the IRS. Douglas simply erased her from the computer. She had to suppress a giggle. She loved Douglas more for it. "Eric, where does that leave us?"

"I like you. I told you that before. I don't believe you had anything to do with it. And if you did, that doesn't bother me either. I don't like the Feds anymore than you do. They're just a bunch of overpowering assholes."

"Then why did you agree to spy for them?" Leah asked.

"Like I said before, if I didn't agree to do it, someone else would have. I guess you could say I'm a double agent." Eric laughed, the idea becoming more amusing all the while.

"What are you going to do now?"

Eric rubbed his chin with his thumb and forefinger. He narrowed his eyes. "Let's give them something to occupy their time, a false lead. Do you have a typewriter?"

"No, I don't."

"That's okay. I can type it at the station when I'm doing my reports. Write yourself a letter from Douglas. Think of a location as far away from where he might actually be as possible. Be sure and include some titillating dialogue. You know, something he might actually say to you. Make it a long letter that says nothing. The idea is to get a location. Since I'll be delivering the letter to them, an envelope won't be necessary. But it will have to have a date and some reference to where he is in the body of the letter. That'll take the pressure off you, and me."

"I still don't know why you're doing this."

"Do you want me to say it's because I'm in love with you?" Eric's voice lowered, giving it a husky quality.

Leah answered tersely, "No. No, I don't." She lurched away from the sofa and Eric, then walked to the patio doors and gazed out, a tormented expression on her face. She scolded herself fiercely.

Eric's voice was soft from across the room. "Okay, then I won't. I'll tell you only what you want to hear. I don't love you, but I want to make mad passionate love to you. No attachments. Just a little tenderness in the night. When you wake up in the morning you can pretend that it never happened."

Leah smiled. She walked over to him and knelt beside the sofa. She took his face in her hands and gently kissed him on the mouth. "You tempt me, Eric."

Her eyes were smoky, her lips parted and moist. "If we made love, I would be pretending you were Douglas. That wouldn't be fair to you."

Eric was tempted to take her any way he could get her. But in spite of that first inclination, said, "He's a lucky man."

Leah rose and smiled tenderly. "Do what you have to do. I'm going to bed."

Eric looked after her for a long while, a strange expression on his face.

Leah walked into her bedroom. She changed from her lounging robe to her nightgown and got into bed. She hadn't closed her bedroom door. She knew what would happen. Eric would search her apartment. She didn't fear him, but at the same time, felt something incongruous about his story. She had no idea what he really wanted. She didn't know for whom he was really working, but she did know that he was a good person. That was enough for her. He was welcome to whatever he wanted. She didn't have anything around that would lead anyone to Douglas, or implicate him in anything. With that peace of mind, Leah went to sleep.

When she awoke the following morning Eric was gone. So was the vase Madame Bouvia had sent her from France.

Leah sat in the Golden Nugget Casino Restaurant next to Jenny. It was Wednesday.

Leah was cheerful as she asked Jenny about her latest conquest.

"Clint called last night," Jenny said sadly. "He asked if I'd consider letting the children live with their father."

"Oh, my God."

Jenny laughed bitterly. "Of course I told him to go get screwed."

"Jenny, I'm so sorry, but better to find out now, than later."

"You know, the problem is, I'm still trying to think of ways around it. I mean, I should never see the bastard again, but I would just die if I didn't."

"Jenny, what are you saying?"

"I thought if I suggested a live-in who could care for the children..." she broke off. "I know I should never see him again."

"He obviously doesn't like children," Leah said.

"I'm not so sure. He has two children of his own. I think it's something else. Maybe guilt. I haven't figured it out yet."

Leah smiled. "I know you will, Jenny. Stick to your guns.

If he wants you badly enough, he'll do it your way."

"I intend to, Leah. In the meantime, I'm going out on the town tonight. Maybe tomorrow night, too. In fact, I'm going to be so busy..." she raised her eyebrows and gave Leah the most innocent of looks, "I just might not be around to get Clint's calls for a good while."

Leah laughed. Jenny could be as coldly calculating as the best of them. What worried Leah was the end result. If she won this game, what would she end up with?

"Have you heard anything from Douglas?" Jenny asked.

"I've sent a telegram to Madame Bouvia telling her that I need to contact him. I didn't give her any details, just that the number I had was no longer in my possession."

"Your situation scares the hell out of me."

"Is that why you don't come over anymore?" Leah asked.

"Hell, Leah, I've got enough trouble of my own. I love you, but self-preservation is an innate thing. Not that I wouldn't do anything in the world for you...it's just that I think that right now, you might invite too close a scrutiny of your friends."

"I found out why I haven't been called in by the IRS. Douglas erased my file from the computer."

Jenny laughed wildly. "You're kidding! Damn, way to go, Douglas."

Leah smiled at her friend's naïve delight. "Not so good, Jenny. It's why the Federal Agents are watching me. They think that Douglas and I are partners in crime."

"Just what crime is he suspected of? Surely a simple erasure wouldn't warrant such attention."

"Eric told me last night that he's accused of stealing Top Secret documents."

"Do you believe that, Leah?"

"I'm not sure. He mentioned something about a special project that he was working on. The two might be connected. I think that if he did take them, it was for a good reason."

"That's just love talking, Leah. It takes a long time to really know someone. Don't forget that." Jenny got up and secured her apron around her hips. She smiled. "Life is just one adventure after another." Her voice regained its natural lilt and Leah couldn't help laughing. Jenny was never down for long. She had her share of problems lately, but it didn't get the best of Jenny.

Leah resolved to learn from her.

Table 5 was open from the graveyard shift. Leah took over from the bleary-eyed dealer who, under the table, gave her a hand signal that she didn't understand. It was enough to signal Leah that something was wrong. There didn't seem to be anything unusual about the betting. The table wasn't stacked high with black chips. Everything seemed to be normal.

The pit boss spread a new deck on Leah's table and she put the old deck in the discard rack for him. She shuffled the standard shuffle and set the deck in front of a player to cut. He cut the deck and clumsily dropped the cards, spraying them in every direction. The pit boss frantically called for security. Two guards came running to her table. The pit boss announced that the table was closed. The guards quickly picked up the cards and the pit boss counted them, checking each card.

The players grumbled and ambled away. The guards remained. Leah was puzzled.

"Hang loose, Doll Face, it'll be a while before this game opens again," the pit boss said.

"What's going on?" Leah asked.

"Somebody at this table's been cheating. I found an extra ace in a deck. Problem is, we've had the same players for hours. Couldn't tell who was doing it. Could be they were marking them, too. We're sending the last three decks upstairs to be checked."

The pit boss gave the guards instructions and they went separate ways. Leah saw them each tagging a player that had been at her table.

Decks of cards were counted and checked before and after they were used in a game. Only two kinds of people would try to cheat a casino, someone very stupid, or very clever. From stories Leah heard of these people, she wouldn't want to be in their place. She had heard that the casinos had their own way of dealing with them.

The morning went by swiftly. Leah's game became routine again. The normal savvy players who sat at the larger minimum games were a pleasure to deal to, in comparison with the many inexperienced players.

Downtown attracted the inexperienced players because the atmosphere was more relaxed. The dealers could, within limits, talk to the players. They could smile and not be accused of collusion, as they might on the strip. Tourists who were not serious gamblers flocked to downtown.

The pit boss walked up to Leah. "Come and see me on your next break."

That kind on directive struck fear in the hearts of the best dealers.

Leah's break came and she walked to the podium. The pit boss handed her a telegram. It had been opened.

She took it and walked out of the pit.

She sat down in the keno lounge and opened it with trembling fingers. *My dear sister, I miss you. All is fine. Have been advised of your situation. Don't buy the house. Stay where you are. See you soon. Love Janet.*

Leah read the telegram again. And again. She was most anxious to see the sender of this telegram, particularly since she didn't have a sister.

The morning's headlines didn't impress Leah any more than usual, the typical government goings on. She didn't pay much attention to that sort of thing. It didn't interest her that the Director of the CIA, Edgar Monahan, had been fired by the President.

Douglas, fortunately, had a good many friends in the Clear Lake area. He had found it necessary to change his residence numerous times. He was now staying in the home of an old friend. There was a private boat slip where he was able to secure the Catalina Express. The house was built on stilts and looked out over the bay. It had been a good place to finish his book. Much precaution had been taken in the transporting of the manuscript. He had been made acutely aware of the dangerous implications of his endeavor. The manuscript had been microfilmed, then the hard copy destroyed. When the Federal Agents had been close to finding him, he panicked and sent the microfilm to his very dear friend, Madame Bouvia. The lengthy time in the mails secured it better than any other way he could have imagined.

It was Madame Bouvia who suggested the false bottomed vase to transport it to the publisher. However, sending it directly to a publisher in such a way would surely make them think twice about their involvement in an already risky venture.

The bomb was ready to drop. The publisher had its advertising campaign designed and newspapers and magazines were lined up to get the information simultaneously. Large excerpts would be splashed over the front pages of every paper in the nation—if all went as planned.

Douglas was an opportunist. He could have accomplished the same thing without a full-length book, but after all, he was a novelist first, a government employee and citizen, second. He wondered how Leah would take the news. There again, he had been forced to deceive her. He wondered how she would like being married to Boston Potter.

CHAPTER ELEVEN

It had been a week since Leah received the strange telegram. She could only deduce that it was some sort of message from Douglas, distorted for the benefit of anyone who might intercept it. And it appeared that someone had intercepted it because it had been opened before she received it.

Leah decided that the only thing she could do was wait for further instructions. She felt more secure now that she had finally had some word.

It was Sunday morning and Jenny was on her way over. She hadn't been to Leah's place in a very long time. Her excited call an hour earlier had left Leah with a warm feeling. She longed for the good old days when they spent so much time together. The bell rang and Leah opened the door to greet her.

Jenny was radiant. She hugged Leah and threw her purse down on the sofa. "I'm in an absolute stupor. You'll never believe what's happened! Clint called last night and asked me to marry him!" Jenny waited for a reaction from Leah.

Leah was not pleased, but she didn't want to put a damper on Jenny's happiness. "Have you come to terms with your differences regarding the children?" The expression on Jenny's face indicated that this wasn't a question that she wanted to answer.

"It will work out. He's changed his mind about that. He wants to marry me, anyway."

"And you've accepted?"

"We're leaving on the afternoon plane."

"What! You can't be serious! He only called last night and you're leaving today!" Leah was the one in a stupor now.

"I know it's short notice, but that's how Clint is. He's spontaneous. When he makes up his mind, that's it."

"Sit down here and tell me your plans, it's ridiculous us standing here. I've made a fresh pot of coffee."

Jenny didn't sit down, but followed Leah into the kitchen and watched her pour the coffee, then, they both went back into the living room. Leah sat on the sofa and Jenny sat on the loveseat directly across from her. But Jenny didn't relax; she sat at attention on the edge of the cushion.

"I've arranged to have movers come in and do the packing. I can virtually pack a few suitcases and be on my way. I had no idea you could just make a phone call and have someone else pack and move you. It's going to be a whole new way of life. How exciting it will be to have money." Jenny blushed. "Not that that's why I'm marrying him...well, you know that. I don't have to explain that to you. But, have you ever thought how it would be to have all the money you ever wanted? I wonder what it would feel like to go into an exclusive store and buy whatever I wanted. Just think, I won't have to worry about the children's education—the best schools from now on."

Leah sat quietly listening. This was so unlike Jenny. She had a bad feeling about the whole thing. Looking at the facts without emotion, Clint had tried to get Jenny to give her children to their father. He only accepted them when he discovered it was the only way he could have Jenny. The children were in for a rough life, Leah suspected. Jenny wasn't being rational, but there was nothing Leah could do about that.

"My dear Jenny, I'll miss you. We've had so many good times together. I can't believe it's good-bye. Who will I tell my troubles to? Who will I call in the middle of the night for advice?"

Jenny laughed. "You exaggerate grossly. It was I who called you. I was the one with all the troubles. You've lead a very sedate life in comparison—until lately, that is." They both laughed at the truism.

"Oh, it's all so crazy. I'm in a wonderful whirl! We'll be married as soon as we get to Abilene. There will be a three-day wait on the blood tests, of course."

"That's ironic. Las Vegas Boulevard is lined with wedding chapels. No blood tests required, no waiting period, just get a license and zap, your married. You certainly are doing it the hard way."

"The only thing lacking is the groom," Jenny said. "He can't get up here just now. That's why he's so anxious for us to get there as soon as possible."

"I wish you a good life, Jenny. It may be hard at first, adjusting to the outside world. You've been in this business a long time. At least the children aren't old enough for it to be a crippling change, but it's bound to be tough on them."

"It'll be okay. We can handle it."

Leah knew she was looking on the dark side of this and resolved not to make any more negative statements. She had said more than enough already. Jenny refused to think beyond her emotions, and Leah decided to be more optimistic.

Leah took Jenny and her children to the airport and bid them a tearful good-bye. It seemed the end of an era. Without Jenny, Leah's life would change drastically. But Jenny's life, Leah feared, would change the most, and not for the best.

Shortly after Leah arrived home from the airport, she received a telephone call from France.

"Madame Bouvia, it's so good to hear from you." Leah wanted to ask immediately about Douglas, but fought to maintain her manners.

"Leah, my dear, I think it's time for you to take a vacation. I'm planning to be in London for Christmas. I've arranged for three tickets to be waiting for you at the American Airlines counter. I know you won't refuse me."

There was a strange tone in her voice. Was it a warning?

"Madame Bouvia, you're too generous. I couldn't possibly get away. The arrangements—"

"Your sister would be most disappointed if you didn't meet her in London."

Leah stopped short. Her mind raced in a million directions. Among other things, she was being warned that the telephone lines could be tapped. The reference to her sister could only mean Douglas. Douglas was waiting for her in London.

"My sister recommended that I stay here. I think her intention was to pay me a visit," Leah said, hoping for some kind of further information.

"That was then. This is now. Christmas in London is memorable. She would never forgive you if you refused, and neither would I, my child. It will be a wonderful experience for the twins. You *must* bring them."

Leah sighed. "I do miss her. When should I come?"

"That's my girl. As soon as you feasibly can. How about tomorrow?" Without giving Leah a chance to answer, she went on. "Dear, be sure to pack enough clothes. It's cold in London. I would suggest that you pack two large bags for each of you. Try to manage enough for a month. They always say pack half as much and take twice as much money, but in your case, I want you to pack twice as much and take *all* your money." There was a long silence.

Madam Bouvia was giving Leah time to comprehend what she was saying, and it came across clearly.

The conversation came to an end with the duchess promising to have Leah met at the airport by one of the staff who traveled with her.

Leah went to the kitchen and poured a Scotch. She rarely drank hard liquor but this was an occasion that called for it. She let out a deep sigh. She didn't entirely understand what was happening, but deduced that she was to take all of her money out of the country with her—from the sound of it, most of her clothes as well. Did that mean that she wouldn't be returning? How could she do such a drastic thing with no direct communication with Douglas? Did she have that much faith in him? She had been frightened to ask questions when it became evident that the duchess was taking precautions against listening devices.

If it hadn't been for the ten thousand dollars that Leah had in her possession, she might not have taken the step, but that did give her some security. If she arrived in London and no one was there to meet her, she wouldn't be stranded. She would have her own means to return or stay for a real vacation. If it meant seeing Douglas again, she would do it. And she was sure it did.

The situation seemed to have a parallel. It wasn't only Jenny, but Leah who was off to foreign lands at a moment's notice. Leah wondered what her thoughts would be if she could stand apart from herself and look on as she herself had done with Jenny. But that wasn't possible, so instead, she withdrew suitcases from the closet and started packing.

Fortunately, Leah was in extremely good standing with the Golden Nugget, and managed to see Murrey that very night. She was given an immediate and indefinite leave of absence. Leah called the airport and confirmed their reservations for the next day. She didn't want to waste a moment. All she could think of was Douglas. The trip to England didn't excite her in the least. It could have been Gary, Indiana. It was the thought of seeing Douglas again that made her heart beat faster.

The next day, Leah went to the bank as soon as it opened and then called the children's school. It was incredible how fast she managed to prepare for a month's vacation. Never having been out of the country before, Leah was unaware of certain requirements which unbeknown to her were being prepared by supporters in the background.

The Yellow Cab sped down Desert Inn Road and turned onto Paradise. Leah glanced at her watch. It was five minutes later than when she last looked. They had plenty of time to make the plane, but she never took a chance on being late. Arriving early was always preferable to her.

The children sat politely beside her, tired from the hectic schedule that was imposed upon them since the evening before. They were still emotionally on edge from the tearful good-bye to Jason, but they were consoled that it wasn't forever. They would be back in a month. It was just that he was such an important part of their everyday lives that it seemed a terrible loss to be without him for so long. And of course Leah couldn't tell them that they would be meeting Douglas. It seemed risky.

Suddenly a siren screamed behind them, then the squad car pulled alongside and motioned the driver over. The driver spat an obscenity.

Leah was shocked to see Eric get out of the car and approach them. He motioned for Leah to roll down her window. She obeyed. She hadn't seen Eric since the night he had slept on her sofa and absconded with the priceless vase.

A broad smile covered his rugged face. "Once again I can be of service to you, damsel."

"Can you?" Leah asked without emotion.

Eric handed her an envelope which she immediately opened. Inside were three leather bound passports, three airline tickets, a large sum of money, both American dollars and British pounds, birth certificates, and snapshots that had apparently been decreased in size and used for the passports.

"Passports! My God! It never occurred to me..."

"Sorry about the birth certificates and photographs, I guess you didn't miss them." Eric grinned.

Leah sighed heavily. "I won't ask one single question. Just...thanks."

"You'll follow me now. There has been a slight change. I'm taking you to a private airfield. You'll fly to Dallas and leave from there via American Airlines. Good luck."

The first leg of the trip was over, and now the

engines of the huge 747 hummed in Leah's ears. A movie was playing on the screen in front of the cabin, but she wasn't paying attention. The twins slept peacefully beside her. It was quiet now. Dinner had been served and the company of travelers around her was quieting down. They would be in the air for approximately nine hours. A seat companion had been telling her about going through customs. She didn't relish waiting in lines with the twins. It was becoming a very tiresome trip, Leah's state of mind adding to the fatigue. She tried to piece it all together, Eric being as much an enigma as Douglas. When he laughed about being a double agent—was he really telling the truth? Was he in fact, a friend of Douglas? Somehow that didn't have a ring of truth.

Gatwick Airport was a menagerie of people. Leah had expected, in her naïvety, to find English people in London, but to her surprise it seemed to be an international assemblage. She fortunately didn't have to stand in line to exchange American dollars for English pounds, and got through customs with no trouble. She found a crowd of people, including what looked like uniformed drivers, displaying large printed placards, and knowing Madame Bouvia as she did, looked for one with her name. It wasn't long before she found it.

Leah hadn't slept much on the plane and fatigue was setting in. The liveried driver sat erect and silent. Leah felt like a puppet whose movements were being directed by an unknown puppeteer. After what seemed an eternity, the driver pulled into a large circular driveway, with bright lights streaming from an expansive canopy. They were in the heart of London. The doorman approached and opened the door.

Leah's driver gave him instructions regarding the luggage and escorted Leah and the children through the lobby and onto the elevator.

"I've been instructed to deliver you to your room and call for you again tomorrow at 4:00 p.m., Mrs. Aston. At that time we will be continuing to our final destination which is between Stratford and Bidford-Upon-Avon."

This didn't mean a thing to Leah. She didn't know where she was, let alone where Stratford or Bidford-Upon-Avon was.

"It is a riverside village called Welford," continued the chauffeur. "I think it's one of the prettiest places in Shakespeare country."

"Oh," she said lamely.

Leah was finally alone. The children had laid down for a nap and she slumped into a lounge chair in the luxurious hotel suite. The telephone rang and she reached for it.

"Welcome to London, my dear." It was the voice of Madame Bouvia.

"Oh, I'm so glad to hear a familiar voice. I was beginning to think I was alone in a foreign land."

"Come, come, my dear. You must be exhausted. That's why I arranged for you to stay over in London for an evening. You'll need to adjust to the time change. How are the children holding up?"

Leah laughed. "Better than I am. They're sound asleep. Madame Bouvia, can I assume that we can speak freely?"

"Yes, Leah. You're out of danger...however, I would prefer that Douglas tell you all about it."

Leah's heart soared. "Oh, I knew he would be here!"

"Not yet."

Leah's heart sank like a deflated balloon. "When will he be here?"

"As soon as he can, dear. Don't worry. Now, back to our schedule. My driver will pick you up at 4:00 p.m. sharp tomorrow. Try to get some rest." And at that she hung up.

Leah lay down beside the twins and none of them woke until the next day.

London was shockingly congested. Every square inch of real estate seemed to be utilized. Buildings huddled together, their rows of smokeless chimneys staring one another in the face.

Breakfast consisted of freshly baked croissants and jelly, strong coffee, and the children had eggs with bacon and sausage. It seemed to be their way to serve two kinds of meat.

More rested now, Leah was getting excited about being in a foreign country. She bought a pictorial guide to London at the lobby gift shop. She wanted to see Trafalgar Square, Westminster Abbey and Buckingham Palace, the Changing of the Guard, and maybe even get a glimpse of the Queen. Even more than that, she wanted to see Douglas. These excursions were not on her agenda at this time but perhaps in the future, she thought. And before she had much time to dwell on these desires the driver arrived to escort them to God only knew where.

They were once again in the spacious car, heading to their final destination. They drove for hours, out of the congested city to a sprawling countryside. Leah kept looking at her watch, but there was nothing to do but practice patience and that was very hard for her.

The *Washington Post* had a reputation for being the first newspaper to ferret out the muck in the capital city. It was inevitable that with the growing number of people involved, a leak would occur.

The premature headlines shocked the nation and caused foreign powers to take notice with a keen interest. "IRS UNDER ATTACK!" The story exposed Boston Potter as not only a renowned and respected author of children's fables, but also as a trusted employee of the IRS for the last seven years. The reporter likened him to Robin Hood, giving his all to his country and his fellow man.

Douglas Lourdes' name was now synonymous with Boston Potter. The story announced the forthcoming exposé on the IRS and went on to say that Douglas Lourdes had mysteriously disappeared.

Boat Lane was lined with timber and whitewashed thatched cottages. Their shiny black Bentley pulled up in front of one of the largest. A domestic, named Hilda, greeted Leah and the children. With Hilda's help they settled in and were served afternoon tea. The children were delighted to find one of their favorite pastimes become reality—a real tea party.

Madam Bouvia telephoned and told Leah that she would be visiting in the evening. Leah had not seen the papers, but became informed through Hilda.

"It's a shame, all the trouble in the States. A good time to be gone from there, I expect," she said in her high-pitched voice.

"I don't know what you're referring to, Hilda, I haven't seen the papers," Leah said.

"*The Daily Express* is full of it. My word, the poor American people! And we thought we had tax problems. I expect a goodly amount of your trusted government officials will be sacked before it's over."

"Do you have a copy?" Leah asked.

The full story had broken now, and excerpts of "Fight Back America" were on the front page. The Attorney General had launched a full investigation into the alleged activities of the IRS. The Ways and Means Committee was on stand-by to interpret tax law which was in question. The Treasury Department, unable to account for their own, was under full investigation. All this was in itself shocking to Leah, but not so much as the author's identity. Douglas Lourdes / Boston Potter—the same person.

For the first time, Leah understood the danger she had been in. But, now, her concern was for Douglas. He had not surfaced. She thought back to all of the deceptions and understood. She couldn't berate him for keeping her in the dark. She had been better off not knowing.

Douglas had been in hiding. His life was in jeopardy as long as the information had not been made public. Now he was safe, but for attacks from newspaper reporters, which was almost as bad. He, along with two bodyguards, boarded the 747 for London.

In the small village of Welford, Leah waited. She wrung her hands and walked the floor. Hilda waited on her and the children, anticipating every need.

It was Christmas Eve and a tree had been erected and decorated. Leah had shopped at Harrods during her one day in London, and had purchased gifts for the children. She had bought Douglas a five-dollar gold piece. She was wondering now if she would be able to give it to him at all. Her mind was filled with apprehension. ESP had escaped her and she had no inner feeling to placate her fear.

A fire burned in the large fireplace, warming the cozy cottage. Leah had just requested tea of Hilda, who thought it strange to want tea at such a late hour.

There was a commotion outside and Leah sprang to the window. At long last! Madame Bouvia and Douglas were disembarking from a sleek black automobile that looked much like the one that had delivered her and the children. Leah darted to the door and swung it open. Douglas stopped in his tracks, as did Leah, and they embraced one another with their eyes.

Douglas broke the spell and ran to her, embracing her in his arms, swooping her in the air, and swinging her joyously in circles.

"It's all over, my love. It's all over. We'll never be apart again."

"You know what?" Leah asked. "I believe you. Maybe for the first time, I believe you."

Madame Bouvia cleared her throat in an effort to be recognized. When she had their attention, she suggested that they retreat to warmer surroundings.

They sat around the fire and ruminated quietly on the shocking decline of the Treasury Department.

Douglas spoke. "Our country, every department of government, must be held accountable. Our forefathers didn't have dictatorship in mind. Democracy: A government for the people and of the people. The people have become lethargic. In a way, I suppose it's our own fault. If we don't take an active interest, and many Americans don't, this will happen again. It's my hope that someday we'll have a simpler tax system. There are too many loopholes now. That's why people were so easily taken in. The tax system is so complicated even tax attorneys are stymied. And too often it's a matter of interpretation.

"Douglas," Leah said, "did you know that agents stripped Jenny's house. They took everything of resale value, toaster, TV, stereo—they even took food out of her cupboard!"

"They were given a free hand, Leah. That was mild compared to what was done to many. A lot of heads will roll in Washington before this is over."

"Is that why we're out of the country?"

"No sense in nesting in a bear's cave. Besides, a long honeymoon is just what the doctor ordered."

A puzzled expression came across Leah's face.

Madame Bouvia came to attention, pulling a document from a folder she had laid beside her. "I have a Christmas present for you both." She smiled as she handed the divorce decree to Leah.

Leah looked up and saw them clasping hands. "I suspect that you two have been in constant collusion."

"We go back a long way, Leah," Madame Bouvia said.

Douglas looked into Leah's eyes. "I'm sorry I've had to put you through so much. Things had to be done in their own way to protect the people involved, including you. It's all going to be different now. We can lead a normal life."

"Tell me," Leah's eyes twinkled, "to whom will I be married? Will it be Jim Henderson, Douglas Lourdes, or Boston Potter?"

Douglas laughed. "I've really given you a hard time, haven't I? You will be married to a very successful author and a man who intends to stay home and write and take advantage of the two lovely children in his household for his inspiration. And it's Douglas. Boston Potter is a pen name. Do you like it?"

"Awfully stuffy sounding."

Douglas laughed. "It's much too late to change it now. Oh, Leah, I can't tell you how good it is to be here with you. We'll stay here for a time, and then we can think about where we would like to live. Perhaps here in England, or maybe in France."

Leah couldn't hide the surprise in her face. "Can't we ever go back to the States?"

"Perhaps in time. When the country belongs to the people again. When they realize their responsibility to one another and the necessity to be actively involved in government, every single man and woman. When man takes responsibility for his neighbor and his country. When we care again."

"Oh, Douglas." Leah's eyes filled with tears. She thought of Jenny and Jason and her life in Vegas, and she thought of the children adjusting to a new country. She imagined what it would mean to live in exile. But when she raised her eyes and saw Douglas looking at her, she knew that the love light in those warm sparkling eyes would make up for any sacrifice she might have to endure.

Douglas reached for her and she blended into his embrace, knowing without a doubt that in an otherwise dark sky, their own special sun was shining down on them.

COMING SOON

Glitz

A novel by Carolyn Slicker DeFever

Leah and Jenny are destined to cross paths again as a bizarre set of circumstances bring them back to Las Vegas...and the saga continues.